A
GOD'S
PROMISE

THEFT. LOVE. RETRIBUTION.

A GOD'S PROMISE

INTERNATIONAL BESTSELLING AUTHOR

KAYLA MAYA

A God's Promise

Copyright 2023 by Kayla Maya

Map art by Cartographybird

Cover art by Saint Jupiter

Editing by Enchanted Author Services

www.kaylamayaauthor.com

ISBN Paperback: 9798376721933

ISBN Hardcover:

[I. Fantasy.   2. Magic—Fiction.   3. NA—Fiction. 4. Ro-
mance—Fiction.]

First Edition

Books by Kayla Maya

The Song and Storm Trilogy

Song of Storms

Song of Crows

Song of Embers

~

The Forgotten Empire Duology

The Aspen Rain

~

Seasons of the Witch Duology

The Winter Witch

The Summer King

~

Saga of the Cursed

Of Gold & Silver

Of Dusk & Dawn

~

The Dragon Empress Trilogy

The Azure Dragon

The Crimson Throne

The Forsaken God

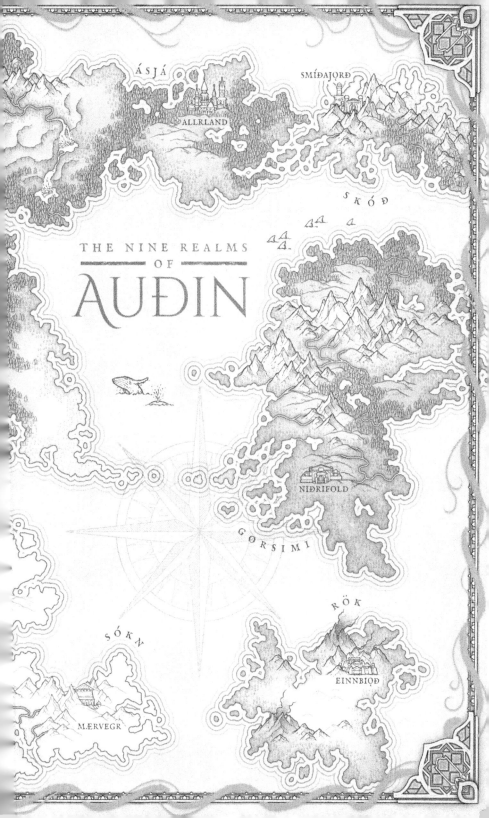

Music Inspirations:

In Another Life—Crown the Empire
Immortalize—Crown the Empire
Villain—Luke Shoemaker
Make Them Suffer—Erase Me
Without Me—Dayseeker
There's Fear in Letting Go—I Prevail
Bow Down—I Prevail
Torch—Black Veil Brides
Infectious—Imminence
Waiting for the Sky to Change—Starset/Breaking Benjamin
Paradise—Future Palace
Just Pretend—Bad Omens
Never Know—Bad Omens
Mercy—Bad Omens
Sweet Dreams are Made of These—Marlin Manson
Show Me Your God—Amity Affliction
Running Up That Hill (Make a Deal with God)—Kate Bush
Blood Runs Cold—Catch Your Breath
Lost—Linkin Park
—Austin Snell
Done With Everything—Line So Thin
Black Thunder—The Hu
Torn in Two—Breaking Benjamin
I Will Not Bow—Breaking Benjamin
Sea of Fire—The Wise Man's Fear

A NOTE ABOUT NAMES

A full glossary of names and terms is provided at the back of the book, which includes pronunciations and definitions.

A spoiler-free Pronunciation Guide for character names and key terms listed in the book. It's found just before the glossary.

For my own companions Poppy and Laila, who don't seem to get the attention they deserve.

ONE

I dropped to one knee to inspect a print in the mud, placing two fingers on the track, feeling the warmth that came from it. The creature hadn't gone far, so I had to make haste if I was going to catch up to it. I slung my bow over my shoulder, reached down into my boot, and gripped my obsidian dagger.

There were far more dangerous creatures that thrived in this wood, and I wasn't one of them.

I crept through the forest as I watched for more tracks and the dangerous creatures that lurked within. I was getting increasingly thankful for this fall weather, as the majority of the trees had shed their leaves, peppering the ground in an assortment of reds, oranges, and browns. It was easier to spot my prey without the forest being as dense as it normally was during the spring and summer months.

I heard the soft, padded paws of an animal as it came towards me, but I hadn't spotted it yet. A second too late, coarse, wiry fur touched my arm, followed by a large, wet tongue.

"Fenrir!" I whispered, keeping my voice low so as not to disturb the wildlife around the area. I pushed him away. "You scared me half to death."

My companion gave a soft whimper before he dropped his head. His tail swished from side to side, ears laid flat over his massive head. I clicked my tongue, upset at myself for getting worked up over not spotting Fenrir sooner. I went to give him a stroke on the head, but I quickly retracted my arm.

Fenrir's black coat was covered in mud, his paws drenched and covered in sharp brambles. I narrowed my eyes at him before I slid closer, acting like I was going to give him a hug. He whimpered.

I gave him a smile before raising my hand and flicking him on the nose. Fenrir yelped and ducked his head, green eyes downcast.

"That's for giving me a scare."

Fenrir's ears flicked forward, the white mask over his eyes making it seem like he was up to some mischief. I paused, turned my head, and caught sight of the animal that had created those prints.

A large buck walked into the area, sporting a rack with antlers that bespoke his old age. The animal favored its left side, ears flicked forward as it listened to the surrounding area. Fenrir stood, but I held out my hand to stop him. He sat back down, observing me carefully.

I reached behind me to my bow, being as quiet and quick as possible so as not to spook the buck. I watched as my prey took a step forward, head swiveling from side to side. I lowered myself, grabbed an arrow, and nocked it into the strings. I heard Fenrir shift behind me.

The buck halted. Ears shifted my way before he slowly turned toward where I was nestled in the bushes. I timed each breath with the beating of my heart, hoping that he had not spotted me yet.

Thankfully, after several long moments, the animal spun away to begin walking back to his destination. I crept closer, my fingers on the string of my bow. I lifted my right foot, angling it towards Fenrir—an old trick my mother once taught me to signal to my wolf—and he responded. He sat up and stalked in the other direction, his paws light on the earth.

I waited, allowing Fenrir time to reach his destination before I made my last move.

I saw my companion's coat for a sliver of a second before the buck did. Fenrir bounded out of the thicket, maw wide. The buck jumped, making a noise before he turned—and I wasted no time. I rose to my full height, my fingers letting go of the string.

TWO

The arrow was fast as it embedded itself deep within the buck's chest, right into the heart. My prey collapsed, head twisted at an odd angle. Fenrir pranced over, his tail wagging back and forth excitedly.

I walked over to our kill, dropping to my knees by the animal's head. I lifted the buck's massive skull and placed it on my lap, my hands running over the fur. Soft, almost dense, it would make an excellent coat, something I would need during the coming winter.

I reached into my boot; my fingers curled around the hilt of my dagger as I yanked it out to start the long, grueling process of skinning my kill. Fenrir waited, lying down with his eyes closed, his huff offering me comfort as I began to work.

I hated skinning my kills in the woods. It was dangerous—far more dangerous than staying out after dark in Ellriheimr. Thieves and bandits hid in the shadows, lying in wait for their next targets. What they didn't know was that I thrived in the darkness. It was the only way I was able to survive by myself over the years.

If it wasn't for Fenrir, I probably would have gone insane long ago. Living alone wasn't exactly the most lavish affair, so having my companion with me kept me anchored to reality and away from prying thoughts.

My mind began to recall a time when, several years prior, a hunter had gone into the woods and never returned. His body was found several days later dismembered with a red skull with an arrow pierced through it painted on his chest. A band of thieves were frightening in itself, but nothing compared to the bears and mountain lions that thrived around here.

A branch snapped behind me, and I paused. Fenrir lifted his head, his ears flicked forward, his golden eyes lost in the surrounding thicket. My grip on my dagger tightened, and I turned my head slightly.

I scanned the area, looking for the source of the broken branch, but didn't see anything that would have been alarming. Stealing a glance over at Fen, I noticed him laying his head back down, eyes closed. If my wolf wasn't worried, then I shouldn't be either. However, I couldn't stop the feeling of unease that crept through me. It must have been a rabbit, or some other animal, but once they caught a whiff of Fenrir's scent, they almost certainly scampered off. Wolves were rare for this part of Röskr, but they weren't impossible to find.

I went back to my skinning; I was not even halfway done with my deer. Another branch snapped, this time closer than the last. Fen's hackles raised, a low growl emanating from his throat.

The hairs on the back of my neck stood on end, the feeling of being watched coursing through me. I began to cut and trim faster, almost nicking myself a few times with my blade. Mother once told me that sometimes it was better to be efficient rather than quick, a skill I had learned and mastered quickly enough.

Just not when I was being watched.

I shifted my weight, digging myself deeper into the buck's sliced-open midsection. I would leave the organs behind for the rest of the predators. I'd rather they be occupied with themselves eating the leftovers rather than me.

Another branch snapped, this time sending Fenrir to his feet as a low growl emanated from his throat. I froze, hearing more branches snap beneath the weight of the other predator.

I rose to my feet and turned just as a large creature barreled towards me. My instincts took over, and I threw myself out of the way. Air hit me as the massive creature sliced through where I'd just stood. I twirled, zeroing in on what was coming towards me. Brown, coarse fur, pointed snout, massive claws, and was easily ten times my height.

My face paled. The brown fur rippled as the beast turned to face me. Black, beady eyes locked on me. Its dagger-like claws sliced the dirt and leaves as it headed for me. *Fuck*. I would rather fight off five thieves than this single grizzly bear.

Fenrir sprang into action, using his back paws as leverage to pounce forward. I sheathed my dagger in my boot, swung my bow from my shoulders, and nocked an arrow in the strings as the bear dug his claws into the earth, stopping himself from hitting a tree. Fenrir landed on the bear's back, his canines biting into the bear's flesh.

The grizzly bear huffed loudly, rising on his hind legs, his head swiveling from side to side to try to dislodge Fenrir from his back.

I aimed, but each time the grizzly swung back and forth, I would aim my arrow directly at my companion. I couldn't afford to miss. I also did not want to hurt my wolf. If I let my arrow fly, I would risk hitting Fenrir. However, if I waited too long, I'd run the risk of losing both the shot *and* my life.

The grizzly barked, driving his back into a tree. Fenrir howled in pain, falling to the ground. The bear dropped to all fours and turned to my companion, his paw raised to swipe at my wolf.

"Don't you touch him," I warned the bear as I let my arrow fly, the arrow hitting the grizzly in the shoulder.

Fenrir gave a slight yelp, trying to stand but falling back to the ground. The grizzly roared, shaking his head as he tucked his ears to his skull and raced forward.

I tossed my bow and reached for my dagger. It would do little against this massive bear, but maybe it would be enough to wound him just enough for me to slip away with Fenrir. I needed to hit him where it counted, right between the eyes. There was a chance I would lose my kill, but in this situation, my life and Fen's were more important.

The grizzly came at me like a stampeding horse. I dug my heels into the ground, holding my dagger next to my ear. He raised his right arm, claws coming towards me, but I ducked, slicing upwards. The blade tore through the bear's flesh.

I rolled away, my dagger cutting into the bear's right leg. Blood spurted out, the sticky crimson dotting my face as I ducked and rolled away from the bear's lunge. I heard Fenrir's yelp, taking my eyes off the bear for a split second, but I snapped back to attention quickly. I couldn't focus on Fenrir just yet no matter how much my heart squeezed at the sound.

The grizzly dropped back down onto all fours and turned towards me. I tried to move away, but I had my back to a tree.

Shit.

The bear lumbered towards me, faster than he normally would. I gripped my dagger to my chest, waiting for him to come closer. I was hopeful that I would at *least* do some major damage by hitting him in a vital organ. The grizzly came for me, and I ducked as his claws ranked over the bark of the tree, right where my head had once been.

I slid away, my foot catching on a root, making me topple forward. I flipped over onto my back as the bear landed over me, roaring in my face, his left paw crushing my wrist with the dagger while the right paw was inches from my head. I gasped, hearing my bone crack from the sheer weight of the bear.

Spittle flew, coating my face as the predator raised his arm, ready to deliver the final blow. I turned my head away, raising my right arm over my face to cover my eyes from what was about to happen.

Blinding white light penetrated my eyelids, and the grizzly bear roared. The pressure from my chest lifted, and I was able to roll away as the bear's paws slammed into the earth right where my head had once been.

I bounded to my feet; the length of my arms covered in runes that bespoke of the ancient gods. The bear roared, stepping back away from me as my runes shone brighter, the light almost blinding my own eyes. The grizzly huffed, turned, and bounded back off into the wood.

I fell to my knees. The light from my runes slowly ebbed, but I could still feel the scorching fire beneath my skin as the magic swept through me—*illegal magic.*

Relief flooded through my veins but was quickly extinguished. Humans like myself weren't allowed to use magic, not that they ever could in the first place. Which made my abilities all the more unnatural. Magic was reserved only for the gods, and they would rather see someone dead than have magic roaming free.

I heard Fenrir's bark and rose to my feet. I raced over to him, my runes all but forgotten as I slid to my companion. He whimpered, his head on my lap, ears laid flat over his skull.

My heart shattered at seeing my boy hurt. He was drenched in blood, his right leg twisted at an odd angle. I noticed two ribs popping out of his flesh. I placed my hand over his head, closed my eyes, and searched my mind for the magic word that would heal.

"*Hvild,*" I whispered.

My runes blazed to life, this time going from the white light to a stunning midnight blue. I watched as my magic seeped into Fenrir, hearing his bones crack back into place. I cringed hearing it, but at least I knew that he was healing. Once he was patched up, I placed my free hand over the one that was nearly shattered from the grizzly's attack from earlier.

Slowly, the rune's light ebbed, and Fenrir was able to stand. He shook himself, tongue lolling to the side as he tackled me, his tail wagging.

"Fenrir!" I giggled, pushing him away. "Down, boy."

I managed to push him away and rise to my feet. I dusted myself off, walking back over to my kill. I grabbed my bow, slinging it over my shoulders, then grabbed my dagger from where I had dropped it during my fight with the bear. I continued to cut my buck. Fenrir was on high alert this time.

I was done within a matter of a hours, the entrails of the buck tossed to the side for other predators. I gestured for Fenrir to grab my satchel from the bushes, and he brought it back without a second thought. I dug into my bag, bringing out the rope and harness that I would use.

"Come." I got down on one knee, gesturing for my wolf to come forward. He walked over happily, turned around, and sat down so that his back was presented to me. I quickly strapped him in before I patted his head and tied the rest of our kill to his harness for him to pull.

I shouldered the rest, wincing at the pain in my side from the injury the grizzly had given me. I'd need to heal myself, but that would have to wait. I needed to get back before dark. I had already healed my hand, which was most important to carry everything back.

"Let's go, Fenrir." My fingers wrapped along the leather and together, we walked away from the wood and into the abyss.

THREE

F enrir and I walked for quite a while before we saw the looming city of Ellriheimr's gates before us. I slid the satchel from my shoulder to the earth, dug through to find my cloak, and clipped it to my shoulders to hide my runes.

If the gods ever found out what I possessed… I shook my head. I couldn't think about that right now.

I shouldered my pack once more and ushered Fenrir forward. He followed happily, but I could sense his unease the closer we walked to the city's gate. Ellriheimr was the biggest city of Röskr. Many cities had popped up through the years, but this was the only place that I could safely hide without worry because this was the largest in the realm and held the most people.

Not only was I a hunter, but a thief as well. I only took jobs that allowed me enough coin to survive off of, and even then, I mainly took jobs that didn't leave the confines of the city.

I wasn't like everyone else; I wouldn't take a job just to get myself some fame—if not death. Having these runes was enough for me.

I walked into the city with Fenrir by my side. The sun was setting, already coating the streets in shadows. People still walked about, but most had begun to hurry along. Mothers cradling children, men holding their purses a little tighter, and guards had begun to filter into the streets. We'd need to be quick if we were to make it home in time before the city-wide curfew.

I stopped, glancing at Fenrir. "Come on, boy. We need to move faster."

He huffed, following me as I began to walk through the streets once more.

A wall built by the previous ruler guarded Ellriheimr long before I was ever born. Since then, no other attacking force had destroyed it. Rather, the subsequent rulers made it stronger. Said it was essential to our survival. I wasn't sure why, though, as all the attacking nations had calmed down centuries before.

The gods built this city as more of a safe haven for us humans, since this realm was created specifically for us. We didn't have magic, nor the gift of longevity; we were mortals.

The buildings were all made of brick. Some were created using silver and iron ore they had procured from the dwarves. Others held some items gifted to them by the elves. The rest were either made by human hands or the aid of the giants.

By now, the sun had nearly rested beneath the world, the moon taking its place. The streets were coated in darkness, and I could almost *hear* the thieves salivating at anyone who traveled the streets unattended, bags filled with coin or other valuables they could procure. Luckily for me, I had Fenrir, and most wouldn't dare cross me.

Most.

I turned down the intersection that was only a few blocks from my home, watching as a few people darted inside, quickly locking the doors behind them. My grip on my leather straps tightened, and I swallowed thickly as I took hurried steps forward.

I wasn't afraid by any means, but today's excursion had taken its toll on me, and I was ready for a hot bath and something warm in my belly.

I saw my home in the distance, and I almost sighed in relief when three dark figures emerged from an alleyway, blocking my path. So close. I had almost made it home this time without being stopped by a group of petty thieves.

Almost.

The leader of the group was a tall young man, his red hair braided away from his face, his chin and cheeks coated in a coppery shade of whisker. He had a scar on his left eye, a longsword strapped to his hip, his shirt sleeves torn clean off to display muscle and the tattoos he had. The other two appeared to be twins, as I could barely tell the difference between them, but it wouldn't matter in the end.

"Dalmar. Gisili. Look what we have 'yer." The red-haired man grinned at me, his arms folded over his chest. "A young woman that strayed too far from home."

"A pretty thing." One of the twins—Gisili, maybe?—licked his lips.

Fenrir made his presence known as he stalked forward, head bowed low and a growl coming from his throat. The twins took a few steps back, but their leader didn't budge.

I narrowed my eyes, my skin itching to use my magic. But I needed to keep myself in check. I stamped down the urge quickly and swallowed, allowing myself a moment to think.

"What brings such a pretty thing like you out at this late hour?" The man tilted his head, inspecting the satchel and the buck's fur I carried along with it. "Hunting, I see?"

"You could say that," I replied. "But I don't think your feeble mind could comprehend—"

He stepped closer, his smile never leaving his face. "What else do you have in that bag of yours?"

"Nothing of importance to you." I gripped my leather straps. "But if you don't move out of my way, my companion here will make sure you remember to stay in your place."

He laughed. "That dog doesn't scare me."

I raised a brow. "Who said anything about a dog?"

His laugh faded as Fenrir took another step forward, what little light left illuminating his features for the three shitty thieves before me. His eyes went wide when my wolf lunged forward, the twins already tucked tail and gone back into the alley. Fen was fast enough that he could have taken a chunk out of each of them, but he was slow in his attempt to harm the thieves.

"I'll remember this." The man danced away from Fenrir's maw, ducking into the alleyway that his goons disappeared into.

FOUR

I'm sure you will," I muttered to myself.

I sighed and continued our trek back to my home. I walked up the steps, dug around for my keys, and unlocked the door. I held it open for Fenrir to skirt past me, the bundle of meat and fur sliding across the floor into the living space. I stepped through, closing the door and placing my forehead to the wood, letting a sigh escape me.

My home was a two-room place with a bedroom and a bathroom. There was a kitchen that was connected to the living room. It wasn't much, but at least it was a place for me to stay. Mother made sure we paid this place off before she died so that I wouldn't have to worry about it. I still did—but not for the reasons she thought I would.

I slid my satchel from my shoulders, letting it fall to the ground. I removed my cloak and turned, seeing Fenrir sitting down, waiting expectantly for his dinner.

I got down on one knee and began to unshackle him from his harness. Once that was done, I dug through the bundle of meat. I chose the biggest of the bunch and tossed it to him. Blood coated my fingers, and I stood. I put everything in an icebox for the next several weeks before I walked into my bathroom.

I turned on the lights, illuminating the space. It was a simple bathroom with a tub, toilet, and sink. I shed my clothing, wrinkling my nose when I caught a whiff of myself. I padded over to my tub, settled down along the rim, and turned on the water. Lukewarm water spurted out of the faucet and into the tub, already getting cold within a matter of moments.

I was thankful that when Ellriheimr was built, the dwarves had been kind enough to draw up some indoor plumbing. While not warm, it was preferable to going out after dark to the bathhouses.

I closed my eyes, dipped my hand into the water, and spoke the words that would ignite the heat within my skin.

"*Fiðri*," I whispered.

I was weary of using my magic outside of my home. Out in the forest, I was primarily alone. Sure, the gods could be watching me through the eyes of ravens or just simply sneak up on me. At least while I was home, I could somewhat relax because I know that the gods couldn't possibly see me through the roof of my home.

The runes along my skin turned back into that blue color, the magic within me sweltering before it swam into my hand, the heat coating my skin. Steam began to rise from the water, and I didn't hesitate as I dipped in. I sighed, the water cascading over my shoulders. I laid my head back, allowing myself a moment to breathe in the steam, the hot water helping my muscles unwind from the day.

After a moment, I sat forward, reaching out to the small table at my tub side, grabbing my soap and sponge. I quickly cleaned my skin until it was pink and raw. I kept my arms over the runes that had been tattooed on my skin for as long as I could remember. Sometimes, I had scrubbed them so much that I wished I could wash them away. It never worked.

Clean, I got out of my tub, walking over to my rack to grab a towel before tossing it around my body. I picked up another and stepped over to the mirror in my bathroom. I stood before it, gazing at my reflection.

I would often think that I had resembled my mother—but sometimes I would look like my father. I had his green eyes, but that was the only thing that tied me to him. Everything else was my mother. From my black-silver hair to my button nose and round cheeks. I even had her fiery determination—something my father once chastised me for before he died.

Nestled on a chain around my neck was a vial of my mother's ashes. Vines from the Yggdrasil tree coiled around it, like it was trying to embrace her even in death. I reached up, running my thumb over the smooth glass.

"Never take this off, Eira," my mother had told me as she handed me the empty vial. *"Because once I'm gone, this is all you'll have of me to remember."*

At the time, I thought it was a silly gesture. My mother was only in her early thirties when I had turned fifteen and she'd given this to me. I thought her invincible until the day I came home from my last hunt for the winter and saw her dead on our living room floor. Fenrir howled for hours, and I held her for just as long, wondering how I should deal with her body.

Thoughts swirled through my mind like the ticking of a clock. Anger, remorse, hatred, and sadness.

How would I survive without my mother? How could I even think to take care of myself? I was barely sixteen; I couldn't fend for myself, not really. What could I do without my mother?

Burying her wasn't an option. It had been already dark by the time I had discovered her body, and it would take a full day before her body would burn to ashes. It was risky business, but we in Röskr didn't believe in burials, anyway.

It's said that once you pass on from this life, the only way to become one with the gods was to be burned. I was never one to follow age-old traditions, but I also wasn't one to go against my mother's wishes.

She had once told me that when it was her time to go, she wanted to be burned, and so I kept my promise to her.

The very next morning, before the sun came up, I hoisted her on my back and carried her out into the small clearing outside the city gates. No one bothered me, but they all knew where I was going by the way I carried my mother's body, wrapped in a cloth with the runes of life and death scrawled in ink along the parchment.

Fenrir and I watched as my mother's corpse burned. We stayed outside for hours, observing the cinders and smoke until nothing was left but her ashes. I scooped them up and placed them into the vial. I've never taken it off since.

I sighed and dropped my fingers from the necklace. I walked out of the bathroom and into my bedroom. It was smaller than my bathroom, with just a single window, a chest to hold my belongings, and a bed. Fenrir pranced into my room, waiting for me. I crawled into bed and held out my arms for my wolf. I was hungry, but the fatigue outweighed my need to eat.

He yelped, jumped into my arms, and snuggled in right beside me like he did every night for the last five years. I buried my face into his fur, inhaling the scent of pine and something else that Fenrir liked to coat himself in. It wasn't unpleasant, but it was better than blood and mud.

I sighed, closing my eyes and willing myself to sleep. I hoped for my sake that I would have a dreamless sleep for once. Hoped that I wouldn't be plagued with the memories of my past, haunted by the fact that I was hiding from the gods.

FIVE

y dreams were plagued with dread and despair. I almost always dreamed of my mother and each time, the setting and times were different. Once, I thought my dreams were so real that I couldn't sleep for days before I ultimately collapsed from exhaustion. Fenrir had been by my side, but other than that, I woke up alone and lost.

Today was no different. I wasn't sure if it was because of the loss of my mother, or the gods were pulling tricks on me.

I knew that they would learn of me eventually. Of the magic I can wield—something a human should never possess, let alone use. I forced myself out of bed, doing my best not to disturb Fenrir as he rested.

I decided that I would go off to the city to find myself some work. Already, my home was filled with food, so I will spend the rest of my time making as much coin as I could to keep the roof over my head. While we had paid the home in full, I still had an upkeep and bills to pay when the tax collector showed up once a month.

This month, I had enough coin to pay and last me half the week, but I would need more for the next month and the next. Yesterday was our weekly hunting trip, and it was mostly so that my companion could be himself out in the wild, something he couldn't do in the city while I was out completing my nefarious work.

Dressing as if there were a fire beneath me, I walked over to my bed, settling down and bending so that I could lace up my boots. I made sure I nestled my obsidian dagger within, but that was the extent of the weapons I would need and carry.

Rifling through my trunk, my fingers touched the slick, cool leather of my gloves. I brandished them, making sure they were high enough on my skin to cover each inch of my arms so that my runes weren't visible to the naked eye. A cloak would not be sufficient by any means once I was out and about. It was broad daylight, an easier time for someone to notice.

I made sure that Fenrir was sound asleep before I left our home. The sun was high in the sky, the bright blue of the heavens streaked through with clouds heavy with rain. Perhaps I should have brought my cloak.

I turned my head, debating whether I should go back inside, but ultimately, I decided it would be best not to go back in. I would find myself back in bed with my companion, sleeping the day away. No, I had things to do today.

I walked into the city. Unlike yesterday evening, the streets were bustling with activity. Shops were opened with their many vendors outside them, yelling and calling for prospecting patrons to come forth to check their wares. It was tempting, but I couldn't afford such luxuries. I had enough to get by, but trinkets and gems were not on my spending list.

The Grand Library of Ellriheimr was the largest building in the entire city—almost as tall as the cathedral at the west end. The library was shorter, but it was wider to house the many books it had procured throughout the centuries.

Outside the doors, an overweight man was standing on a few boxes, holding out a flyer that I couldn't quite make out.

I shuffled closer, my interest piqued the moment I heard someone's name.

"Oeric…" the man's voice boomed, creating an audience for a couple of blocks. He spread his arms wide, holding up the flyer I still couldn't see. "…was once a kind and just god—until he lost his eye."

Ah yes. I rolled my eyes. *As if talking about the eleven gods of the Nine Realms meant something to these people.*

They had left centuries ago, not once coming back down. The Nine Realms thrived without them as they loafed around in Ásjá, drinking and whoring to their hearts' content. Of course, there were still some people who worshipped them, dedicating their lives to the service of the gods.

Or so I was told, anyway. Mother hated the gods as much as I did. It's the main reason she hid me and my illegal magic for as long as I could remember.

She had said there was another reason, but she had never specified. I also never pried further.

Never trust a god, Eira. They'd sooner put a blade through your heart than a grain of salt in your hand.

I snorted. Those were the words I lived by, but the eleven gods have never resurfaced, so it wasn't like I would ever speak to one, let alone even *see* one. It was an odd phrasing, one I had admitted to my mother, but she would scold me for thinking such things.

"They built Röskr to house the mortals," the man continued. "It was from our savior that humans survived the Last War. Today, my friends, I saw a sign that another war is coming, one that will be the end of everything."

A collective gasp raced through the crowd, and I crossed my arms, brow raised. I had heard this prophecy for so long that it was almost ingrained in my memory.

Ragnarök.

It was a myth, a legend really. No one had seen the gods in centuries, and the other creatures of the realms stayed within their borders. Oeric made sure that no one could leave their realms, all ties to the Yggdrasil severed completely. It was a way for him to ensure Ragnarök would never happen, but many still believed it would come. They just didn't know when.

I turned away from the madman with the flyer, returning to my main course: the library. I sifted through the crowd of people eager to hear the crazed man's words, a few knocking into me like they couldn't even see me. It was different—knowing I held magic. I never considered myself to be human because of the power I could use, but there was nothing else that I could call myself.

I certainly wasn't as tall as a giant, nor was I a dwarf that dug for gold and ore. I could use magic like the elves, but I didn't have pointy ears or an elongated chin that made me look like I was frowning all the time. A demon was way out of the picture. I would assert that I was a witch from Eiði, however, the entire species had been extinguished long before I ever came into being.

Even then, the teachings and legends never said anything about runes being carved into their skins. I held no place in this world.

I pushed all thoughts from my mind as I ascended the steps, dodging a group of women clutching books to their chests, their giggles coursing through me.

I felt a pang in my chest at seeing the women laughing together. I was a loner by choice. Don't get me wrong, I wanted friends as much as the next person, but it wasn't in the cards for me. I was an anomaly, and with these runes… companionship simply wouldn't work in my favor. Besides, I had Fenrir.

The library was indeed spacious. It was one of the last few remaining in the entire Nine Realms. Oeric had destroyed all other libraries, leaving this one for the mortals to read through and learn. I assumed it had something to do with us worshiping them.

The library's main quarter was a massive, oval-shaped space. It held a seating area with plants, desks, and chairs. Along the right side of it were dozens of shelves filled with tomes. To the left of the quarter was a desk with an older woman seated behind it, her hair tied up into a tight and clean bun, her fingers shuffling through papers.

Further in were endless shelves and darkness. There were pillars that held up the building, coupled with a dozen or so windows that let the light filter in. A white birch tree was nestled in the middle of the library, leaves full and golden.

It was a way for the humans to connect with our one great tree, the Yggdrasil. Carved into the bark of the tree were the runes of each realm, the middle being Röskr: the home of the humans.

I ignored the librarian, breezing on in. I knew where I was going; it was almost like breathing. I halted by the tree for a moment, my hands running up the bark, my fingers tracing over the runes of my home realm before I dropped my hand and continued on my path.

Towards the end of the massive library was a long, almost haphazard bookshelf hallway. Not many trekked this far as they were afraid of it collapsing on them, while others would wander through it just for the hell of it. I, however, came here for a different purpose.

I glanced around for a moment, hoping no one was in the vicinity before I shifted my weight and walked in. Shadows curled closer, almost as if ghostly fingers embraced me like a long-lost lover.

I thrived in the shadows; it was like a second home to me. I walked three steps and then stopped, turning my head slightly.

My gaze caught on the book I was searching for.

The History of Röskr.

I grabbed the book and pulled it free from the shelf—right as a hand shot out of the space where the book was, holding a piece of paper. I would have been startled if I hadn't done this so often. I reached out, took the paper, and then replaced the book before I stuffed the paper into the sleeve of my gloves.

We exchanged no words, no names, places—nothing. It was the most efficient way of doing these nefarious jobs. But it also meant that I'd received a random one.

I bit my lip and stared down at the folded piece of parchment. My fingers twitched. I wanted to open it, but I needed to wait until I got home. It was safer there.

SIX

I opened the door to my home, instantly greeted by Fenrir, as he jumped from the floor in the living room. He pranced over, tail wagging and tongue lolled out to the side. I stroked his head before tearing off my gloves. They made my skin itch.

The parchment fell out of the glove when I tossed it on the ground, and I groaned. I walked over to my couch, settling as I gestured to the rolled-up letter on the floor. "Fetch."

Fenrir barked at me before he turned and walked over to the glove. He placed a paw on the glove, gently using his nose and teeth so as to not damage the paper. Once it rolled out, he grabbed it between his canines, walking back over to me slowly and carefully.

I took the parchment from his mouth, wrapping my arms around his neck. I snuggled deep into his fur, loving the way he smelled so much like the earth and wilds beyond the city. I would never take him for granted. I lost my mother and father, but I wouldn't lose Fenrir. Not if I had anything to say about it.

I unrolled the parchment to read what this new job would be.

Find the ring. West end district. Half past midnight. Karsten.

Could it have been anymore vague? The west end district was for the highborn nobles and where the Jarl of Ellriheimr lived. I also knew it to have the highest security.

Of course I had to have received the hardest of jobs in the entire city. I could not understand what it meant by "find the ring."

Rings weren't hard to come by. You could easily have them made. Which begged the question of what *kind* of ring this was. Many of the old relics were destroyed long ago, around the same time Oeric had closed off the realms. The ring could hold magical capabilities, but humans couldn't wield magic.

Save for me. Not that I would tell anyone that.

"What am I going to do, Fen?" I asked my wolf, who had settled at my feet.

I was no stranger to the hard jobs, but I also would need to find a way to inside the west end, which was also just as hard. I was in the South District. It wasn't the poorest by any means, but it also wasn't the richest either. I sighed, massaging my eyes as if that would solve all my problems, when I heard a knock at my door.

I rolled the parchment back up and tossed it behind the couch. I couldn't risk anyone else seeing it. While it may have been daylight outside, it was still risky to have your business out and about. There was no telling who would see and think you were up to no good.

The knock came a second time, and I rose. Fenrir followed closely at my heels. He wasn't growling, so it wasn't any of our enemies, of which we had many. A third knock came, this time more forceful.

"I'm coming!" I shouted. I stomped the rest of the way over, throwing open the door, right in a guard's face.

I blinked. "I'm sorry. I meant no—"

"Are you a single woman?" The guard's words were short and clipped, hinting at his annoyance.

My mouth dropped open. "Excuse me? What kind of question is that? Who comes to my home and—"

"Jarl Lott has requested all eligible women come to his ball tonight. I was told by several of your neighbors that you were… single."

I tried to hide my embarrassment as I peeked my head out into the street. The passersby ducked their heads and shuffled quickly to their destinations, avoiding eye contact. If I wasn't in the presence of this guard, I'd… do what, exactly?

"Miss?" The guard tilted his head, moving in my line of sight.

I blinked, tearing my gaze away from the people who had just sent this guard to my door. "I'm sorry. What did you say exactly?"

He raised a brow at me. "Jarl Lott has requested all eligible women to attend to his ball tonight."

"Not that part, the other part."

He looked exasperated with me, but I didn't care. What luck had this guard stepped into? Here I was wondering how I would get into the West District and find this ring, and my solution just knocked on my door. Surely this wasn't a coincidence?

And even if it were, was this a prayer from whoever had sent me that paper? There was only one way to find out for sure.

"I'll accept it." I smiled up at the guard, ignoring what he had just told me a second time.

The guard watched me carefully, like I had accepted the invitation so easily. Surely, I could have told him no and had him leave my home, but then I wouldn't have this chance to sneak around and get what I needed from them.

"The West District will be open for all women. But your *dog* needs to stay here," he grunted, sliding a side eye at my companion.

Fenrir barked, jumping forward with a snarl. The guard took several steps back, almost falling off my steps in the process. I got down on my knees, wrapped an arm around his massive neck, and smiled at the guard.

"Fen doesn't like to be referred to as a dog," I told him simply. "He's a pure-blooded wolf."

The man quickly collected himself, clearing his throat and walking away without another word. The people in the streets had all but stopped to see what was happening, and when Fen and I turned in their direction, they ran for the hills like I had set a fire beneath them.

"Well, Fen," I said as I scratched him behind the ears, "guess I'm going to a party tonight, huh?"

EIGHT

I wasn't one who typically liked parties, especially ones you had to dress up for. I preferred fighting with that bear again over drinking a cup of firewater. I also didn't have a single thing to wear for this shindig.

Honestly, this whole thing was strange to me, but if it was a way for me to get into the West District, I would have to take it.

I walked back into my room. I had closed up most of my mother's belongings, burning them with her so that she could have something in the afterlife. I kept some of her stuff, but the majority had long since been scorched to ashes.

I wasn't proper by any means, but my mother had made sure that I knew my manners around others, nobles especially. They were rare in this district, but they weren't in hiding. They'd rather spend their days holed up in their massive homes rather than out and about.

I bent down by my bed. Fenrir followed me, but he seemed none too happy with me going out alone. He always came with me. The only exceptions were like today when I went to the library to procure this job for us.

Many associated him as being merely a wolf-dog, never a full wolf. They weren't... the greatest of pets, but with enough love and devotion, they were the most loyal and kind animals around.

Reaching underneath my springs, my fingers wrapped around something leather, and I pulled it. A small trunk slid out, covered in dust and smelling like rotten wood. The hinges creaked when I opened it, dust spiraling out and coating both me and Fenrir. I coughed, waving my hand in the air to dispel it, then I reached inside it to pull forth what I had come for.

My mother's black wedding dress.

It was the nicest thing my mother ever owned, being what she wore when she married my father. It wasn't traditional of course. It was long and made out of the finest silk imaginable. My father must have paid a pretty penny for this, as it was defiantly not made within the confines of Röskr.

The bodice was cinched a little too tightly, just enough that my breasts would bunch up a little to make them seem fuller. The dress fanned out at the hips, but not so much that it would appear as if I was holding something beneath it. It had sleeves, but they were see-through so I would need to wear some black gloves to make sure that my runes weren't visible. There was a cape with it, but I tossed it aside, as I would not need it.

I took out the dress, standing up to lay it flat on the bed. I turned to close the trunk but saw a picture nestled in the bottom. I hastily dropped to my knees, taking the picture in my hands as gentle as I could. The picture was of my mother and father on their wedding day.

I had only seen a picture of my father once, back when I was curious to know why he wasn't around when everyone else had theirs. Mother had explained that he had gone off to war and never returned. I ended up finding a picture of him later that day and went to show her what I had found. She scolded me and then removed the picture from my grasp. I'd never spoken about it since.

Now, looking at this picture, it was hard not to see just how in love they appeared to be with each other. My father had long red hair that was shaved on both sides, a braided tail swung over his shoulder. He was covered in tattoos, but his weren't like the ones I held on my own body. His beard was wrapped with small beads, a smile on his face as he held my mother's hand.

My heart stopped as I continued to gaze at the picture. I was the spitting image of my mother, right down to every last detail, save for my eyes. Her hair was longer than my father's, braided with beads, feathers, and all manner of other objects. She wore the cape. In her hand she cradled a bouquet of flowers, ones not native to Röskr. They almost resembled the Midnight Florence, which thrived within Möl.

Fenrir whimpered, his tail tucked between his legs as he walked over to me, ears laid flat on his head as he plopped down beside me, his eyes taking in the image I held in my hands. I couldn't help the small smile that rose to my lips when I noticed poor little Fen in the picture, almost hidden beneath the folds of my mother's dress.

Fat tears dripped onto the picture, my eyes not being able to focus. I wiped my eyes with the back of my hand, while the other still clutched the picture. I had allowed myself not to grieve for so long. I believed that if I just kept moving no matter what, I would be able to get over my emotions, but I was so very wrong.

Now, seeing this picture of my parents, it struck a chord within me. It was almost like I was seeing them with fresh eyes.

The sound of the nearby clock tower's bell chimed, and I dropped the picture. The glass shattered at my feet, and I scrambled to try to reclaim the pieces, the shards cutting into my hands and legs, but I didn't care. I couldn't save the glass, but at least I could save the picture. I dusted off the shards, cradling the picture of my parents to my chest, even as blood oozed from my fingers.

The bell chimed a second time, signaling that it was near time for me to get ready and go. I had a long walk ahead of me, but I couldn't force myself to move.

I sighed and placed the picture on my nightstand, grabbed the dress, and began to change. The dress was a little tight on my hips and chest, but there was no time to find an alternative. I just had to focus on reaching my destination as quickly as possible. I ran my thumb over the vial wrapped around my throat, almost choking with emotion.

Mother never wanted me to live this life. She had told me for so long that I deserved better, that I should leave Ellriheimr and go somewhere else.

But where else would I be able to go? Traveling between realms was forbidden, and even if you could travel, you would need every ounce of magic you could use. I was human, and I could not.

Almost as if in answer, the runes along my arms blazed to life, blinking as if they were trying to say otherwise.

I chewed my bottom lip. I couldn't focus on leaving. At least, not yet.

I grabbed a fistful of my hair and tossed the heaping mass out of the dress. I would do nothing with it. This dress would be enough. I didn't exchange my boots, but I did leave off the cape in favor of my gloves. It wasn't the best, but at least it was better than nothing at all.

Fenrir watched me from our bed, his eyes following me around the room as I got ready. I dug through my trunk, finding the sheath I could use for my dagger. However, this dress didn't sport a slit on the side for me to quickly access my blade, so I would have to once again settle with it nestled in my boot.

Once I was done, I tucked the parchment into my sleeve, gave Fenrir a kiss on the head goodbye, and began my long trek to the West District.

NINE

Already, the streets were beginning to fill up once more. The guards were out in abundance today, as well. Everyone knew how dangerous it was for a single soul to be out in the city without a weapon, so it stood to reason that the Jarl would have his men out and about to protect the women that would be making their way to his home for this party that had yet to be named.

I followed at a slow pace. I wasn't overly eager to arrive, but I also didn't want to be the last to do so, either. I wanted to get there with enough time for me to search the premises.

I had until half past midnight to get this ring. I assume the name Karsten was the man who possessed it, but the letter had been so vague, it could easily mean that the ring belonged to the man who had sent me off on this heinous mission.

I was making ample time. A lot of the women would stop to chat or complain about their feet hurting.

I secretly grinned each time I passed a gaggle of girls. They seemed so intent on this party that they had no need for self-preservation. I was no fool; I was observing my surroundings.

With each moment the clock ticked, the closer it grew to darkness, to bloodshed. The guards knew this, as every so often I would watch them force the women to walk.

Jarl Lott had something up his sleeve for sure, but I wouldn't focus on that detail. I had to remain steadfast on my mission. Perhaps afterwards I could investigate his affairs, but certainly not now. The minutes stretched on, and I was beginning to get rather bored walking by myself.

The home of the Jarl soon rose above the other buildings. A rather too large house, if you'd ask me. I'd never seen another Jarl's home before, but my mother would tell me that they would grow immensely, depending on who lived there.

There was a longhouse set in the middle, with two more on either side connected by a small, covered hallway. There were two more longhouses that were placed on top, making it triple its size. The grounds were crawling with women and thralls.

My steps slowed as I neared, the girls around me walking a little faster to reach the Jarl.

"Get moving," a passing guard scolded me. "It's already dark out."

"I know." I shot him a glare before I continued on. I heard him mutter under his breath, but I couldn't catch what it was that he said. Best to leave it for now. I had bigger fish to fry.

I glanced up at the sky, seeing the once baby blue morphed into the darkest ebony, stars twinkling into existence. The moon was full but partially covered by the clouds. Shadows blanketed everything around me, and I couldn't help but feel enveloped in them, almost like they were embracing me like a long-lost friend.

I stepped onto the grounds of the Jarl's home, hearing the sounds of drums and music pouring out of the front entrance. I lifted up the hem of my dress, careful not to catch myself on a step and fall over. It would be an unpleasant business, and I couldn't risk wasting any more time than I already had.

The bottom longhouse was filled with food, dancing, and music. A long table spanned the entire length of the room. Food that would have taken me weeks to fill, if not longer, was on every inch of it. Barrels of mead and other drinks were on the other end of the room, men standing by it pouring themselves their own tankards.

I licked my lips. Mead sounded great right now. But I had to focus.

Easily slipping into the shadows, my black dress blended in seamlessly. I watched as women mingled, giggled, and acted like fools around the others present. I stopped short, almost running into a man with red hair tied into a bun at the nape of his neck, his skin crawling with tattoos of ravens and trees. He noticed me, brow raised in question.

"What are you doing in the darkness?" he asked me, perplexed.

I cleared my throat, fanning my face. "I may have drunk a little too much. I was thinking of going to the second floor, as it may be a lot quieter."

"Hm." He studied me, those dark blue eyes washing over me. "I don't think the second floor would be the best for you. That's where the dancing is."

"Dancing?"

He turned to me, both brows raised now. "Do you not know how? It's one of the main reason for this—"

"Oh, there you are, my darling!"

The man and I turned at the sound of the unfamiliar voice. An arm wrapped around my shoulders, drawing me to the person's side. My instinct to draw my dagger rose in my mind, but I stamped it down. No need to let anyone know that I was packing and get sent away before finding that ring.

I glanced up at the man with his arm wrapped over my shoulders and almost swooned at the sight of him. He was a little on the shorter side but still several inches taller than me. I could feel the muscle that was beneath his shirt. The front portion of his blond hair was pulled back, the sides braided and coated in various beads and twine. The rest of his hair cascaded just underneath his neck. His blue eyes were almost as dark as the night sky, with a twinkle in them that captured me.

His entire body, or what little I could see, was covered in various tattoos. There were so many that it was hard for me to decipher each and every one. He had a crooked nose that had seen far too many fists, and his sharp features were covered with blondish-red stubble.

"I was wondering where you'd gotten off to." His voice was low, husky, almost like he was saving it just for me. "I've been looking everywhere for you."

The red-haired man observed me for a moment before his gaze strayed over to the blond Adonis beside me.

I should have pushed the man away, should have told him to get off his high horse, but I was too enamored with his handsome face that I couldn't even think of anything that *wasn't* him. Worse still was the scent of him. He smelled of frost, pine, and merlot. A scent that both intrigued me and terrified me.

The other man squared his shoulders, arms crossed over his chest. "I didn't take you for being a lady's man, Karsten."

Karsten.

I now looked at the man beside me with fresh eyes. Was this who held the ring?

I shuffled a little closer into his side, making it seem as if I were warming into his embrace, when I was really looking for the ring on his fingers. I searched the hand around my shoulders before peering up at Karsten through my lashes, pouring on the seduction.

My heart fell. There weren't any rings on this man's hands, so would that mean he was the contact? If so, how had he been able to seek me out so quickly? Was I that obvious?

"I thought single ladies were the only ones coming," the other man continued. "Not ones already tied to someone."

Karsten's embrace on me tightened, and I sucked in a breath. "Yes, but this one I fancied."

"I don't think the Jarl would—"

"Ah." Karsten dismissively waved the other man away. "Lott will get over it. It's not like he doesn't have *three* longhouses filled with women eager to bed him."

I stifled a gasp. Just who was this Karsten man that thought he could talk about Jarl Lott in this way? It was a death sentence to say such treasonous things.

Karsten glanced down at me, cracking a grin. "Come now, darling. Shall we go somewhere… quieter, perhaps?"

I opened my mouth to say something, but he reached down, took my hand, and ushered me away. I could feel the other man's eyes on me, but I didn't dare turn back to look. Doing so would make him even more suspicious than he already was.

I followed Karsten around the room, opening a door that led further into the longhouse. I dug my heels in, but he was far stronger than me. I tried to reach for my boot, but each time my foot connected with a step, my hand would slip, and I would miss the handle of my dagger.

He opened the door to another room, this one awash with brightly lit colors. At least fifty or so people were out on the floor dancing and drinking, and some were even having more fun in the shadows away from prying eyes if their moans and gasps gave any hints.

I dug my heels in for a second time, finally able to slip my hand through this mysterious man. His touch was almost euphoric, his scent so damn dangerous that I was afraid to get lost in that smell. I crossed my arms, glowering at him like I'd seen Fenrir do a hundred times before.

"Who are you?" I demanded, narrowing my eyes.

Karsten held out his hand, that wicked grin spreading over his lips again. "Dance with me."

My glower slid from his outstretched fingers to his face, my heart beating like a caged bird as my features softened. I was always a sucker for a pretty face. While my experience with men wasn't the greatest, I always found myself admiring them from afar.

Still, I jutted my chin. "I don't think so."

He took a step closer, lowering his head slightly. "I know what you're searching for. If you wish to acquire it, you'll need my help to do so."

I studied him for a second too long. This definitely wasn't a coincidence anymore. This "Karsten" knew what I was here for, which meant that he was the reason this party was in full swing. It was probably the easiest way to get people into the Jarl's home. It was smart, but was I willing to go this far into the World Serpent's den?

I glanced at his fingers, weighing my options. This handsome stranger was my only hope of finding this ring and getting paid. I finally let out a resigned sigh, placed my hand into his, and allowed him to take me out onto the dance floor.

TEN

My experience with dancing was far worse than it was with men. Mother had tried to teach me several times, but I had always made up some excuse to never learn. She had insisted it was essential, but I told myself that I would never use it in this life.

I was so wrong.

Karsten rested a hand on my hip and captured my other, while my remaining hand laid on his shoulder. We swayed to the music, but each time I moved my foot, I would crush his own. I caught him wince a few times, his grip on my hip tightening a little whenever my foot connected with his own. I would have felt bad for him, but to me, he was holding me hostage.

"You said you wanted to talk." I ducked my head, hoping no one would notice me or recognize my face. "So talk."

He tsked. "So forward, darling."

I bristled, my lips curling in disgust. "Don't call me that."

"All right, love. What do you want to talk about?" A shit-eating grin formed on his face.

I stamped down my irritation but held my chin up so that I could look him in the eye. "Who are you?"

"You already know my name. Karsten," he chuckled.

I narrowed my eyes. My right boot connected with his knee. "Sorry, *Karsten*. My foot slipped."

"Indeed," he quipped with a wince.

"I won't ask again," I told him, more insistent this time. "Who are you?"

He sighed. "My name cannot be disclosed at the moment, but I was the one who had need of your skills."

I frowned at him. "That's not how that works. Those papers are random. You couldn't have known it would have been me."

"Oh, but I did." He glanced around, his other hand slipping into my own, so now he held both. "Come. This place isn't safe."

"What do you—"

He pulled me away from the dancefloor and straight towards the shadows. *Oh, hell no.* I immediately put on the brakes, trying to slip free from his touch.

There was only one reason why a man would want a woman alone in the shadows. My runes began to blaze to life through the fabric of my gloves and I startled, trying to calm down my racing nerves. I couldn't let anyone see my magic, especially not here.

Karsten spun me forward, my back to the wall, his hands on either side of my head as he leaned in, his lips dangerously close to my own. "Listen to me carefully," he whispered, "because this is the only chance we have of getting back my ring."

I swallowed, my eyes never leaving his lips. "O—okay."

A couple walked by us, and he dipped his head into my shoulder and neck, his lips touching the sensitive parts of my skin. My knees grew weak, and if it weren't for the wall, I would have fallen to the floor. Once the couple left, he drew back, his eyes boring into mine.

"Jarl Lott has my ring, but we have until half past midnight to get it," he said, all seriousness again. Not even a hint that he knew what he was doing to me present.

"Why such a specific time?" I gestured toward everyone around us with a nod. "This place is crawling with distractions."

"Because once we exceed that time limit, I must return to my realm."

My mouth formed an O. "*Realm?* Where are you from?"

My gaze traveled down the length of him. He wasn't tall enough to be a giant, nor was he short enough to be a dwarf. He didn't have elongated ears, and he certainly wasn't a god—at least, not that I could tell.

He didn't acknowledge my question. "The Jarl keeps his belongings on the floor above us. One of us needs to distract him so the other can get the ring." His eyes dropped down to my chest, lingering there before he looked at my lips, then my eyes. "You should be able to seduce him long enough to for me to slip through and get my ring."

"Seducing isn't part of the job description." I wrinkled my nose at him. "You hired me as a thief, nothing else."
He chuckled. "You are a little spitfire. I love that."

I narrowed my eyes at him. "I don't care what you think or have to say. I'm not seducing him."

"Not with those gloves you're not." He gripped my arm, his hand going to my glove. "If you showed some skin perhaps—"

"*No.*"

I swiftly drew away from him and wrapped my arms around myself. These gloves were the only thing that held my magic at bay. If this man saw them... I shuddered. Karsten withdrew, his eyes narrowing as he inspected my gloves. For a moment, it looked like he noticed the white light beneath them, but he shook his head as if to clear it instead.

"*Fine.*" He set his feet apart and crossed his arms. "I'll distract him while you get the ring."

I blinked, glancing around the room. There were so many people that it would be hard for me to go unnoticed. Especially when his guards were posted around every corner of the room, watching everyone. "How am I supposed to get into his room?"

He shrugged a shoulder. "Perhaps if we'd stick to my—"

"We're not," I interjected.

"Well then, you'd better think of something before—"

"Karsten!"

We both froze as a man walked over to us. His long red hair was streaked with more gray than red. His clothes were embroidered with every rune imaginable, a silver crown placed upon his brow, a cape draped over his shoulders. His hands were covered in jewelry, and I inspected each and every one of them, judging there value.

Jarl Lott.

Nothing screamed important to me, and clearly not for Karsten either, as he didn't react to the many rings, which led me to believe that the Jarl wasn't wearing this fabled ring.

I inched closer as Karsten smiled broadly, clapping the Jarl on the shoulder and gesturing to the people in the room.

"Quite the party, eh?" Karsten smiled.

Jarl Lott laughed. "It was your idea, after all, old friend."

I waited in the darkness, watching as Karsten spun the Jarl around and walked him in the opposite direction. I slinked along the wall, keeping myself as flat to it as possible. Many of the couples that were hidden in these shadows were far too busy with each other that they weren't paying any attention to their surrounding.

A shout, followed by a slew of curses, rang out, and I halted. I angled my head slightly toward the noise, searching the area for what was causing the commotion. Two men were fighting each other, a woman crying a few feet away. The guards near the doors sprang into action, trying to staunch the brawl.

I used that distraction to my advantage, almost jogging to the door that led into the third and final longhouse of the Jarl's domain. I wasn't exactly sure what to expect, but at least I was away from Karsten's sinful face.

I opened the door, slid on through, and began to ascend the stairs.

ELEVEN

I took the steps two at a time, hoping that there would be no one in Lott's private quarters. I would think his wife would be there, but he hadn't remarried since the last wife left him for another man. While common for a Jarl to remarry, it appeared to me that Lott rather preferred the bachelor life.

I made it to the top of the stairs, almost sighing in relief when I saw there were no lights on. Then I heard a voice from up ahead and stopped mid-step, eyes wide. Had I just been caught?

"Are you sure about this?" A woman's voice, strained and filled with emotion. "Your father won't know?"

"He won't," a male's voice soothed her. "I promise."

I frowned at how familiar he sounded. I stalked up to the door, looking through the slit to see a lit candle on a nightstand. Sliding through the open space, I noticed a man and woman kissing on the bed that belonged to the Jarl. The woman moaned, dipped her head back as the man devoured her skin, his mouth exploring every inch of her.

I glanced around, hoping to find something to hide behind so as not to get caught. I found my salvation when I noticed the curtains to the windows were spread wide, and I slowly inched my way to hide behind it. There wasn't any light in this room, so this was my safest bet.

The downside? I was now seated front and center before this show.

The man ran his fingers along the woman's body, cupping her core as he moaned. She sighed, holding his shoulders and bringing him closer to her. He removed his hand from between her legs, then grabbed her ankles and turned her around. Then he grasped her hips and pulled her closer to him, off the bed, her rear end on full display for his indulgence.

He gave her right cheek a good smack before he reached out and grabbed a fistful of her hair, thrusting as deep inside her as he could. She gasped but arched herself so that she could take more of him.

Bile rose in my throat, and I closed my eyes. I didn't want to be privy to this sightseeing, but it was either endure in my hiding spot or tell Karsten that the deal was off.

I wasn't a stranger to sex; I knew what it was. I just never found anyone I wanted to be *that* intimate with.

I opened my eyes, hoping that at least one of them would be done. I was wrong. The man held onto her hips, pounding into her relentlessly. She cried out, clawing at the sheets, panting as he rammed into her with so much force it made me wince. How could something that hard feel so good?

The man's breathing quickened, each thrust getting him closer to his goal. He gasped, his body convulsing as he rammed into her for the last time. His grip on her hips relented, and he released her hair so that he could run the palm of his hand along her back. Once his breathing slowed, he slid out of her and reached down to gather up his clothes that were on the floor. She turned slowly, legs still open for him to continue.

Gross.

The woman watched him with hooded eyes. He tugged on his pants, pulling his shirt over his head as he walked back over to her. He grabbed her knees and shut her legs, bringing her closer to him. He kissed her, sucking on her bottom lip.

"I'd love to have a round two, my dear. But if we don't go now, my father will surely notice our absence." He dropped her knees and held out her dress.

She sighed and took it from him. "I don't see why you even bother. Jarl Lott doesn't like me."

"Ah, my love." He took her face in his hands. "I don't care what he thinks of you, and you shouldn't either."

She clicked her tongue, slithering into her dress. "You should. You're to become the next Jarl. He's already chosen your wife for you and—"

"Once he finds out you're pregnant," he cut her off, "he will make sure you're my wife. Why else do you think we've been doing this for so long?"

She pouted. "I want to be more than just your wife."

"And you will be." He kissed her temple before slapping her on the rear end. "Now, let's get going."

I waited for several more agonizing minutes before I found the courage to slip through the curtains. I scanned the room, trying to adjust to the surroundings.

If I were a Jarl with far too much jewelry, where would I keep my belongings? I slinked over to his nightstand where the candle was, lifting the wick and sliding open the drawer. I rifled through, looking for a false bottom or something else to indicate something of value was hidden beneath the layers of wood.

Finding nothing, I slammed it closed and walked around to the other nightstand, doing the same thing I did prior. Nothing. I dropped to the floor, lifted up the blanket, and looked around to see if I could spot anything. Once again, my search was fruitless. Frustrated, I blew air out through my teeth and stood.

The Jarl's room was *enormous*. There was a king-sized bed, a door that led into the bathroom, another door that held a closet, and then a bunch of furniture.

It would take me far longer to scout for it, and I didn't have enough time to begin with. I walked over to the vanity next. Makeup, rollers, and other women's essentials were tucked inside, but nothing else of value. I set down the candle, hands on my hips as I tried to think of another area that would possibly hold the Jarl's belongings.

By no means was Lott stupid; quite the contrary, in fact. He'd no doubt hidden his most valuable object, and done it well. Which would make this all the more difficult.

I smacked my lips and began to feel around the vanity. A lot of the people I had stolen from previously always used false bottoms. Not many thieves around Ellriheimr were aware of this, and many jobs had fallen to me simply for my knowledge of such. I sometimes thought I was chosen for those roles rather than it being randomized.

My fingers finally ran over a slight bump, and I stopped. I prodded the area for a moment, running the tips of my fingers along the seam. Aha! Eureka! I raised my leg to grab my dagger, my lips curving into a satisfied smile as I got to work.

Each creak of the wood was like each beat of my heart, erratic, almost like a butterfly caught in a jar with no means of escape. I had to hurry. I wasn't sure how long I had been gone, but Karsten surely couldn't hold off Lott for long. I jiggled the dagger again, the bottom coming away, much to my relief.

I slid out the contents of the hidden drawer. Papers, a necklace, and a few rolled up pieces of parchment.

My heart fell. Had I been wrong? Was the ring not in here? I shifted through it. This was the last spot. Once this was thoroughly searched, I would need to leave. I was already spreading myself way too thin.

To my luck, I found a small, black box nestled within the papers and other jewelry. I placed it on the top of the vanity and closed the hidden drawer. Lifting the box and opening it just a fraction, my eyes rested on the largest rock I'd ever seen. A large, obsidian gem nestled in the middle of a metal band covered in runes, a few resembling the very ones branded into my skin. But the rest were unrecognizable.

I tucked the ring back in the box, stuffed my dagger into my boot, and shoved the box in my dress between my breasts. It was the last place anyone would look, and if I was quick enough, I would manage to get out of here unscathed.

I pushed away from the vanity and slinked my way down the stairs. Hopefully, this time I wouldn't run into anyone.

Too late.

"I need to retrieve something." Lott's voice emanated from the door in front of me. My only exit.

"Surely, it can wait." Karsten's voice. "We've much to discuss."

"It'll have to wait," Lott chided. "I need to make sure I have something."

I heard footsteps, my heart palpitating. There was nowhere for me to run, to hide. All I could do was stay still. However, if I did just that, then I would get caught. The ring would be taken from me—and with it, my only hope of gold. The sound of a key turning made me jump back a step.

Shit, Eira! I racked my brain, hoping for a solution. *Think.*

The runes beneath my gloves began to shine, almost like they were telling me to use them. I chewed my lower lip, my right foot tapping as the knob clicked and the door began to open.

"Hræzla."

Lott walked into the stairwell, climbing the steps two at a time. I held my breath, waiting for him to notice me. He breezed by me, not even batting an eye. I sighed heavily and instantly froze as Lott halted. He turned, his eyes scanning the stairwell, looking for the source of the noise.

I didn't waste a second. Once he turned his back and ascended the stairs, I raced through the door before one of the guards closed it. I walked a little bit away from the commotion, glancing around the room. Karsten was nowhere in sight.

I made my way down the second floor of the longhouse, ensuring that I didn't accidentally bump into anyone on the stairs. While I may be invisible, I could still touch and feel, so I had to be careful.

I waited for the door to open to the bottom floor before I slid through it and into the main hall. Most of the participants were now sitting at the large table, eating and talking amongst themselves. My stomach growled seeing all that food, but I couldn't waste a moment of this. Food would have to wait.

The moment my foot stepped out of Lott's longhouse and onto the grass around his home, a hand gripped my wrist.

I spun around, my dagger already poised and ready. Karsten held my hand above my head, the tip of my dagger resting against his throat, right where I could see the vein. If I just moved the tip a little more to the right—*wait*. How did he know I was there?

Karsten wagged a finger at me and tsked. "My naughty little spitfire. Just what do you think you're doing?"

"I could ask you the same thing," I sneered.

He grinned, dropping my wrist to take a step away from me. "Where's my ring?"

I blinked. "What ring?"

"Eira—"

I froze. "H—how do you know my name?"

He shrugged. "Word gets around. I was told you were the best thief in all of Ellriheimr." He nodded towards my gloved hands. "I also know you're harboring illegal magic."

"How—"

"I've done my research."

I narrowed my eyes at him. If he so much as told someone, the Jarl himself, I would be killed—or worse, sentenced to the gods. Karsten seemed to notice my hesitation and sighed, taking a careful step towards me.

"I'm not going to tell anyone," he said.

"You're not?"

"I won't if you give me my ring." As if to emphasize his point, he held out his hand, palm up.

I hesitated, weighing my options. He already knew I had the ring, and he knew where I was when I was invisible. He knew my name, knew everything about me. It was unsettling, but I couldn't deny the fact that if I didn't give him this ring, my life would be in his hands.

I reached into my chest, pulling out the little black box before setting it in his hand. He pulled back, opening the box to look inside. Then he slipped the ring onto his finger. The gem embedded in it glowed slightly before returning to normal.

"Ah." He cracked his neck and rolled his shoulders. "Much better."

I narrowed my eyes. "How did you—"

Karsten tossed a coin purse at me, and I scrambled to catch it, almost falling down in the process. Tugging it open, my eyes widened. This was far more gold than a single person would ever need. This would last me months, if not more.

I gaped at the loot, blinking several times before glancing up to say thank you to Karsten, but he was already gone, leaving me alone in the back of Jarl Lott's longhouse.

TWELVE

O ver the course of the last several days, Fen and me did absolutely nothing. It was glorious. The first two days were filled with me wrapped in my blankets, never leaving the house, much to Fenrir's displeasure. On the eve of the third day, the tax collector came. I gave him enough coin for the next two months and sent him on his way. On the fourth day, Fenrir began to scratch at the door, begging me to let him out.

I slid from my bed to the floor, legs crossed as I opened the pouch Karsten had given me. It was still filled, almost as if I hadn't taken anything from it for the whole week. This was far more than I should have received, which unsettled me slightly.

Was he going to frame me for stealing his coin? If so, what was his goal? I had given him his ring before the time was due, and I was compensated. Albeit a bit more than usual.

Fenrir whimpered in the living room, and I sighed. Rolling to my feet, I grabbed my dagger and left the comfort of my room. My companion was sitting by the door, his tail thumping. He noticed me and immediately brightened.

"You know, Fen." I grabbed my cloak, clipping it to my shoulders before I walked over to him. "I really don't feel like going out today."

He huffed, scratching at the door and plopping back down, waiting for me to open it. I rolled my eyes and opened the door.

Fenrir wasted no time before bounding out of the house, his paws not even touching the steps. In seconds, he was prancing into the street.

Closing the door behind me with an amused eyeroll, I descended the steps to follow my companion. Fenrir didn't tarry long. He was already running a few paces in front of me before he circled back, nipped at my heels, and then raced faster.

I halted when I noticed the direction he was going in. He was leading me towards the gates of the city, right outside to the forest we came from almost a week prior with our kill. I had hoped to simply amble around the city, not venture out into the forest.

I sometimes forget that Fenrir is a full-blooded wolf and as such, he needs more room to roam that isn't my small house.

Indulging him, I followed. He pranced, yelped, and howled as we continued on our walk. *Only for a little bit*, I told myself. *At least until Fen's desire to roam is sated.*

We walked through the gates of Ellriheimr, taking the path that would lead us into the depths of the woods. It would take us about thirty or so minutes to reach our destination, and that was pushing it. My feet felt like lead, a burning desire to run in the opposite direction almost overwhelming.

Why was I feeling this way? What could possibly affect me enough to make me want to tuck tail and run?

I shook my head when I heard Fenrir yelp excitedly. Shaking my head, I turned to where he was yelping, seeing a small herd of deer that were heading in the direction of the forest. Fenrir didn't waste a single second as he bolted for them.

"Fenrir!" I called to him.

My wolf didn't slow; he likely didn't hear me as he ran as fast as he could towards his prey. I ran after him, ignoring the blast of frigid air that seeped into my cloak, chilling me to the bone. When had it gotten so much colder?

My pace slowed when I entered the forest. The ground was covered in permafrost, snowflakes swirling down from the clouds, dancing along the wind currents.

"*Eira.*"

I spun around, my heart hammering in my chest. I scanned the area, searching for the source of who had just called my name. I was alone in the middle of the thicket. Fog swirled around me, swelling up from a forest full of foreboding shadows.

"*Eira.*"

The runes on my arms began to glow a light blue, almost in time with my heartbeat, if that was at all possible. Instinctively, I reached up to grab my necklace, hoping the ashes of my mother would help soothe me.

I was never one to get spooked about things that went bump in the night, but there was something about that voice that unsettled me. About the darkness that was swiftly closing in.

"*Eira.*"

A twig snapped beside me, and I jolted, side-stepping away and withdrawing my dagger without missing a beat. I hadn't lived this long without being efficient.

An object whizzed down from above, narrowly missing me. I jumped back, my eyes searching the forest floor for what had just almost hit me. A lone pinecone rested in what appeared to be a nest of brown needles, a few raven feathers peppering around it.

Pebbles began to shake, the ground quaking beneath my feet. A yelp off in the distance made my head snap up and dread pool in my belly.

Fenrir.

Abandoning the pinecone, I raced deeper into the forest, into the swell of shadows and freezing mist. I heard the sound of my wolf's yelp a second time, this one closer than the first. I broke into a clearing, a felled deer lying beside Fenrir.

Everything in my body froze as my eyes landed on the behemoth before me.

A human—no *monster*—had his back towards me, crouched down as he poked at my companion with a finger. Fenrir growled, his canines narrowly missing the monster's flesh.

Fear for my wolf overtook my need for safety as I took a harrowing step forward.

"Hey!" I yelled, brandishing my blade.

The monster froze, slowly rising to its feet before it shifted to face me. My mouth dropped open, and I took a step back. This creature resembled a man. He had to be at least two to three times the size of a mortal man. His nose was malformed, crooked like it had been broken but never fixed. One eye was bigger than the other, and he only had one ear. He had a large belly, a cloth covering the most sensitive part of him.

One word sprang to mind when I continued to size up this beast.

A troll.

This was truly the most grotesque creature I'd ever seen.

Fenrir's yelp brought me back to the present, and I snapped to attention. The troll arched forward, his feet slamming into the earth, the ground quaking underneath me.

I unclipped my cloak, the fabric snapping in the wind as it fell off my shoulders. I braced myself, holding out my dagger. The troll lumbered forward, knocking trees down as he ran for me. The runes along my skin blazed to life, a deep red this time.

An idea formed, but I would need Fenrir for it. My gaze slid to my wolf, who yelped at me.

I narrowed my eyes. Then I raced forward, kicking up needles and leaves in my wake. The troll roared, arms encroaching closer to grab me in a bone-crushing hug. I slid on the ground, using my blade to slice through his flesh. A gruesome howl of pain tore through from his throat.

"Are you okay, boy?" I didn't look over at my wolf, but I heard him whimper, and my heart shattered upon hearing him hurt. I got down to one knee, placed my hand over his shoulder, and said, "*Hvíld.*"

Fenrir bounded to his feet almost instantly, growling and snarling, jumping forward to open his maw and take a bite out of the troll.

I twirled my dagger and crouched. I used the tip of my blade to dig into the dirt, creating the rune that resembled the same as a flame. The troll came for me, blood oozing from his new wound, arms at his sides with his head bent as he charged.

I placed my hand on the rune, closed my eyes, and spoke the words for flame.

"*Fiðri.*"

Fire erupted around us, shielding both me and Fenrir. The troll hit the wall of flames, crying out as it scorched his skin. The air filled with the stench of charred flesh.

I grabbed my dagger and yelled, "*Now!*"

I bent down, and Fenrir used me as a bridge. His paws hit my back and shoulders, jumping over the wall of fire, his maw held wide to deal a blow. His canines sank into the troll, and the creature howled in pain, desperately trying to pry off my wolf.

"*Skoða.*"

I arched my arms forward, like I was going to smack my hands together. A cascade of water tumbled forth, hitting the troll square in the chest. Fenrir dislodged himself from the creature, this time going for the legs.

My arms fell to my sides, sweat beading along my brow. I wasn't used to exerting myself so much. Magic wasn't to be used lightly, and I was breaking the rules continuously. If I kept this up for much longer, I wouldn't be able to stand, and we'd run the risk of the troll tearing us to shreds.

If only I had my bow, I thought bitterly.

Still, seeing a troll this close to Ellriheimr, let alone Röskr, was worrisome enough. Was this a coincidence? Was there a tear in the realms that allowed this creature to come tumbling forth? More importantly, did the gods know?

Fenrir barked at me, his body circling the clearing as the troll roared. I had one more failsafe I could use, but that would no doubt zap me of the rest of my magic for a while. I gripped my dagger, closed my eyes, and whispered, "*Fiðri.*"

The blade blazed to life with my flames, the heat almost a little too intense as I took a step towards the grotesque creature.

This was going to be a stupid idea, but I had no other options. With Fenrir by my side, I rushed at the troll.

The creature came for me, eyes alit with fury. Blood drenched his fur, the holes in his skin from my wolf's massive jaws. Charred parts of his body hung down, water droplets sizzling as it hit the ground. The blade was still blazing with fire, siding the hairs on my arms. Fenrir barked, ducked, and dug his fangs into the troll's leg. The creature shrieked, his arm connecting with my side and sending me flying into a nearby tree.

I fell to the ground, my vision blurry. My dagger was embedded into the troll's arm, the creature waving his arm around to try and dislodge it. Flames crackled, roaring over the troll, burning him even as more blood spilled. Fenrir slid over to me, covering me with his body, his paws right next to my face.

I watched blearily as the flames consumed the troll, the creature falling forward to the ground in a slump, dead. The dagger was still lodged into his arm, the flames dying out with each breath I took from the magic inside me.

I panted, rising to my feet. I winced, using the tree beside me to hold myself steady. Blood was pooling down the side of my face, dripping into my eye. I didn't have enough magic in me to heal myself, so I would need to allow myself time to heal naturally before my magic regained its strength.

I hobbled over to the troll slowly. Fen stayed right with me, never leaving my side. He would occasionally brush against me, but I was in far too much pain to focus on anything that wasn't returning home.

I grabbed my dagger from the troll's arm and placed it back into my boot for safekeeping. Hopefully we didn't encounter any other dangers while on our way back because at this point, I would readily just keel over and die.

"Come on, boy," I groaned, running a hand over my face. When I pulled it away, it was slick with sweat and grime, making me grimace. "I need something strong to drink."

THIRTEEN

I stayed in bed for the next several days recuperating. My magic still hadn't recovered from the battle with the troll back in the woods. Fenrir hadn't left my side, occasionally fetching me something to eat or drink. Sure, there wouldn't be hardly anything left for me to sip on, but at least it was something to tie me over. I rolled over onto my back, staring up at the ceiling.

Today was the day I would gravitate from my bedroom to the living room. I had barely been able to clean myself, and what little magic I had in me was used to heal. It wasn't much, but it was enough to mend me together. I still had that nasty cut along my brow, but thankfully it was healed nice enough that I was no longer bleeding. I would have a nasty scare, though.

With as much effort as I could muster, I forced myself out of bed and got dressed. Being cooped up all day was boring and depressing.

Fenrir followed at my heels, helping me along like I needed him as a crutch. I smiled down at him, relieved to see him healed and alive. I don't know what I would have done if he had been seriously injured. I'd have probably gone insane.

"Come on, boy." I gestured for him to follow, like he needed prompting. "Let's go for a walk."

At the mention of those magical words, he yelped and jumped. I giggled, ran my hand through his fur, grabbed my cloak, and together we walked out into the city. It was a little early for me to go out drinking, but I felt the need to do something today. I told myself that I would never celebrate today—not since my mother passed well over five years ago. I tried to force myself once, but I couldn't stop thinking about what my mother and I would be doing on this particular day.

Fenrir and I walked through the streets. I watched our surroundings, careful to keep my runes hidden. Tattoos were abundant, but no one held the old language on their arms like me. It's what drove my mother into protecting me for so long.

If Oeric knew what I held, he would surely send the whole realm after me.

We soon reached the mead hall, and I almost sighed in relief. I would need many to get over this pain, both physically and mentally. I opened the door, letting Fenrir go ahead of me before I let the door close and walked into the hall. It was filled with men, drinking to their hearts content. There were a few women, ones who were probably Shieldmaidens, female warriors. They were rare, and most of them were off the coast of Röskr, along with the male warriors.

The hall seemed to grow quiet the moment I walked in. All eyes turned towards me, their drinks and conversation long forgotten as they watched me walk over to the bar. I made it a point to remain hidden or remain at home to the point where most who noticed me thought me nothing more than an outsider.

I took up an empty seat, with Fenrir settling at my feet. A tall, red-haired man walked over, holding a flask in his hands. He arched a brow when he noticed me, settled in the middle of two larger men whose muscles could crush my skull with a single glance.

"Mead, please." I paused. "The strongest you have."

The man nodded and wandered off to get the drink. I sighed, rolling my shoulders back as I scanned the room. Most of these men looked worn and ragged. They must have just returned from one of their pillages. There weren't many villages for them to conquer, as Röskr was the smallest of all the Nine Realms and didn't have any oceans.

The man came back with a tall mug of mead. He placed it in front of me before he went to attend to another man that called for something to drink. I tipped my head back, downing the mead without a second thought. I gasped, holding in the flavor before I breathed out, setting the mug back down on the counter.

"Thirsty?" a familiar voice asked me.

Karsten.

I bristled. Karsten settled in the seat beside me, lifted up his hand, and two more mugs of mead were placed before us.

He grabbed his, taking a long swig, his eyes watching me from the rim. I narrowed my eyes but didn't acknowledge his presence as I grabbed the other mug from him to take an additional drink for myself.

He pointed at his brow. "You have something there."

Ignoring him, I took another sip of my mead. My brow itched, almost like it was responding to Karsten's voice. I wasn't going to give him the satisfaction of seeing me squirm, no matter how sinfully handsome he was. I may have been a sucker for a pretty face, but I also wasn't stupid. Karsten was trouble.

He leaned closer to me, his lips turned up into a grin. "I'm surprised you haven't healed yourself already."

I froze. Did he just say—? No, he couldn't have, at least not in public. Irritation filtered through me as he brought it back up. He already knew I wielded magic, so why bring it up now? Because I hadn't healed myself properly yet?

I set the mug down. "I should get going."

Karsten's hand snaked out, his fingers wrapping around my wrist, holding me there. Fenrir rose, growling low in warning. I didn't tell him to hold off, at least not yet.

His eyes dropped to my arms, covered by my gloves and the cloak. "I know what you are."

I swallowed. "I don't know what you're talking about."

Karsten chuckled. "I have a proposition for you, Eira."

I tried to piece everything together. Karsten saw me while invisible, he touched me while also in that state, he knew my name, and he knew that I had dangerous magic. Which begged the question, who was he? He could very likely be one of the eleven gods, but which one?

"What do you want from me?" I asked him.

Karsten's eyes bored into my own, watching me. He released my arm, settled into his chair, and raised his mug of mead. "I only come because I have a job for you."

I crossed my arms. "And you couldn't do it the way you had before?"

"No. This job is of the utmost importance. I am in need of your skills."

I snorted. "Surely there are others."

"There are," he replied. "However, none passed my tests and none of them have *magic.*"

I ducked my head. "Don't say that so loud."

He grinned, running his finger along the rim of his mug. "Will you at least hear what I have to say first before saying no?"

I watched him. "Do I have a choice?"

Karsten shrugged a shoulder. "Depends."

I pinched the bridge of my nose, growing irritable. For the love of the gods, why was he making this more difficult?

"Fine." I scowled. "What do you have to say?"

He grinned playfully, leaning forward. "I need you to steal something for me."

I wrinkled my nose. "Again? What is it this time? An earring?"

"It's something far greater than that," he replied. "An old relic."

My brows knitted. "An old relic? Those have all been taken away from Röskr the moment Oeric banned travel between the realms."

"Indeed, he did. But what I desire is in another realm."

I snorted and rolled my eyes, conversation already all but forgotten now. "Good luck with that, pal. No one has the ability to jump through the realms anymore. All the passageways have been destroyed."

"What if I told you that there was another way?"

I shot him a glare. "Then I would call you a fool and a liar."

He withdrew from me, hand over his heart like I had struck him. "Oh, my dear little hellfire. You have no idea just how spot on you are."

"Hm."

"I will pay you triple what I gave you the night you stole my ring back," he said.

Temptation flared in the pit of my stomach, but so did remorse. I couldn't allow myself to get dragged into this type of job. It was unethical, one that would certainly get me killed. Besides, how would I be able to travel through the realms? All means of travel had been destroyed, and unless you were a god, you couldn't leave your realm. It was even hard for gods.

I turned to him., my fingers drumming along the countertop. "And how will I get to this realm? I can't travel between the threads of reality."

"Ah." Karsten smiled and tapped his chest, right where my necklace was. "But you can."

I grabbed my necklace, suddenly self-conscious about it. "What does my necklace have to do with it?"

"May I?" He held out his hand, palm up for me.

I narrowed my eyes, stuffing the necklace underneath my shirt. "I don't think so."

"Very well." I didn't respond, so he continued to prattle on. "The vines that are connected to the vial were once part of the Yggdrasil. With those roots, you hold a sliver of magic from our world tree. It will help you travel between the realms."

I blinked at him. "I don't believe you."

"Well then." He jumped from his seat and held out his hand for me. "Allow me a moment of your time then, my hellfire. I will show you the truth."

I narrowed my eyes at him again, an expression that I was growing accustomed to in Karsten's presence. I tipped back my head to down the remainder of the mead, wiped my mouth with the back of my hand, and slid from my chair. I ignored his out-stretched hand, instead crossing my arms.

"You have one hour to prove me wrong," I told him. "After that, we're done."

"Challenge accepted."

FOURTEEN

I followed Karsten for quite some time. We'd barely spoke more than two words since we departed from the mead hall. Fenrir remained at my heels, hackles raised as he watched Karsten closely. We were walking towards the eastern district, one of the lesser districts in the city and home to many thieves and bandits.

I never strayed too far out this way. However, each step Karsten took was calculated and cool, never stopping for more than a second before he continued on. I followed him, but each time I stumbled, a deep pain would slice me in two. I needed to heal, but I couldn't do it in Karsten's presence.

"You're awfully quiet back there." Karsten didn't halt his progress as he led me and Fen further into the eastern district.

I raised my brows at him, fully aware that he couldn't see me doing it. "Did you want me to say something?"

"Nothing in particular," he intoned. "I am curious to know, though, how you can use magic—"

My hand snaked out, wrapping around his wrist. "Don't say that word."

He grinned, and his eyes turned down towards my hand that was touching his wrist. "I never agreed to not saying it, little hellfire."

I bristled. "Stop calling me that. I have a name."

"Ah." He whistled, gently prying my fingers from his wrist. "That's right. How could I forget? *Eira.*"

The way he said my name was like a symphony. It sent goosebumps along my skin, the hairs on my arms rising.

Gods, I thought. *Why was this one handsome? Couldn't he have been a fat, hairy man?*

"You coming?" he asked me.

I blinked, face flaming in embarrassment. My feet moved of their own accord, arms crossed over my chest as I kept my distance. I hated that he had this effect on me. My heart would race, my skin would flush, and all I could think about was how handsome he was.

Next time, I was going to make sure that my next employer wasn't so distracting.

"So, where are we going?" I asked.

He turned his head just enough so that he could see me out of the corner of his eye. "There's a tree that we're heading to."

I frowned. "A tree? I don't think—"

"This tree holds the power to travel between realms," he interjected.

"How?"

We walked through the eastern gate and into the fields beyond. The forest was further away on this side, with more rolling green hills and less wildlife.

However, settled atop a small hill was a singular aspen tree. Unlike the rest of the foliage during this season, the leaves were in full bloom. The colors resembled an iridescent golden yellow, black spots dotting the bark of the tree. This looked to be a regular tree, but it was ten times taller than a normal tree.

Karsten didn't stop, and I had to jog to keep up with him. Fenrir saddled on behind me, head cocked to the side as he watched the tree we were coming up upon.

Amazed by this tree, I could only gaze up at it in awe. It was far too late into the year for this tree to have all its leaves, not to mention look as if it wasn't at all bothered by the frost on the ground and the cold breeze that swept through the area.

Still, I held my breath. Just because this tree was taller than most and held all its leaves didn't mean it was magical.

It was hard to explain the view in itself, but I would justify it as… an uncommon occurrence. I climbed up the hill, almost falling backwards when my foot caught on a large rock. If it wasn't for Fenrir behind me, I would have fallen flat on my back. I *really* didn't want to get hurt any more than I already was.

Karsten placed his hand on the bark of the tree, waiting for me to clamber the rest of the way up the hill. It must have been nice for him to have such long legs that would allow him to walk ten times faster than me and not appear as if he broke a sweat doing it.

Finally, I made it to the top, panting. My entire body screamed in pain at me, begging me to use what little magic had replenished to heal myself.

Almost as if responding to my body, the runes began to glow.

Shit! I scrambled to hide my gloved hands beneath my cloak, hoping Karsten hadn't seen. I didn't trust him yet. He *knew* about these runes, but I wasn't going to let him see them.

Karsten gestured to where his hand rested on the bark, a lazy grin on his face. "We'll travel using this."

I eyed the tree. "How? It's just a tree."

He patted the bark. "With that necklace you're wearing."

My hand reached up to grab my necklace, narrowing my eyes at him in the process. What did the necklace my mother had given me have to do with this strange tree?

He took a step closer. "That vial has a rune etched into it. That rune, coupled with the vines of the world tree, will give you enough magic to travel between the realms."

Hope blossomed in my chest at the prospect of leaving this place. There was nothing wrong with Röskr, but the idea of being able to travel sent a tremor through me.

Mother had once told me that she had been to several realms and had wanted to take me there to explore. That was back then, back when she was still alive and when travel was not forbidden. What were the other realms like? How did they differ from my own? All these questions and more sprang to my mind, but I stamped them down quickly, not wanting to seem too eager.

Still… I held up my necklace to inspect it. I had honestly never really paid any attention to it since the day my mother had given it to me. Back then, I thought it merely a gift, something to cherish, not something that would help me *travel*. However, the closer I inspected my necklace, I noticed small indentions in the glass. It was a rune, but one I'd never seen before.

My fingers itched to remove my gloves and look at my runes, but I couldn't do that with Karsten in front of me.

I clicked my tongue. "And you're *sure* this will help us travel?"

"I am many things, Eira, and honest is among them."

Eying him, I wasn't entirely sure I could believe him. Back in the mead hall, I had called him a fool and a liar, and he told me that he was those things and so much more. So why would he flipflop? Was he trying to get me to trust him?

He cleared his throat. "We don't have all day."

I narrowed my eyes and slipped the necklace from my neck.

I didn't need the money because I had plenty. Although, what was wrong with having more than enough? I didn't know or trust him, but the thrill of adventure called to me deeply, like a nagging voice in the back of my head.

Should I stay or should I go? I held the necklace out to him, and he stepped back, hands held up.

"You need to be wearing it for it work," he explained.

"Why? I can't read the rune." I held it out to him.

Karsten took a step closer, his eyes sweeping over my glass vial. His brows knitted, and he grabbed it in between his fingers, looking for the rune in question. He clicked his tongue and nodded to himself.

He walked back over to the tree and placed his hand over the bark. He gestured with his other for me to follow his steps. I walked over, resting my fingers along the cold wood. Karsten saddled closer, and I flinched away from him.

His hand snaked out, grabbed my wrist, and yanked me back over to him, his lips almost touching my ear.

"Repeat after me," he whispered. "*Nál.*"

I closed my eyes, taking a deep breath. "*Nál.*"

The ground beneath our feet began to quake, the cold wind stirring, catching the leaves from the aspen. The rustling leaves began to encircle us, whipping in my face, the wind almost choking me.

My necklace began to glow brightly, the same shade of blue my runes normally changed to. Karsten's eyes flashed in triumph, his smile broad as the tree began to shake.

The bark of the tree began to splinter and crack, forming a wide door. Karsten removed his hand from the tree, entering the depths of it. I hesitated, my hand still splayed on the bark. Fenrir headbutted me, whining as he glanced around us all the vortex of leaves. We were essentially trapped.

"Well, Fen," I swallowed. "It was nice knowing you."

I removed my hand and stepped towards the opening in the tree. A deep, almost enchanting forest stared back at me, filled with fireflies and croaking frogs. Karsten was nowhere in sight.

I reached down to grab a fistful of my wolf's fur before I jumped in.

FIFTEEN

The feeling of falling came to me first and foremost, before a prickling sensation started in my neck all the way down to my toes.

Where was I? I felt like I was floating, like I was streaming through a vortex that led me into oblivion.

It was bright, with vibrant colors streaking around me. I reached out, my fingers slicing through the cold, water-like substance. A gaping hole emerged from the colors, swallowing me whole only to spit me out on the other end.

I rolled to a stop a few inches from someone's feet. I sat back on my butt, scared for a moment before I realized that it was Karsten himself.

He held a hand out for me, but I smacked it away to take a look at my new surroundings. I was in that same enchanting forest I had seen, except I was *in* the forest. The area held nothing but dense foliage, no sunshine coming through the leaves or needles. The grass was green and lush beneath my fingers, almost wet as if it had just rained prior to me coming here.

There was a break in the forest just beyond. I could see something glistening, and my eyes widened. A lake? Or an ocean perhaps? Fireflies, rabbits, and other wildlife frolicked in this area, and I turned to show it to Fenrir.

My heart sank, and I jumped to my feet, looking around the area for my companion this time rather than for sightseeing.

"Fenrir!" I yelled.

"Your companion is back in Röskr." Karsten crossed his arms, his feet set slightly apart.

I whirled. "Why? Where is he?"

"The wolf has no magic in him," he explained. "Without a sliver of magic, he's not able to travel between the realms like you or I can."

"Okay but *how* can we do this?" I was still very much upset that my wolf wasn't with me, but there was nothing I could do about it now seeing as now I was in a whole other *realm*.

Karsten gestured at the forest around us. "When my father decided to close off all the magical gateways, he made sure that only his children and the other six gods could travel through the Bifrost. It was also because—"

"*Whoa!*" I held out my hands, stopping him in his tracks. "Hold up. Did you just say your *father* closed off all the gateways?"

Karsten clicked his tongue. "You still haven't figured it out yet? I thought it would have been obvious by now."

I narrowed my eyes at him, taking in his appearance again, this time with a fresh set of eyes. There were exactly seven main gods in this entire world.

There was Oeric, the main god, also known as the All Father, and he had a wife named Ansa. Then there was their son Eirik. There was Carin and Ivar, two siblings that were sired by the All-Father that were equal parts god and witch. Tyra was the goddess of Móðr. Njal guarded the realms from sworn enemies. Roar was another one of Oeric's children, but he was born from a mother that was a giant. Inkeri guarded the sacred apples, and lastly were Kol the trickster god and Magnar, the son of Oeric and Ansa—the god of thunder he was called.

He had said "his father", so that left out the majority of the nine gods. All that left were Roar, Eirik, and Magnar.

It was obvious that he wasn't Magnar; the legends them-selves spoke about him being a mighty warrior that carried around his fated hammer created for him by the dwarves. He could well be Eirik, but for some reason, Karsten really didn't fit the description either. The only son left was Roar.

And yet, deep down, I knew exactly who this god before me was. It was evident now, thinking back on it. The tricks he played with Jarl Lott, the way he reacted when I had called him both a liar and a fool.

Kol.

I crossed my arms over my chest, scowling as everything about this guy clicked into place. I had been messing with the god of tricks and mischief. How fortunate for me it would seem.

"Ah," Karsten—Kol—smirked. "You figured it out finally."

"I did," I spoke evenly. "However, Oeric only has four sons. Magnar, Eirik, Ivar, and Roar. You, are not one of his sons."

"Someone knows their history." He smacked his lips together. "I'm highly impressed."

I rolled my eyes. "Hardly."

"You know me at least," he teased.

"Both of your parents are giants." My brows knitted. "You are not a giant either."

"Watch and learn, my little hellfire." Kol's smile was wicked as he ran a finger over the obsidian ring, the same exact one I had stolen for him from Jarl Lott's longhouse. His image shimmered, his body growing slightly taller than before. Tattoos spiraled along his arms, a snake's head peeking out of his shirt, curling around his neck to rest just below his ear.

Kol spread his arms out wide. "*Now* do you see me for who I truly am?"

There honestly wasn't anything different from before. The only new thing was that he was taller, and his tattoos were far more intricate than before; that snake was something new itself. I also recognized it as Kol's symbol—one he often associated himself with.

I turned away from him, my eyes zeroing on the glistening lake in front of me. I began to walk in that direction, ignoring him as I went. I didn't have time for games, but in truth, I was scared. It took a lot for me to be frightened, but seeing a god, that was something else. He also knew my secret.

A fluttering of wings made me stop, ducking when a pine-cone whizzed by my head. I yelped, jumping back as a raven soared over my head, landing in a tree to preen its feathers. Nestled in the middle of its forehead was a runic symbol, and it was glowing a bright gold.

My heart stopped. There was only one person on this entire planet who could command those ravens, one that was to be feared.

Oeric.

Kol seemed to notice our new companion, and he gripped my upper arm, leading me away from the raven's prying eyes. I turned my head around so I could see, watching as the raven hopped to another branch, black eyes never leaving mine. It spread its wings wide, cawed, and took flight.

Kol watched the raven leave before he wretched me back into the forest. I huffed, trying to get my arm free from his grasp, but the pesky god was not budging.

"Let me go," I hissed.

"He knows we're here." Kol's voice had changed, a hard undertone to it. "We need to leave."

I stopped my squirming. "*Leave*? But we just got here!"

Kol's grip on my arm tightened, and he brought me closer to him, our noses almost touching. His eyes bore into my own, filled with mischief and cunning and something else. Something I couldn't name. Awe, maybe?

"I showed you another realm. Wasn't that the deal?"

I blinked, forgetting that his fingers were touching my skin. I swore. He was right. I had told him that if he could prove himself, then I would help him. He did, so now I would have to own up to my own bargain. I had given him an hour, but in reality, he had given me so much more.

"Fine." I wretched my arm from his grasp. "I'll help you."

Kol's expression changed the moment we heard another caw from a raven. He didn't waste a second as he grabbed my hand again and ushered me back over to the aspen tree. The very same tree we had come in from. We reached the tree, Kol's fingers splayed over the bark.

"*Nál.*"

Just like before, the trees around us began to sway, the leaves encircling us. I gasped, this time from the intensity of this magic. It was far stronger than my own, and it sent a warmth through me like never before. Was this the true magic of the gods?

The bark of the tree splintered, a hole opening up for us. I had expected to see the lush rolling hills of Röskr, but instead I saw a mountainous region covered with forest and rivers. I blinked, trying to think about this new realm, but Kol didn't allow me a second to waver before he placed his hands on my shoulders and pushed me in.

SIXTEEN

I was never one for screaming, but today was a different day for me. I was tumbling through the air, the sky rolling around and around, clouds forming anew as I continued to fall through.

My hair whipped in my face, my necklace dangling on the chain, acting like it was about to swing off my neck.

"Eira!" Kol cried.

I turned my head toward the sound of his voice, but it was hard to pinpoint where it was coming from. The wind rushed into my ears, making it hard for me to hear anything that wasn't the wind and my screams. I kept turning my head, my arms spiraling as I tried to flap them like a bird to stop my fall, as ridiculous as that sounded.

Something red glinted in my field of vision, and I turned in that direction, eyes wide. A large crimson dragon soared towards me. The body resembled a serpent, with a wedge-shaped head that held elaborate horns, pointed to a fine tip. It opened its massive mouth, fangs on full display.

The age-old runes on my arms responded to my fear, shining with that brilliant white light. The dragon roared, the light hitting it straight in the eyes. It soared beneath me, its tail catching my feet, causing me to spiral. I screamed, the mountains coming closer and closer by the second.

I tumbled backwards, watching as the dragon slithered from beneath me.

I reached for my necklace, cradling it in my fingers. If I was going to go out like this, then I would do so holding onto my mother's ashes.

I couldn't fight off a *dragon*. I was lucky enough that I had killed that troll, but I was also on solid land. The dragon spun, and I landed right on its back, my arms wrapped around its massive neck.

The dragon soared down to the mountains, and all I could do was hold on for dear life. Letting go was suicide, staying with it was suicide. No matter how I looked at it, I was going to die. Whether in the jaws of this creature or by falling to the rocky surface below—it had yet to be seen.

The dragon landed, sliding along the mountain face, hitting the surface on its back. It cried out and slithered around like a snake, with me still clamped on its neck for dear life. The dragon began to shrink, golden sparkles exploding in my field of vision and I gasped, letting go of the dragon's neck—and falling straight into the arms of Kol.

I blinked, scowling up at him. His right arm was around my back, the other underneath my legs. My arms were wrapped around his neck. I flushed and released him, but he still held onto me. He shook his head as if to clear it from some fog before he set me on my feet.

I fell to my knees, the palms of my hands slapping the mountain's surface. I panted, sweat beading along my brow. The dragon had been Kol the entire time? Was that even possible? I jumped to my feet and spun around to face him.

"How did you do that?" I demanded.

He raised a brow at me. "And here I thought you were smart enough to know your legends."

"Cut the crap." I was irritated. My heart and body still felt like I was falling through the sky, so I didn't have a second to calm my nerves because they were already shot. "How can you do that?"

"I'm more than just a trickster," he told me. "I may not be able to command armies or wield a magic hammer that controls thunder, but I can shapeshift into anything I so please."

"Anything?"

"You need only ask."

"Hm." I would need to delve deeper into the lore of my own people.

I never paid much attention to the stories my mother told me when I was a child. I never believed in the gods, not until the day

I had seen Oeric for the first time, coming to Röskr to close the gateway.

It was then that my mother told me to never show anyone the runes on my skin and forbade me from ever traveling between the realms. Not that I could anyway.

I turned my back to him, walking over to the edge of the cliff to gaze out beyond it. It looked like we were on the tallest of the mountains in this realm, this cliff overlooking *everything*. There was a massive river that cut through the mountains, forests on the right side and hills on the left.

"Where are we?" I asked.

Kol saddled up beside me. "Gørsimi."

The Realm of the Giants.

My eyes took in the scenery, but there wasn't much for me to see, being so high up. If this was the realm of the giants, then what realm had we entered before this?

I racked my brain but came up with nothing. I was still too wired up from almost falling to my death to even think.

It's probably why I wasn't all that fazed that a literal *god* was my companion and he shapeshifted into a fucking *dragon.* How much worse could it get?

"We were in Möl before this," Kol told me.

The Realm of the Elves.

"It was beautiful," I said.

Kol turned toward me. "Are you ready to listen to what I have to say now?"

I crossed my arms. "Depends. Are you going to force me through another gateway?"

He glanced around. "I don't think so. My father's ravens aren't here."

My arms dropped. "You keep saying 'father'. Why is that? It's not in the texts that Oeric had a fifth son."

"Because the legends don't like the god of tricks," he replied, voice flat. "It's a long story, one we don't have time for. Are you going to listen to me or not?"

I sighed and waved my hand at him dismissively. "All right. Go ahead."

He nodded. "I need you to steal Inkeri's Apple."

"You want me to do *what?*" I bristled, taking a step closer to him. "Are you insane?"

He raised his hands, halting my movements. "Just hear me out."

"I can't go to the Realm of the Gods!" I shouted at him. "I'll get killed."

"Not if you're smart," he said.

I huffed and turned my back to him. I could not believe that I had just entertained this idea.

Just a few minutes ago, I thought Karsten was an okay guy. Broody, sure, but otherwise harmless. But now I had just learned that he was one of the eleven *gods*. For all I knew, he was working for Oeric, drawing me into a trap so he could kill me for the illegal magic I possessed.

"I'm willing to pay you three—no, *five* times what I paid you to get my ring," Kol continued. "I can offer you more in exchange if need be."

I titled my head to glance at him over my shoulder. "Why can't you steal Inkeri's Apple? Why do you need my help?"

He scratched the back of his neck. "It's complicated."

I turned to him, brow raised. "Is that so? How?"

Kol had the audacity to look embarrassed at my question. "Look, how about we go back to Röskr? I'll let you have a few days to think this over before accepting my offer."

Eying him, I could sense he wasn't being entirely truthful. In fact, he looked slightly guilty. I reached up to touch my mother's ashes, drawing comfort in their presence.

What would my mother have done in this situation? Simple, she wouldn't have done anything. She didn't have age-old runes embedded into her skin, and she couldn't use magic like I could. But still, something bugged me. Why, out of so many people, would Kol choose me?

"Shall we get going?" he asked me.

I gave a slight nod, glancing around at our surroundings. There wasn't an aspen in sight. In fact, this area was mostly mountain. "How will we get back?"

"We don't need a tree." Kol reached over to touch the rock-face behind us. "This will suffice."

My brows knitted. "But there's not a rune on it. How will I be able to speak the word?"

He dropped his hand. "Do you not remember it?"

I wrung my hands. "Yes... and no?"

Saying those words made me feel dizzy. Who knew traveling between realms would take this much magic from me? I could use at least three to four magical runes before tiring versus traveling twice. The second time, I hadn't even said the rune; Kol had.

"It's fine. I don't need your magic. I have my own." He turned away from me. I watched as he grabbed a dagger from his belt, using it to slice his palm open. With his other hand, he dipped his fingers into the blood, using it to create the rune that was etched into my necklace. He placed his uninjured palm on the rock's surface, right next to the rune he had created. "*Nál.*"

The ground quaked. I couldn't help but stumble forward toward the rockface. Kol's hand snaked out, catching me around the waist to keep me from falling. The rock wall crumbled, creating a similar portal that we had entered the last few times.

The scenery was of Röskr—or rather, the walled city of Ellriheimr. I noticed Fenrir lying beside the tree, eyes closed and tail swishing back and forth.

I didn't even wait for Kol, I jumped right through the portal. I fell face-first, but thankfully I landed right on Fen's furry body. He yelped and jumped up, growling low in his throat. His growls halted when he noticed that it had been me who had landed on him, and his expression changed as he tackled me.

"Oh, Fen!" I giggled, tucking his massive head under my arm. "I'm never traveling the realms without you again."

"It's best to say that you won't be traveling at all." Kol stepped through the portal, arms crossed over his chest. "It's extremely dangerous."

I gently pushed my companion's head to the side to prevent being licked, hearing his whimpering. "Why? I know how now."

He jabbed his thumb toward the closing portal. "Because you'll get found out. Those ravens weren't just any ravens; they were my father's most trusted sentinels. It's safe to say they know you exist now."

I swallowed. "Will they come looking for me?"

"Not if you keep your head down," he said. "If you jump through to another realm, I can't guarantee that Oeric won't find you."

I stood, my hands fisted in Fen's fur. "But he will find me eventually?"

"If you don't stay here."

Letting go of Fenrir's fur, I took off my gloves, holding out my arms for Kol to see. "He'll find me because of these, won't he?"

He stepped closer, inspecting my arms. He took my right arm, his thumb roving over the intricate design of the old runic language—the language the gods spoke.

Kol's eyes turned up to meet mine. "Do you know how you got these?"

I shook my head. "I... I don't know."

He raised a brow. "Amnesia."

"I would have known if I had suffered from that."

Kol dropped his hand from my arm. "Not necessarily."

My heart jumped. "What do you mean?"

He clicked his tongue. "What do you know of these runes, Eira?"

I blinked. "Nothing really. The only thing my mother told me was that I needed to remain hidden from you and the rest of the gods. She said that it was dangerous but would never tell me why other than the fact that I'm human."

"The only ones who can use this type of magic, other than my people, are the people of Eiði. But they were forbidden from leaving their realm the same time the humans were forced to stay, not that it mattered."

"What do you mean?"

"Humans can't travel through the realms unless they have magic or have something like this." He lifted his hand to show me the ring I had stolen back for him. "Relics contain old magic. It's also the only way a human can go between realms. For you, the magic is already embedded into those runes."

I swallowed. "Does... does that make me someone from Eiði then?"

Kol's laugh was dry and humorless. "No. I can tell that you're not one of them. However, seeing you with those runes poses a lot of questions."

I grabbed my gloves and put them back on. "Who would have the answers then?"

"Your mother."

"And she's been dead for years," I sighed.

Kol's expression softened. "I'm sorry."

I waved away his sentiment. "It was a long time ago. I don't worry about it anymore."

"And yet,"—he drew closer—"you still grieve the loss as if she just died."

I frowned, my body stiffening. "No, I don't."

"You do." He turned, preparing to leave. "Oh, and another thing."

"What?"

He winked. "Happy birthday, my little hellfire."

SEVENTEEN

appy birthday, my little hellfire.

There weren't enough words to describe how I felt when those words left Kol's lips. I hadn't thought much about my birthday, mainly because it was a few days before my mother's death.

I tried not to think about it, and I almost always forgot about my birthday.

I was twenty-one.

I wondered how Kol knew about my birthday but thought better of it. He was a god, so he would know a whole lot of things. Not to mention that he'd said more than a handful of times that he had "done his research" on me before hiring me to invade Jarl Lott's longhouse. So if he knew about me, it stood to reason that so did Oeric. The only thing about that was, he didn't know who I actually was. But today, he would learn my face and would use that to scour the realms to find me.

It wasn't every day you found yourself working for a god, but it also wasn't every day you had the chance to do something out-of-this-world impossible.

I realm jumped today.

I lowered my head back down on my couch, eyes closed as I remembered everything I had seen in Möl, The Realm of the Elves.

I sucked air in through my teeth, seeing myself standing in that enchanting forest again, looking around at how beautiful and filled with magic those woods were. I only wished Fenrir had been with me; he would have loved it.

Then there was Gørsimi, the Realm of the Giants. That place had been mostly mountains with sparse foliage and several rivers, but other than that, there wasn't much that I could have seen. It may have been because I was falling through the sky and almost got eaten by a dragon that was actually Kol that whole time.

I was hungry for more. I wanted to know everything about the other realms.

Snorting, I stood and grabbed my gloves from the desk beside my door. Fenrir sprang to his feet, prancing over to me. I stroked him and together we walked out into the streets.

Snow was now falling, fat snowflakes of frozen water cascading from the sky. The streets were coated in white snow, tracks leading to and from the intersections. It was less busy today, with almost everyone probably holed up in their homes so they didn't have to be out in this cold weather.

I pulled the hood of my cloak up over my head, gesturing for Fenrir to follow me. We stepped out onto the snow, my boots crunching over the frozen wasteland.

It wasn't a long walk from my home to the library, so I would be home before too long. Normally, I would let Fenrir stay home, but being separated from him for those few hours I had spent with Kol in those other realms made me realize just how much I appreciated my companion. He was all I had left of my family, and he would stick with me.

I passed a few guards, but most of them were far too busy keeping themselves warm and dry by hanging under the awnings of buildings. We soon came upon the library, that same guy from a week prior still perched on his miniature stand, holding out flyers and crying about the second coming of the gods.

If I hadn't just spent time with the god of tricks, I would've still scoffed at him and went on my merry way.

Now, however, I wanted to learn more. Although, I doubted that Kol being here in Röskr would cause Ragnarök. We ignored him, taking the steps two at a time until we reached the doorway.

I was surprised to see that the library was mostly full of people today. Normally, there would be some people, ten at best. Now, it was crawling with visitors. I wasn't exactly sure why, but I assumed it had something to do with this weather.

It was cold out, and these people would rather sit by the fireplace and read a book than be out in that terrible chill.

I shouldn't mock because I was about to do the same thing. I ushered Fenrir forward, and he followed close at my heels. A child smiled, pointing at my wolf. His mother gasped, picking up her son and scurrying away with him.

My brows knitted. I didn't know what would warrant that to happen. My Fen was well-known in these parts. He would often come home some days with children at his heels, playing around with them. Some of the vendors in the city would hand him some meat or another treat.

He was a beloved beast of the city, so this was strange.

Ignoring that weird reaction, I walked through the library in search of the books I wanted to read. It wouldn't take me long to find them, as I was familiar with this place. I spent a lot of my time in this place, gathering information and getting my jobs through here. Finding a few books on the realms wouldn't take me long.

As I suspected, it didn't take me long to find what I was looking for. My fingers skimmed the spines of the books, the tips of my fingers now coated in grime and dust from the novels being shelved for so long.

Each book was a tome of each realm, with the last book titled: *The Nine Realms of Auðin*. The book next to it was called: *Myths and Legends of Auðin*.

Interesting.

I glanced at Fenrir, watching as he napped gracefully at my feet, waiting for me to finish what I was doing here. I knew a pretty good amount of everything about our world, but what else could I learn along the way?

I bit my lower lip in contemplation. Images of both Möl and Gørsimi flashed across my mind, and it helped with my resolve.

Grabbing all the books on the shelf and hobbling over to the counter, I hoped I wouldn't drop anything or kill someone with these hefty books. The librarian stamped something into a book, pushing it aside to work on the next one. She didn't notice me, at least not until I slammed the books on the counter.

She jumped, hand to her heart. "By the grace of the Áræði!"

I grinned. "No, it's just me."

She scowled, standing with her arms crossed over her chest. "And what on this Irithia are you doing with all these books, Eira?"

Shrugging my shoulders, I leaned over the counter to gaze at what she was working on. "It's about to get worse. I thought some nice reading material would do me some good."

She raised a brow, taking a book in her hands. She read the title before she opened it, skimming through a few pages. "You just so happened to pick up a book that pertained to each realm in Auðin?"

I gave another half-hearted shrug. "I'm bored, and this seemed interesting."

My heart sped up when she frowned and chose another book, thumbing through the pages. Had Jarl Lott made a rule that no one could take out these certain books? Absurd obviously, but why else would this librarian be so suspicious about all these books that I had chosen?

Traveling between realms was forbidden; everyone knew this, so what harm would befall someone by reading about these eight other realms? It didn't make any sense, but I made a mental note to ask Kol about it later. *If* I wanted to even do this job for him.

I jabbed my thumb out to the doors that led out into the city, my other hand resting on my belt. "So, um, can I take these and go? It's about to get dark, and I don't want to get caught up in more than just snow and ice."

The librarian looked as if she wanted to argue, but she clicked her tongue and began to stamp the front pages of the books.

She placed them in a leather bag and held it out to me. I reached out to take it, but then her eyes strayed to my gloved hands, and her brows drew forward in confusion. I quickly took the bag and slung it over my shoulder, tapping my hip for Fenrir to follow.

I could feel the prying eyes of the librarian following behind me, and I quickened my pace until I reached the safety of the outside world once more.

EIGHTEEN

I placed the bag on the table in the kitchen before I went to my bedroom to relieve myself of my cloak and gloves. I hated wearing them, but it was a far better alternative than long sleeves.

Once I got that put away, I headed back out into my kitchen. The fire in the hearth was dimming, the flames slowly dying. Walking over, I crouched down before it, my fingers touching a piece of log that hadn't ignited yet.

"*Fiðri.*"

A small flame danced off my fingers, instantly catching on the log. It crackled, popped, and shot off cinders as the logs settled, the flames dancing along the bark. I stood, holding out my arms so I could warm them up before getting to work.

Fenrir didn't waste a single second as he laid by the fire, going to sleep almost immediately.

Settling in my seat, I brought over the books, reading through the titles. There were exactly nine realms in the entirety of Auðin. Each realm had their own people, vegetation, and monsters. I had already seen some of both Möl and Gørsimi, so I pushed those books to the side for now.

Picking a random book, I looked at the title: *The Realm of Móðr*—better known as hell itself.

I flicked the book open, seeing the map of my world. Röskr was in the middle of the world, with Ásjá, the Realm of the Gods, above it. Then the other realms were evenly spaced out around my little one, almost like they were protecting it from something.

I breezed through the two realms I had been to, skipping over Röskr as well since I lived here. I knew this place like the back of my hand, so I wasn't exactly sure what I would be looking for if I had never left this place. I knew all the legends, all the lore, everything.

I read the beginning title of the chapter, intrigued already: *The Goddess of Móðr*. I knew little about the goddess who ruled over hell. The only thing I knew about her was her name, Tyra. I began to read the passage, my fingers sliding along the page.

The Goddess of Móðr is half goddess and half giantess. She is split into two parts, one of beauty that rivals all others, and the other that is rotten, flesh slipping from the bone to show off the marred and dead features.

Smart, cunning, and equally evil, Tyra was chosen to reside beneath the earth to hide, ultimately creating the Underworld for her to rule and watch over.

There is very little mention of this goddesses, only short tales spun by wary travelers and half-drunken men. However, many believe that if your soul does not die on the battlefield, it will be cast down into the Underworld under Tyra's rule.

Interesting.

I thumbed through the rest of the chapter, my eyes skimming over anything I didn't care enough to read. At least until I found what I was searching for. *The Realm of Móðr.*

The Realm of Móðr is vast and endless. It was divided into sections for Tyra's rule. She chose these sections, giving each person who died a specific place. One of those sections was called The Shore of Corpses. Here, adulterers, traitors, and murderers were sentenced for all eternity.

Móðr is a placed filled with ice and snow, cold just like Tyra's soul. After she was born, Oeric decided that ruling over the coldest realm would stop her from gaining much control over anything else.

She ruled over the dead, conjuring up her own army.

I closed the book and pushed it away from me, biting my thumbnail to the quick.

I knew that most realms held a dark backstory, one that was hidden when Oeric forbade it long ago. Now, I strongly believed that the All-Father was up to something, but I just wasn't sure what yet. There was no reason for him to seal off the realms and ban travel. However, based on my two realm jumps, that clearly wasn't the case.

Travel *wasn't* banned. Far from it, in fact. Maybe Oeric made it seem like that on purpose? What would he have to gain from doing that?

I reached for another book, my fingers touching the cover of one as a knock at my door made me nearly jump out of my skin. Fenrir lifted his head, ears forward.

I waited for a moment. Lo and behold, another came, and I sighed as I stood up to go and see who it was. Fenrir didn't move, but I could see that he was still on high alert just in case he was needed to protect me.

Opening the door, the last face I had ever expected to see was Kol's. Frowning, I went to slam the door in his face, but his boot came out, stopping the door from closing.

I narrowed my eyes as Kol slithered into my home, arms crossed as he inspected my living space.

I closed the door, leaning my back against it. "What are you doing here?"

He turned, hands in his pockets now. "I just came by to see if you'd thought about my offer." His eyes slid over to the books on my table. He walked over, picked one up, and read the cover before he placed it back down, his fingers drumming over it. "But I'm quite curious to see why you have every book of the realms in your home."

"The librarian said the same," I told him. "She seemed suspicious."

"Because no one is supposed to be asking questions about the realms."

"Why?"

Kol turned and walked over to Fen, who had gone back to sleep. Upon hearing someone coming over, my wolf lifted his head.

Kol squatted down, running his hand over my companion's fur. I noticed something silver gleaming in his hand and went to ask, but Kol was quicker. Without a word, he clipped the object to Fenrir's ear, but my wolf didn't make a single noise.

I walked over, trying to see what it was that he had done to my wolf. "What are you doing to Fenrir?"

Kol gestured to my wolf, who now sported a metal hoop on his right ear. I got down to my knees to inspect the weird new object. It was elegant craftmanship, the edges smooth. There were runes engraved into it, but I couldn't read it. I could read *some* of the Old Language, but not all. Mother never got that far before she died.

I ran my hand over the engravings, trying to piece together what it could mean, but came up short. I turned my head up to look at Kol, my eyes narrowed. "What does this say?"

"Since you complained when you realm jumped, I decided to find an old relic that held magic in it." He gestured to Fenrir's new earring. "This holds magic in it. Now that your wolf has magic with him, he can realm jump with you now."

My eyes went wide, but they instantly squinted at him. "You're being awfully generous. What's the catch?"

He held up his hands. "Haven't I always been generous?"

"Hm." I stood, hands on my hips. "I don't believe you."

He cocked his head toward the table in my kitchen with the books laid out. "Mind if we sit and chat? We need to discuss what's to come."

Walking over to the table, I moved my books to the opposite end before I sat down, my hands on the table. Kol didn't even wait for me to tell him to sit before he took his place at my table, once more grabbing a book to inspect. He opened it, flipping through the pages.

I sat back in my chair. "What did you want to talk about?"

Kol closed the book and set it back on top of the rest. He pointed at my arms and the runes that I hadn't even tried to hide from him. "First off, you asked me what those were."

Suddenly self-conscious, I slid my arms under the table on my lap. "I did."

He held out his hand. "Mind if I see them again?"

I hesitated, chewing my bottom lip. I'd never shown anyone my runes before, and only my mother knew of them. She worried that if someone knew or found out, I would be taken or worse—killed. She never told me why, just that it was because humans weren't supposed to possess magic.

However, Kol already knew, and he held some answers. Granted, he had just told me yesterday that it was my mother who held all the answers.

Slowly, I lifted my arm and placed it across his palm. "You said that only my mother knew the answers."

"I lied," he said matter-of-factly.

I rolled my eyes. "Why am I not surprised?"

He ran his other hand up along my arm, tracing the runes that were tattooed onto my skin. His touch alone sent shivers down my spine, made my knees weak.

Gods, why does his touch ignite my soul? I thought to myself.

He shouldn't elicit anything from me and yet I had to clench my legs to keep from squirming.

He released my arm. "I lied because we were out in the open. Those ravens are Oeric's shadows, and they will report back to him about what they've heard."

I swallowed. "You said that we were alone."

He shrugged. "I wasn't completely sure, but I had to be safe just in case."

Seemed reasonable, but I was still pissed about the whole situation. "So, what are these runes, and why do I have them?"

"As I mentioned before, these runes are part of an old tongue that was used by the Völva, back when they used to live in Eiði. They were mostly human, but the vast majority of them were half god and goddess. Back then, magic wasn't seen as a curse. In fact, it was the opposite. They were worshipped. However, the only people allowed to have the runes and to use them were known as the Völvas."

"You said that name twice now," I commented. "But you never specified *what* a Völva is."

He crossed his arms. "Seeress."

I blinked. "A Seeress? I thought those were all—"

"Dead?" His brows raised. "Exactly."

I ran a hand over my arm, right along the marks on the tattoos. "So, I'm a Seeress."

He shrugged. "I speculate it, but I'm not certain. Your mother was human, therefore she had no use for magic. Someone else placed those runic curses on you."

"Who would do that?" I asked.

"Who knows," Kol replied. "Your mother must have angered the gods or your father. Either way, they enacted a punishment, which was those runes."

"Except the punishment befell me," I sighed.

He nodded. "It would appear so."

I chewed my lower lip. "Do you think we can get them removed?"

"Perhaps. But the Áraeði are vengeful gods, and they won't allow this to go on for much longer. Those ravens didn't find us by chance. You were being followed."

I sat forward. "Followed?"

"Have you noticed any birds or ravens this past season? That might help me break down the timeline."

My eyes narrowed. "Why are you suddenly interested in helping me?"

Kol stood, pushing the chair back to the table, his hands resting along the backrest of it. "Because it's in *both* our interests."

"Seems like it's more for your benefit rather than my own," I sneered. "Let me guess. You'll help me figure out my runes and why they were given to me and in exchange—"

"You'll steal Inkeri's Apple," Kol finished for me.

There really was no way around this, was there? I could readily deny him, and he would leave... only to come back again and again.

I really didn't want to get any closer to the eleven gods, but I also couldn't live the rest of my life watching over my shoulder, waiting for Oeric's time to strike. Kol was cold and calculating, using my runes to his advantage.

If I wanted answers and a way to get off Oeric's radar, I would need Kol's help. To receive that, I would need to help him in return.

"So, what is this apple you're so fascinated with? Why is it so important for me to get it for you? I mean, you're one of the main gods, so why can't you just go up there and retrieve it for yourself?" I asked him.

He hesitated for a moment before he shrugged. "As you know, I'm world-famous for my bag of tricks. It's not often that I don't get blamed for other's wrongdoings. But if someone else does the job for me, the blame goes elsewhere, and I'm allowed to do what I please."

"So, you're risking my neck for your own sake?"

"No." He seemed hurt by that comment. "Quite the opposite. Once I get blamed and they find out it wasn't me, I'll point fingers at the real culprit."

"Which is me."

"Obviously, I'll choose another to blame, Eira."

I gestured to him and then to myself. "You seriously can't believe that I would help you with this. Not after what you just said."

"I'm a fool and a liar," Kol replied. "But the one thing I can promise is that I always keep my word."

"Which doesn't speak much," I muttered.

He turned, his hand on the knob of my door. "Study up on what Inkeri's Apple does and I'll return in a few days with a firmer idea. I promise that I won't let harm come to you in any way, Eira. There are far more forces in this world that would rather see the gods fall to their knees than you'd think."

I rose to my feet as Kol left my home, slamming the door behind him. Grumbling, I kicked my chair back and sat down, my back to the rest and my arms crossed.

Fenrir didn't move from his spot in front of the fire, the gleaming red-gold of the flames dancing along his new relic. My eyes strayed to the tomes on my table, my fingers itching to grab another to read. But that would come at another time. For now, I needed to rest for what was to come.

NINETEEN

The next day, I decided that I would go out with Fenrir to the markets. All night, my dreams were plagued with monsters, skeletons with glowing blue orbs for eyes, wielding axes and swords. Another dream was me being eaten by that same dragon that Kol had shapeshifted into.

I'd kept Fen up the whole night, so he lagged behind me, head low but keeping pace like he always did no matter what.

Almost a week ago, if not longer, it was warmer, with only the cool wind and falling leaves signaling the coming winter. Now, the whole scenery had changed. The streets were coated in a thin layer of ice and snow, the populace bundled up and shuffling to their destinations. My breath came out in frosts, the hairs on my arms standing up each time a gust of wind tore through my cloak.

The markets were basically empty this morning. The rest of the deer I had killed and skinned was mostly gone now. A few slivers of meat remained, so that was the cause for this mini excursion out into the city. I preferred to hunt, but after that grizzly and the troll, I refused to go back out into those woods if I didn't have to.

I passed by a few of the vendors, checking their wares. I still had plenty of coin left over from what Kol had given me a week ago, so money wasn't an issue.

The issue I did find was that these vendors' stalls were mostly bare. I loved vegetables; they were probably one of my favorite things to cook with, especially carrots. And my usual vendor was empty save for a beet, three potatoes, and a single bundle of rainbow carrots. Nothing else remained.

The vendor, an older man by the name of Ric, nodded his head at me, smiling with those almost black, yellow-stained teeth. "It's been a while, Eira. How have you been?"

I dug through my purse and handed him a little more than normal, taking everything he had left and stuffing it in the satchel around my shoulders. "Fine for the most part. I've just been hanging around."

Ric eyed my coin purse that was nestled in the palm of my hand. "Got a decent paying job this time?"

I shrugged, tucking my purse back on my hip for later. "The job paid well enough." I turned, looking at him over my shoulder. "I should get going now. I don't want to miss anything else the vendors have to sell."

Ric waved me off, standing up to pack up his belongings. With each season that came and went, he had grown frailer and older.

I cared about Ric; he was the closet person I had to a friend in this city without Fen. He always saved me the freshest vegetables, and even when he didn't have enough for himself, he would offer me the rest. I always declined his offer, as I made more than enough to pay for my fair share.

A few other vendors were packing up for the day, the clouds above opening up with more bouts of snow.

I drew my cloak closer, pulling up my hood to stave off the chill of the wind that bit at my cheeks and nose. This was promising to be a dreadful winter, and it wasn't even late December yet. I wandered through the remaining stalls, buying three apples and a few more vegetables from another vendor before I spotted the last remaining stall in the street.

Fenrir's ears perked up when we walked closer, his nose sniffing the air. The meat man, whom I'd lovingly named Solis, was bent over a box of knives and other kitchenware. He lifted his head when my wolf and I stopped before him.

His brows raised. "Well, if it isn't Eira and her companion Fenrir."

I grinned. "Nice to see you again, Solis. Anything left from today?"

He gestured for me to get closer as he rose to his feet and began to rummage around in another box he had hidden behind his small stall. He pulled out three rabbits, holding them by their legs as he held them out for me. "I have these three left."

My eyes roved over the rabbits. They were far smaller than the ones I normally hunted. These looked no more than a few months old and still young and small for their age. There wouldn't be much meat on them, but at least it would be enough for tonight. I would have to go hunting in the morning.

I took the rabbits from him, tying them to my satchel as I dug out some coin to give him. He took my payment before beginning to dismantle his stall like the others before him. I stroked Fen's head, offering him a small smile as we began our trek back home.

The snow was beginning to fall faster and harder, the small flakes now turned into fat, heavy ones. The streets were already covered, the tracks from other people already beginning to fill up with more snow and ice. I quickened my pace, and Fenrir bolted forward, his paws digging into the snow to create tracks.

Everyone was already inside their homes, nestling in for the long winter ahead.

Fenrir was already on the steps of our home right when I passed the wrought iron gate. My boots crunched on snow, and I took two steps before I decided to knock the sides of my boots on the wooden stairs to help dislodge the snow. Once my soles were cleared, I unlocked the front door, Fen wasting no time in sliding in between my legs to get inside where it was warm.

I closed the door behind me, locking it. Shedding my cloak and gloves, I unlaced my boots and set down our spoils for the day. Thankfully, I had left the fire going with a pot of water resting above it. Steam curled up from the contents, and I went through my satchel of goods. I put aside the fruits I had gotten, laying out my vegetables.

Grabbing my dagger, I sliced through my carrots, squash, and a weird green vegetable that the other vendor told me was good for stews. The mushrooms and potatoes were left on the side, as they would go in later.

Once my vegetables were all in the scalding hot water, I began to shed the fur from the rabbits. In the safety of my own home, I wasn't worried about how long it would take for me to skin these animals. Still, there was hardly any meat on these three.

Walking over to where I kept the last of our deer, I gave the rest of it to Fenrir, who huffed at me gratefully before he started to eat by the fire.

Once the rabbits were skinned and the meat was chopped up and set in the pot, I sat down at the table. Reaching out to the books, I brought them closer to inspect the titles to see which one I wanted to read. Of course, the tome titled: *Myths and Legends of Auðin.*

I cracked it open, thumbing through some of the obvious chapters I'd heard about from my mother when I was a child. Those stories were ingrained in my memory, so there was no need for a refresher. I did halt by the lore of Kol's origins but decided against it.

I had other things to read about first, and that was… what was the name? Seeress? I remembered that it started with a "V" so I would search the index.

Völva.

That's it! I began to flip through the chapters until I found the page where the chapter was titled: *The Origins of the Völva.* Excellent, this would do and then after this, I would find out why Kol was so hellbent on taking Inkeri's Apple.

The Völva, also known as the Seeress, in Viking settlements were harbingers of ancient magic called Seiðr. Unlike the Áræði, the Völva's used magic from runes that were embedded into their skin. Even with the runes, the Völva's had to say the magic runic names before casting magic.

The Völva's originated first in the Realm of Eiði, also home to the lesser gods, Vætt. The very first Völva was one of Oeric's own Valkyries. When the All-Father had discovered his Valkyrie's magical properties, he sent her to live alone in Eiði with the Vætt.

After years of living on Eiði, the Valkyrie bore a child, a daughter with runes embedded in her flesh. This girl became the first known "Völva" in the eyes of mortals. This Völva would grow to bear more children, every third daughter having the Seiðr.

I stopped reading for a moment, running my hand through my hair. So, a Valkyrie, one of Oeric's most trusted warrior, was the first Völva, at least to the Áræði. To the humans, it was the

Valkyrie's first daughter that became the first Seeress. However, this book clearly stated that every third daughter would inherit the Seiðr.

I was an only child. My parents never had any other children because my father died shortly after my second birthday. My mother never disappeared long, a few days at most, but I would have known if she had fallen pregnant by another man. I never noticed, and she never said anything about it either. The only other explanation was that she had children before she met my father, which was a possibility.

Perhaps I was an exception? To the ancestors, maybe they believed that it was every third born daughter?

So many questions and yet so little to answer them. These books offered little to no insight, and it was beginning to wear on my mind and heart heavily. Maybe now it was time I read about Inkeri's Apple to get a feel for what I was about to walk into.

I opened the page for the chapter about the apples when I heard something sizzling by the fire. Closing the book, I glanced over at the fire to see that some of the stew's broth was spilling over into the logs, making that hissing noise.

I got up and stirred the pot, removing it from the fire and setting it on the table. Fenrir was asleep, letting out soft snores. Filling my bowl, I sat back down to eat my fill. Each time I lifted my spoon, all I could think about was the first Seeress and the magic she possessed. It was strange to think that someone could be born with magical runes.

Once I was full, I put my pot of stew away for tomorrow's meal and headed off to bed. At the sound of my footsteps, my wolf perked up, now awake.

Fenrir yawned, scratching himself before he followed me lazily. He took his usual spot at my feet, and I curled up into a ball, my mind a jumble of nerves. Tomorrow was a new day, and hopefully, I would get some answers.

TWENTY

I t was still snowing by the time I awoke the next morning. It was also far colder than before. I started the fire, using my magic to rekindle the flames before I dressed for the day. Making sure that I was bundled up in the warmest of furs, I left my cloak but put on my gloves just in case.

I opened the door, peeking outside. The snow hadn't stopped since yesterday, so there was a good nine inches and climbing. Grunting, I held the door open for Fenrir, my companion jumping right into the snow flurry, rolling around like he was having the time of his life.

"And to think I thought you hated snow," I grumbled to him.

Fenrir barked at me before bounding after me when I began walking. Today, no one was out. Thankfully, this would be a quick enough trek to the forest, but the snow was almost to my knees, so I would have a hard time keeping quiet.

I hoped to get another buck today, something that would last us another week or two before we had to venture out again. Of course, once this winter storm gave way and there was no more snow on the ground, I would wager we'd venture out again just to stock up for another impeding winter. The vendors would have nothing left this season, the rest in their pantries for themselves.

I had tried to grow a garden once, but it never really panned out. Hunting was more my forte, and it was something my mother taught me by the time I could walk and hold a bow. I was a skilled archer; I never missed. But that didn't mean I always got my kills. Sometimes, my shots would land, just not in the spots where I wanted them to.

When my prey would scamper off into the woods, I would follow the trail of blood. Nine times out of ten, there would be no other predator taking my kill for themselves. That one time every so often was another predator that would steal my kill, and I would leave them be in search of another.

My steps were light, my chest rising and falling with each breath that I took. I was beginning to sink, using all my energy to get my feet back on track. Even Fenrir was having trouble keeping up, his tongue lolling out as he had to jump every so often to keep walking.

I halted, listening to the forest around me. I so hoped that there wasn't another grizzly or troll. At this point, I'd just let them kill me because there was no way in hell I would be able to defend myself from an attack, not when my feet were covered in heavy snow.

Thankfully, my ears didn't pick up anything out of the ordinary. I did hear a raven off in the distance, but I doubted it was one of Oeric's shadows. I wasn't sure how long it would take them to reach Röskr from the other realms, but it had to be at least long enough for me to be safe.

I made a quick mental note to ask Kol about the Shadows later, but right now I would focus on finding me and Fenrir a kill.

After an hour of being out in the forest, I finally found something worth killing. A small herd of deer wandered by, but there wasn't a buck in sight.

My heart fell slightly. I hated killing the female deer, as they were the ones that rebuilt the population rather quickly. Not to mention she could have a calf and I wasn't about to lower the deer population. However, it was either them or me, and I would choose myself first and foremost. Life was tough for all of us, but sometimes, the most difficult choices had to be made.

I unslung my bow, nocked an arrow, and let it fly.

I dropped the satchel of deer meat on the table, sliding into my seat with a heavy sigh. Fenrir hobbled inside, weak from the snow and running. He dragged the rest of the deer behind him, lying flat on his stomach with his massive snout held open to cool himself off.

"I know," I panted. "I'm tired too."

Fen whimpered but said nothing more. I allowed myself a moment to collect myself before I got up, walked around the table, and unlatched him from his reins. He sighed, rolling over onto his back with his paws in the air and his tongue lolled out.

It wasn't long before he began to snore, and I couldn't help the giggle that rose to the surface.

I decided to leave the meat on the table for now. It was mostly frozen anyway, so I didn't have to worry about getting cold quickly. The thought of a hot bath was enticing, but I was sweating in my gear. All that work and I was working up a sweat. Thankfully, we had made it back in time before we both collapsed from exhaustion.

Perhaps once I was cooled off and irritable, I would take a bath and then a nap. There wasn't much else for me to do besides read, and even then—

"Hellllooooo."

Kol.

I didn't even hide my groan, and I made sure it was loud as hell as I stomped over to my door, throwing it open to see the trickster god standing before me.

"What do you want, Kol?" I wasn't in the mood for his antics, and I sure as hell was not going to entertain him.

He grinned broadly. "I just came by to see if you want to join me in a little, oh I don't know, adventure?"

I narrowed my eyes. "What sort of adventure?"

He clicked his tongue. "So rude."

"I'm in no mood," I said flatly.

Kol breezed in and I slammed the door shut, resting my back against it as he walked over to the fire to warm his hands. Fenrir didn't even move an inch, his snores reaching each crevice in our house.

"I can see that," Kol retorted.

"What do you want?" I asked a second time.

He stuffed his hands in his pockets. "I'm about to head into the Realm of Skóð."

I blinked at him; my interest piqued. "The Realm of the Dwarves? Why would we need to go there?"

Kol's eyes drifted to the dagger strapped to my side. "If you're going to help me steal Inkeri's Apple, you're going to need a stronger weapon than that."

I frowned, removing my dagger to glance at it. "What's wrong with it?"

Kol's hand snaked out like a viper, his fingers curling around my dagger. He held it up in the light, inspecting it. "It's obsidian."

"So?"

"Obsidian is made up of rock and glass. This dagger is mostly rock with pieces of obsidian in it." He handed it back to me. "Good against most things, but not so good against trolls, giants, and the like."

I sheathed my dagger, annoyed. "So, what does my dagger have to do with anything?"

"Like I said, if you plan on helping me steal Inkeri's Apple, you'll need something far stronger than a rock and glass dagger."

My brows knitted. "I never said I would fight anyone or anything."

"You also never fully agreed to this arrangement. However, I have a feeling you would regardless to get out from beneath the thumb of the All-Father. I'm sure by now he knows about you from that little stunt you pulled with the troll in the woods and the realm we visited with the elves."

My heart froze. I already knew this as he told me some days prior that I had been followed. However, I heard the deep undertone to his voice and knew that it meant something different than before. "Oeric knows about me?"

I wasn't about to ask how he knew about the troll. If the Shadows had seen, then Oeric would definitely know about me. I'm not sure how Kol knew about the troll, but I would ask him about that part later.

Kol shrugged. "It's a safe bet. He hasn't asked me anything yet, but he *is* the All-Father. He got rid of his eye just so he could see glimpses into the future."

"What will the dwarves do with my dagger anyway?" I asked him.

"Not sure. Best I can gather is they'll make it strong enough for you to use against a stronger opponent."

"Fine." I turned to my bedroom. "Let me put away my—"

Kol's hand reached out, his fingers wrapping around my wrist as he tugged me forward, my other hand resting along his chest. My eyes widened, the warmth that I felt seeping into my flesh, making my knees weak and something twinge in my navel.

It was almost like his touch was electric—in all the good ways.

Gods, I thought. *Give me strength.*

I cleared my throat and removed my hand from his chest, the other one still clasped in his hand. He seemed to realize what he had done and unlatched me like I had burned him. He didn't utter a word as he took a step back from me, his eyes on the roaring fire.

"I'll be out here. Take as much time as you need," he said.

Face flushing, I started to walk backwards from where he was. "I won't be but a moment. I just need to change out of this gear." I paused. "What's the weather like in Skóð anyway? Is it anything like it is in Röskr?"

Kol shook his head. "It's the exact opposite."

My legs basically didn't need any prompting as I sprinted into my room, slammed the door shut behind me, and began to change into something warmer. He did say that it was the exact opposite of how cold it was here, so I could only assume it was summertime or springtime. Either way, I was going to jump headlong into something warm.

Once I had shed my cloak and my other garments, I changed into what I would normally wear. Long pants and a sleeveless shirt with fur-covered armor on my shoulders. Of course, I would need to wear my gloves, but that was nothing compared to being out in the cold with snow and ice. I would take what I can get.

Walking out of my bedroom, I noticed Kol shifting through a few pages of the books. He lifted his gaze to meet mine for a second, almost like he was assessing me before he placed the book down.

"Ready to go then?" he asked.

I grabbed my bow and arrows and whistled for Fenrir. He bounded up almost instantly, yelping as he danced on the balls of his paws. "Let's get going."

TWENTY-ONE

I *really* should have thought this plan over before accepting the offer to jump to another realm. Trudging through the snow that now reached almost to my knees, with nothing to cover myself but my gloves, I was miserable. My arms were wrapped around myself, head ducked so that the snow wouldn't collect on my lashes.

"You do realize that you can control magic right?" Kol pressed on, leading us outside the city gates. "Why don't you just use it to warm yourself up?"

Because I'm an idiot, I thought to myself.

"I thought you could just jump us into another realm. I didn't think I had to walk through snow to get to that blasted tree again," I said instead.

Kol looked amused at that comment. "I may be a god," he said. "But even I have my limits."

"So jumping without a portal isn't one of them?"

He didn't stop as he turned his head to glance at me from the corner of his eye. "I would focus on heating yourself up, Eira. You're turning as blue as a Frost Giant."

I hated to admit he was right, but I also couldn't fathom saying those words. I couldn't feel anything anymore, so that was a sign that I needed to get warm before hyperthermia set in.

I closed my eyes, calming my nerves. *"Fiðri."*

Almost instantly, my body began to warm, almost like a fire was scorching underneath my skin. Each time a snowflake landed on my flesh, it would sizzle and dry instantly. I glanced over at Kol who had now stopped, watching me intently, almost like a science experiment.

My face flushed. "What?"

He blinked, almost like he was in a trance before he shook his head and turned around. "Nothing."

I wanted to pry some more but decided against it. Thankfully, I noticed the aspen tree off in the distance. Just like before, it appeared almost untouched by the winter elements. The leaves were full and bright, the ground around it covered in snow.

Quickening my pace, I did my best not to lag behind both my wolf and the trickster god.

A sound similar to a knock came from a distance, and Kol halted when he heard it. His shoulders drew forward, and he glanced up at the sky. I followed his gaze, trying to see what it was that he could see.

"We need to hurry," he said flatly.

He quickened his pace. I tried to catch up, by the snow was up to my knees now, so I wasn't making much progress. I may be warm now, but I was still powerless against the deep snow and biting wind.

I eventually made it to the tree with Fenrir by my side. He shook himself from the snow, his tail wagging slightly as he waited for me and Kol.

"Are you or am I...?" I asked.

He placed his hand on the tree, ignoring me. *"Nál."*

Fenrir hit my side, keeping himself close to me as the tree began to shake and stir. The ground quaked, but with all the snow, it did little to move the pebbles beneath. Instinctively, my hand reached out, fingers digging into my wolf's fur.

Fen was my comfort, my *home*. I couldn't—*wouldn't*—do this without him by my side.

The bark splintered and cracked, opening up to a world that looked similar to one we had visited previously. Kol put one foot through the portal, holding out his hand for me. I allowed Fen to go through first, sighing in relief when he jumped through with ease. So that ring Kol had given him actually worked. Good.

I walked forward, ignoring his offered hand and jumping through.

At first, I was worried that it would be like last time and I would be falling through the sky, but the moment my feet touched down on solid ground, I felt at ease. Fenrir was running in circles, chasing his tail before he threw himself down into the dirt, rolling himself around.

Kol was right; Skóð really was the exact opposite of Röskr. My realm was heavily wooded with rolling hills and rivers, with cities and towns dotting the regions. Skóð was nothing but mountains. All I could see for miles upon miles were more mountains. Small, big, medium—they ranged from all sizes.

I knew little about the other creatures of the realms, but from what knowledge I did have, I knew that dwarves thrived beneath the surface.

Kol dusted himself off, running his hand over the rock wall behind us, closing up the portal. He seemed troubled about something, but he walked around Fenrir's frolicking form to stand beside me.

"Enjoying the view?" he asked.

"Depends." I glanced at him. "Was that one of Oeric's Shadows?"

Kol nodded. "It was. It seems he's watching you after all."

I swallowed. "You said that he gave up his eye to see the future, so shouldn't it stand to reason that he knows what we're doing?"

"*Premonitions*," Kol corrected. "I wouldn't be plotting this if I knew he would have already known what we were doing. It's why he's sent his two Shadows after us. He doesn't know what we're up to, but he knows that something is up."

"Oh."

"Come on." He started to walk away from the edge of the cliff. "We should get going."

I gazed out at the mountainous range once more before turning to follow. I whistled, and Fenrir ceased his dirt bath to follow, albeit reluctantly. Kol walked across the mountain's path, placing his hand on the rock surface like he had before. His mouth moved, but I wasn't close enough to hear what he said.

The ground quaked, and I would have lost my footing if it wasn't for Kol. His hand reached out, holding me steady as the rocks began to tumble forth, creating a door that was lit by glowing lanterns and fireflies.

Every time he touched me, it was like an electric shock that zipped into me. I wasn't sure if he could feel it, but it was a little unsettling to say the least. I'd never felt this with another before, so why would I feel this sort of connection with a god? *Especially* the God of Mischief?

The gods were cruel indeed.

A dwarf appeared at the opening to the cave, arms crossed over his chest. He had red hair that was done in braids along his back. His beard was equally as long, also sporting a few braids and beads. He was draped head to toe in armor, a hammer resting on his shoulder.

I'd never seen a dwarf before, only hearing such tales about when they came over to Röskr to help build up the city of Ellriheimr. I knew that they were short, I just never realized *how* short they actually were. He was maybe up to my hips, if not a little bit shorter.

The dwarf's eyes narrowed as he noticed Kol. "The God of Tricks has returned, I see." His focus turned to me, and he gave a slight smile. "I see you brought with you a woman, as well."

Kol winced, and he withdrew his arm from around me, standing up to his full height. "Brokkr. It's so good to see you again."

I flushed, sliding away from him a fraction. "We're not... together like that."

Brokkr didn't seem fazed. "What a shame. You're such a pretty thing. Although," he mused, "I don't blame you. No one wants to lie with someone who lies and cheats."

Kol huffed, gesturing to the open door in front of us. "Eira here needs some gear. Can you help her out?"

Brokkr clicked his tongue. "Gear? That depends, what are you going to use it for?"

"Killing monsters," I told the dwarf. "I... killed a troll a few weeks ago. This,"—I withdrew my dagger—"didn't really do anything against it."

Brokkr held out his hand, and I placed my dagger into it. He noticed that I was wearing gloves, a question forming in his eyes before he lifted up the dagger to inspect it. "This is an old dagger. Where did you get this?"

I shrugged. "It belonged to my mother."

Brokkr's expression softened. "Well, I can try and enhance it. However, it will take a while to do so." He waved us over. "Come in."

Kol didn't waste a second as he walked through the door. I glanced down at Fen, and he looked up at me, our unspoken bond palpable. If Brokkr noticed my wolf and why he was here, he didn't ask. Instead, he closed the door behind us and began to walk away. We followed, my fingers itching to get my dagger back.

"Those gloves," Brokkr said. "It's strange to see someone wearing them in this weather."

I swallowed. "It's quite cold back in Röskr."

"Hm."

The path was windy, spiraling downwards rather than up. It was cool as well, but it was still a whole lot better than the blistering winter we had just left behind. Just thinking about it now made me shiver. I was so not ready to go back just yet.

The path opened up, and I stood overlooking a ginormous city.

There were rock bridges that connected each entrance, almost like veins within a person's body. A molten lava fall was off to the side, spilling into a river that ran like it was water. Homes were built inside the mountain, going up and down and around. It stretched on for miles.

Brokkr spread his arms wide. "Welcome to Smíðajǫrð."

TWENTY-TWO

S míðajǫrð. *The City of the Forge.* What an interesting name. I could hear the pounding of metal, listen to the music that rang through the mountain, the clattering of armor, and the shouts of victory.

I was mesmerized by this city. It was nothing like I'd ever seen before, and it was immensely beautiful. *Otherworldly.* Traveling through these realms was indeed a welcoming experience.

"My forge is this way." Brokkr gestured for me to follow, and I turned to do so.

Fenrir lagged behind, taking in all the sights and smells around him. Just like me, he'd never left the safety of Röskr, so this was as new to him as it was for me. I would relish this moment, commit it to memory because it was likely that I would never get the chance again once this was all over.

Brokkr led me deeper into the mountain, and I caught a glimpse at various forges. Several dwarves were in these rooms creating and bending metal to their will. Some worked with gold, others silver, sometimes both at the same time. Kol was nowhere to be found, and I wondered if it was because of something

Brokkr had said to him. It seemed like they shared a history, one that was deeply rooted in a myth I had yet to learn or know about.

Brokkr's forge was massive in comparison to the others I had seen thus far. Part of that molten lava fall was filtered into this room, resting in a cauldron that was embedded with runes. There was a massive wheel in the center, another cauldron of water, and two stations for two people to bang on the metals.

There were two people in the forge when Brokkr and I walked in. I recognized Kol almost immediately, standing beside another dwarf that was pounding on a sheet of metal that resembled a sword.

This new dwarf was the same height as Brokkr, except he was covered in grime and soot. His hair was black and tied behind him, his beard only touching his chest rather than Brokkr's knee-length one. His blue eyes were sparkling when he lifted up the sword from his anvil.

Kol noticed us and turned. "About time."

I frowned. "Sorry. It's not every day a human travels through the realms."

"Oh ho!" the other dwarf chortled. "I like this one."

Brokkr chuckled. "Yes, she's a little spitfire, isn't she?"

The blue-eyed dwarf sauntered over, holding out a gloved hand. "I'm Eitri."

I took his offered hand. "Eira."

"So, Eira, what brings you to the city of Smíðajǫrð? It's not every day we get visitors, let alone the human kind." Eitri turned back to his forge to see that Brokkr had already placed my dagger on the table beside the water cauldron. "What's that?"

"Eira's dagger," Brokkr replied.

"Let me see it." Eitri walked over, running his hand over my mother's dagger. I wonder why these dwarves were so fascinated by this weapon. It wasn't special to anyone besides me. "This... this looks like Astrid's dagger."

My heart stilled. Did he just say my mother's name? Was it possible that this dagger was created by the hands of these two dwarves? "How... how do you know my mother?"

Even Kol seemed intrigued by this new development. He walked over, curious to know as well.

Eitri placed the dagger back on the table. "We created this dagger specifically for her. It was her gift. I never thought I would see this again, let alone even touch it."

"Ah." Brokkr ran a hand through his beard. "I was wondering why that dagger looked so familiar."

Eitri turned to me. "The fact that you possess this dagger means she's gone."

Brokkr gestured the vial of her ashes clasped around my neck. "That necklace you're wearing also belonged to Astrid. I made that for her as well."

I reached up to take the necklace in my fingers, running my thumb over the engraving. Not only had she asked these two dwarves to create her dagger, but she also had them make this vial for her as well. Why had my mother done this? What was she planning on doing?

I took a step forward. "You knew my mother? Truly?"

"I wouldn't say *knew* her so much as *of* her," Brokkr said. "Oeric was pretty explicit when he said that no one would say her name."

Oeric knew my mother? I reached out, trying to find something that would make it so that I wasn't falling on my face. The closest thing was Kol, and his arm once again wrapped around my waist to hold me steady. Eitri saw my expression and brought over a chair, helping me sit down.

"You act as if you didn't know your mother knew Oeric," Eitri said.

I shook my head. "No, why would my mother tell me such things? Unless…"

Unless she was hiding that very fact from me. What was my mother's goal in all this? She never told me about her past. She made it seem like her life never started until the moment she had met my father and had me. But what if after all this time, my mother was hiding her real identity from me?

It would stand to reason because she didn't want Oeric to find me, especially since I held ancient magic. Magic that belonged to an extinct race of people.

Brokkr cleared his throat, his eyes sliding to Kol, who had remained silent the entire time. "Why don't you show Eira around the city, hm? With the both of us working on this dagger, it will be ready in no time."

I sat forward, reaching for my coin purse. "How much do I owe you?"

Eitri held out his hand, pushing my purse away. "Don't worry about payment. Astrid was a good friend of ours, so this is in her memory."

I frowned. "But you said you knew *of* her, not that you *knew* her."

Eitri flushed. "That's what I meant."

I wanted to ask him what he meant by that, but Kol held out his hand for me, and this time I took it, allowing him to help me up.

Why would he say that only for him to contradict himself later on? Was he trying to spare my feelings or keep me from learning the actual truth, whatever it was? Fenrir raced in a circle for a second before he followed us out of the forge.

TWENTY-THREE

There wasn't much else to look at in Smíðajǫrð. This place was mostly made up of forges. But it definitely beat being back home in Röskr. It was scorching in here, and I wanted to take off my gloves, but I feared what the dwarves might say or do if they discovered that I possessed magic. For all I knew, they had already told Oeric where I was.

"You're awfully quiet," Kol said beside me.

I scoffed at him but remained silent. What else was there for me to say? I had just learned that my own mother knew Oeric and had these two dwarven brothers create an item just for her long ago. What could I say?

Kol stopped, and I ran right into him, almost falling on my back in the process. "I have an idea."

I raised a brow at him, regaining my footing. "Is that so?"

He spread his arms out wide. "How about we go realm jumping? You can choose the realm."

My eyes narrowed in suspicion. "That's awfully nice of you. What's the catch?"

He placed his hands over his chest in mock hurt. "Why do you always assume that I am evil or have ill intentions? I can assure you, my hellfire, that I am none of those things and all of those things."

"Uh, huh." I sighed. "How about someplace warm? I'd rather not deal with anymore cold until we go back to Röskr."

"We can go back to Möl," he suggested. "Oeric's Shadow should be gone by now."

My skin itched underneath the gloves, and I realized just how much I was sweating in this place. With all this lava and the forges going, it was almost unbearable.

I found it hard to believe that these dwarves really were acclimated to this type of heat. I could be wrong, but damn, it was sweltering in here. Still, something else plagued my thoughts. My mother had come here once. She had gotten that dagger and this necklace made just for her.

Was my mother a Völva? It stood to reason that she was, and they lived in Eiði.

"What about Eiði?" I said finally.

Kol blinked at me. "The Realm of the Vætt? Eira, I don't think—"

"How about just Möl then? Forget I said anything." I quickened my pace, narrowly missing running over Fen, who stopped to sniff at the ground. I knew Kol wouldn't approve of the idea, but why did I care what he thought anyway? I didn't need him to realm jump anymore. I could do it myself.

Kol sighed, his expression soft as he took a step towards me. "Eira, Eiði is gone."

I paused. "Gone? What do you mean?"

"Surely you speculate that you're the sole Seeress, right? Oeric killed off the last of their kind long ago. That realm is desolate. No one lives there anymore."

My hands closed into fists, and I stomped my foot. I seemed like a child, but I didn't care. This was far too important for me, and I needed answers. "Take me to Eiði."

Kol studied me for a long moment before he led me back up the mountain to where we entered. He placed his palm on the rock wall, the wall crumbling around us to create a door. We walked through and back out into the day. It was cooler up here thanks to the elevation and how high up we were. I slid my arms out of my gloves, letting the wind cool my skin.

I peered over at Kol, who was glancing around, probably looking for more of Oeric's Shadows. "Hey, Kol?"

He glanced at me. "Hm?"

"What did Brokkr mean when he said—"

"Don't listen to him," Kol interjected. "He's a dwarf."

I frowned. "But he mentioned—"

He sighed. "Gods fall in love with mortals all the time and when they do, they bring them back home to show the All-Father. So, when you came with me, it stood to reason that they assumed I was courting you to bring back to Ásjá."

I flushed. "Do… you bring women back often?"

"No." He walked over to the rock wall that we traveled to. "Mortal lives are fleeting, and I refuse to allow myself to love anyone that'll die before myself."

I slid closer. "But don't we gain eternal life in Ásjá?"

He placed his hand on the wall, fingers splayed. "Inkeri's Apples are the only thing that give us gods our youth and magic. It won't work on humans because there's not a sliver of magic in your veins. So even if you were to eat an apple or be near one, you'd still age normally."

"Have you ever fallen in love before?" I asked.

"*Nál.*"

Kol didn't respond to my question. Instead, he said the words for the portal to open, and a new image shone through. I was surprised to see that it was another forest, this time brighter, almost like it was Röskr. I glanced over at Fenrir, and he bolted without me saying a single word, jumping through the portal.

"Ladies first." Kol gestured to the portal.

I placed my hand on the wall, putting one foot into the new realm, the other half still with Kol. "I didn't mean to—"

"Do not apologize," he said quickly. "Let's just wander for a bit and come back."

I clamped my mouth shut and ducked into the portal and into this new realm. I landed on my feet with an oof. I was in a forest covered with green foliage and lush grass. I saw a few insects, but there was nothing else that would tell you people lived in this realm. It looked like nature had taken over, a few houses around obscured by trees and other roots.

I returned my gaze to Kol as he dropped in from above, the portal already closed. Fenrir was nowhere to be found. Panic set in, and I began to look around frantically for my companion.

"Fen!" I yelled.

Kol rested a hand on my shoulder. "He'll be fine. There's nothing dangerous in this realm. He knows your scent, so he'll find his way back to you."

I shrugged out of Kol's hold and began to walk around. I don't know where he had dropped us off at, but it was nothing but a wasteland of greenery. None of the homes in this town were unscathed by these trees.

He jabbed his thumb in the other direction, where a small market had once been. Stalls were upturned, baskets taken over by roots, and the spoils were long gone. "I'm going to go look for something over here."

"Like what?" I asked.

He shrugged. "I don't know. I've never been in this realm before, so I want to check it out too."

Without another word, he walked away. I watched him leave for a moment before I turned back to the house that was beside me. It felt weird of me and shameful to go into someone's home, but it's not like there was anyone else alive to say something about it.

Glancing around a third time, I walked up to the door—or what had been a door. It was caved in, barely held on by the hinges. I reached out, touching the door, and it gave way, falling to the ground. I ducked inside, looking around the home. It was… mostly empty.

There was a kitchen, a living space, and a singular bed that was pushed to the side. Everything in the kitchen was rusted out and dusty, with some of the metal caved in like someone had hit it several times. The bed was all but covered in dirt and mud, and a nest of fur and bones were the only thing left. There was a table, however, and rested on its top were several books.

Walking over, each step prompted the floorboards beneath me to creak. Reaching the table, I inspected the books. I lifted one up, my hand running over the cover of it, dislodging dust and dirt. It wasn't a book but a *journal*. I cracked open the journal, reading the first page.

Dear journal,

Ragnar said hello to me today. I know that I shouldn't get too excited, but I just can't help it. All this time he hasn't said a word to me, instead courting my sister, the next Völva. But not today. No, he said one word to me and made eye contact.

I dare say nothing to Mother, and I know I won't say anything to my other sisters and friends. They wouldn't believe me; they'd

*call me a fool for thinking that a man such as he would ever give
me the time of day. Perhaps tomorrow, I will be bold enough to
give him a smile.*

I closed the journal, setting it in my satchel. I wasn't going to
lie, it was a little weird for me to take this journal, but this was
the only thing close enough to a family I held. If my mother was
indeed a Seeress, then it stood to reason that she lived here before coming to Röskr.

For all I knew, the girl writing in this journal was a cousin or
aunt. I ran my hand over another book, reading the title.

"*Eira.*"

I paused, my hand mere inches from the edge of the book to
open it. I swallowed and turned. I recognized that voice. It was
the same one I had heard back in the woods… the same one I had
heard in the forest back home.

I shook my head. There was no way that it would have followed me here—

"*Eira.*"

Okay, now I was convinced. I tore my gaze away from the
books and walked out of the house and back into the woods. Kol
and Fenrir were nowhere to be found, and I didn't want to bother
the god into asking if he'd heard what I had.

"*Eira.*"

I turned in the direction of the voice, hesitating. Kol did say
that nothing in here would harm us, but what was the cause of

this voice then? So help me gods, if it was another troll, I was just going to let him have me and be done with it. I had no method to defend myself, so this would be utter suicide.

Following the voice, I marveled at the forest around me. It was almost untouched, growing as if humans and gods had never once thrived here. I still hadn't seen any wildlife yet, and I had yet to decide if that was a good thing or not.

A flapping of wings behind me made me jump, and I nearly screamed.

"Daughter of the Wolf."

My heart was thudding in my chest as I turned around, seeing a massive raven perched on a branch, watching me intently. Just like the last one I had seen, a golden rune blaze along its brow, large pool of black eyes never leaving me.

Did this raven just call me "Daughter of the Wolf"? If so, what did that even mean?

"Daughter of the Wolf."

I took a step forward. "Who are you?"

The raven spread its wings wide, making a knocking noise, hopping from branch to branch.

"Eira! Duck!"

Kol's voice.

I blinked and did what I was told without a second thought. A ball of flames soared through the air, hitting the raven in the chest and sending the creature flying.

Kol and Fenrir raced over, the god sliding in the dirt. I saw his mouth move but couldn't understand or hear what he was saying; it was like my ears were no longer working.

When I didn't answer him, he pulled me up, grabbed my hand, and yanked me forward.

I couldn't react, couldn't think, couldn't even breathe as we raced through the forest back to where we had come from. I noticed the house I had been in, followed by the empty market Kol had gone through.

He spun me around, my back to the tree as he placed his hand on the side of my head.

"*Nál.*"

I opened my mouth to say something, but Kol didn't waste a second before he pushed me through the portal, jumping in after me with Fenrir in tow.

TWENTY-FOUR

I landed on my butt, with Fenrir on my lap and Kol to my right. He sprang up, closing the portal before Oeric's Shadow could see where we were. He reached down, grabbed my wrist, and hauled me to my feet.

"Why would you follow that voice?" Kol's tone had grown harsh, almost like he was upset with me.

My brows knitted. "What else was I supposed to do?"

"*Avoid it.*"

"I've heard that voice before," I told him. "Back in Röskr. When Fen and I had found that troll."

Kol blinked. "You heard that voice before?"

"Yes. Twice now. He called me…" My nose wrinkled as I tried to remember what the raven had said. "Daughter of the Wolf."

Kol's brows drew together, but there was a subtle twitch to his lips. "Daughter of the Wolf? I've never heard of that before."

"Neither have I."

He looked as if he wanted to say something more but decided against it. Instead, he strode back over to the entrance of the dwarf's city. "Let's go see if Brokkr and Eitri are done with your dagger. We have another pitstop to make after this."

"Wait." I reached out to take his arm, but he was already strutting down the stairs.

What had gotten him so worked up all of a sudden? I glanced down at Fenrir, finding he looked just as perplexed as I felt. I decided to shove it aside for now and follow.

I walked down the stairs with Fenrir at my heels. The door to the mountain closed on its own, sealing us inside once more. It didn't take me long to get back to the dwarven brother's forge. I wasn't too busy sightseeing this time, so I didn't stop to marvel at the scenery.

"Is the dagger done?" Kol's voice drifted out of the forge. "I'm on a time crunch now."

"Yes, it's done," Eitri replied. "But I don't see why you asked about this ring."

I rounded the corner and entered the forge just as the dark-haired dwarf handed Kol my dagger. He then brought out a small pouch and placed it on the palm of Kol's hand.

I blinked and pointed at the pouch. "What's that?"

Kol turned, tossing me the pouch. "Your new ring."

"My *what?*"

I caught the leatherbound item. Opening up the pouch, I dumped out the contents in my palm, seeing a small silver ring with a green gem in the middle of it. My eyes went wide as I turned to look over at Kol.

He tapped the ring. "You're going to need it."

I held it in between my fingers, inspecting the craftmanship. It looked almost fragile yet sturdy as my thumb ran across the engravings. I glanced up at him. "What's this for?"

Kol stuffed his hands in his pockets. "Well, I'm sure by now Oeric knows what you look like, so we're going to have to change your appearance."

My eyes went wide. "*Change* my appearance? How can you do that?"

He sniffed. "I cannot, but I know someone who can."

My brows rose. "Who?"

He glanced at his fingernails, looking as if he were inspecting them before answering my question. "An old friend of mine."

I opened my mouth to ask him what he meant, but he turned to the dwarven brothers. "Thank you for making those items for us. We'll be on our way."

I frowned. "I'm not going anywhere until—"

Kol grabbed my wrist, turned me around, and forced me to walk with him. I dug in my heels, but the god's grip was far stronger than mine.

"Kol, so help me gods—"

He turned to me. "Don't say another word, okay? I'll explain everything when we get there."

"I don't think—"

"Just trust me, Eira."

Trust? Did he really tell me to trust him? There was no way I could readily trust him so easily. I barely knew him and had only spent a little bit of time in his presence, most of it for his benefit rather than my own.

Kol knew things. About me, my magic, maybe he even about my mother or why the raven had called me "Daughter of the Wolf" back in the forest of Eiði.

At the end of the day, I needed him—for his information and nothing more. "Fine," I said, voice flat. "I'll go along with this plan, but I don't trust you."

Kol didn't say anything, just tugged me further. Fenrir gave a low growl at Kol's touch along my skin, but my wolf remained calm as we walked up the steps that led to the entrance of this cavern.

"I didn't even get a chance to say goodbye," I muttered under my breath.

"You'll see them again," Kol told me. "But we need to go."

I didn't question him, even though everything inside me boiled over, wanting to know what he had meant when he had that ring made for me.

The leather bag was still clutched in my hand, the weight of that single ring weighing heavily on my heart.

I was acutely aware of Kol's fingers wrapped around my wrist. My skin was on fire wherever he touched, sending jolts of electricity through me. I'd never felt this before with anyone, and yet I felt this towards a god of myth and lore.

Was it because he was a god? Or was it because of something else? Whatever it was, I could walk up the stairs myself, and I did not need him to guide me.

I dug my heels in, trying to wrangle free from his grasp. "I can walk myself. I don't need you to help me."

Kol released his grip on my wrist. "That wasn't my intention."

I breezed by him, ignoring the buzzing I felt whenever I got so close to him. It was a weird sensation, one that I hoped would go away—and sooner rather than later. After a moment, I heard him follow me.

I opened the door, inhaling the scent of open air and feeling the sun warm my skin. It was a shame that we would leave this place. I wasn't sure where we were going, but wherever it was, I hoped it was a place as warm as Skóð.

Fenrir brushed up against me, and I reached down to scratch him behind the ears.

Kol placed his hand over the rock wall, the rune glowing a midnight blue. The rocks crumbled, a shimmering portal opening up to reveal another forest, this one similar to the one I had seen previously. I saw the glistening lake off in the distance and instantly knew where it was that Kol was taking me.

Möl.

The Realm of the Elves. He stepped away from the portal and I walked in, landing on my feet in the grass. Fenrir bounded beside me, tail wagging as he inspected the area, his nose taking in all the scents. My vision blurred, legs shaking as I leaned against a tree for support.

Kol placed a gentle hand on my elbow. "You've used far too much magic today. We'll have to stay here for the night for you to regain your strength."

I blinked at him. "What magic? I haven't used any of it today."

"Like I said previously, you don't have to consciously use magic for it to be used. Just traveling between realms is enough. While it is my magic that has been transporting us, you're still using a slight sum of yours. That's another reason why I had that ring crafted for you."

My brows knitted. I had completely forgotten about that stupid ring. I didn't see how that happened, as I still had it clutched in my hands. Fen pressed into my side again, whimpering.

I held up the leather bag. "So, why this ring?"

"Oeric knows what you look like now, and because of that, it'll make you getting into Ásjá much more difficult. That ring I had made for you holds magic and creates illusions. My friend will add their magic to it and help make you a new appearance when you wear the ring. It'll also help you in case you used too much magic and need some more in a pinch."

Interesting.

I fingered the pouch. It's so strange that something so small could hold so much power. It was really amazing, to say the least. I stuffed the bag in my pocket, a wave of nausea coming over me and I had to lean on the tree, using it to help me up. Fenrir whimpered, nudging my hand with his head.

"Eira?"

I opened my mouth to say something, but nothing came out as I toppled forward. Fenrir yelped, and Kol reached out to grab me, but I couldn't keep my eyes open for much longer.

Before I knew it, everything went black.

TWENTY-FIVE

arkness. All I could see was darkness. I wasn't sure where I was, what I was doing, or why I was doing such things.

What I *did* know was that I had blacked out and now I was here, standing in the dark.

I glanced around me, trying to see if I could find any identifiable markers that would help me to understand where I was, but I couldn't make out a single thing. Slowly, fireflies began to fly around me, creating enough light for me to see.

One thing I was certain of was that I was in a forest. I could see the trunks of trees, the shadow of leaves, and hear the rustling of the wind. I placed my hand on a tree, feeling the rough bark beneath the palm of my hand. The fireflies danced, winking in and out of view. A few of them nestled along the ground, creating a path with their glowing butts.

I began to walk down the path, using my hand along the trees to help guide me along with the fireflies. The forest seemed to get thicker for a moment, leaves on the smaller trees brushing along my arms and legs. Then, all too quickly, the path opened, and I was standing in the middle of a clearing.

There were millions of fireflies, blinking in and out, creating enough light that I had to squint my eyes. A waterfall was cascading into a lake, surrounded by flowers and grass. In front of the waterfall and lake was a boulder. On top of that was a massive white wolf.

This wolf was unlike anything I'd ever seen before in my life. The creature was easily ten times larger than Fenrir, with ears that were coated in thick, coarse fur with slightly grey tips at the top. Large cobalt-eyes were set in a massive head. Bright blue runes were etched into the wolf's white fur, shining brightly as if the sun were coming from them. In the middle of the wolf's forehead was a crescent moon.

The wolf lowered its head, maw held open just enough for me to see the massive canines in those black gums. "Welcome, Daughter of the Wolf." The voice was feminine, with a hint of a deep accent.

That name again. What could it mean? Surely, being in the presence of this wolf meant something similar to why those ravens were calling me that back in the forest of Eiði.

I took a slow, tentative step forward. "Who are you?"

"Do you not know who I am?"

I paused, shifting through all the lore and knowledge my mother had given me throughout the years. Nothing about a massive white wolf ever sprang to mind. However, I couldn't place my finger on why the eyes of this wolf seemed to eerily familiar.

It was like I knew these eyes, had gazed into them a thousand times, but I couldn't place where.

I shook my head. "No, I'm sorry, but I don't."

Sadness clouded the wolf's eyes, but she snorted and gazed behind me into the darkness, almost like she was lost in thought. After a moment, she turned back to me, blinking slowly. "I'm surprised."

My brows knitted. "Just now, a few moments ago, you called me 'Daughter of the Wolf'. What does that mean?"

The wolf lowered her head onto her paws, watching me carefully. "That is for you to find out."

I stomped my foot in frustration. "It seems I never get answers lately. This,"—I held out my arms that were covered in runes—"happens to be one of the things I must question lately. Nothing is adding up anymore."

The wolf licked her lips. "Knowledge is power, dear one. If one seeks it, they will stop at nothing to learn the truth. It's a unique skill and yet not many possess it. Many are content in the unknown."

"Not as many as you'd think," I said.

She lifted her head. "And what do you hope to gain from this knowledge? Once you learn the truth, they will come for you, and they will stop at nothing until you are gone."

"*They,*" I frowned. "You've said that twice now. Who are they?"

"Enemies," she growled. "The very same ones that we tried to shield you from many years ago."

I blinked, my mind spinning. What was this connection I had with this wolf? None of this made sense, and I was beginning to get increasingly irritable. A branch snapped behind me and I turned, the hairs on my arms raising.

"I don't have much time." The wolf jumped from the boulder and walked over to me.

I knew I should have been afraid, but I couldn't find it in myself to move or shy away. In fact, I felt drawn to her.

Maybe it was because of my relationship with Fenrir, or maybe it was because I felt a kinship with this beautiful wolf. Whatever it was, I would find out.

"Be one with yourself, dear one." She lifted her nose, touching my forehead. "Tread lightly."

"What do you—"

Another branch snapped and I turned my head toward the sound, eyes searching the woods for what it could be. I was in the middle of an unknown forest, surrounded by wolves that could easily eat me. Fear gripped me like ghostly claws, choking me and burning me from the inside out.

Taking my dagger out of its sheath, I slowly made my way toward the noise. I brushed away brambles and leaves to find a massive print in the mud, left by whatever creature had been here moments before.

I glanced back at the white wolf, shocked to see that she had already left, the fireflies dying at my feet, flickering slightly. I took a step forward before I stumbled and toppled to the ground. I sat up just as the maw of a massive black wolf leapt towards me.

I covered my face in my hands, screaming and waiting for the cold claws of death to take me away.

TWENTY-SIX

I gasped awake, hand over my heart, the other clenching the blankets beneath me. What on earth had just happened? My hair was matted, clinging to my forehead from sweat, the nightgown I wore drenched.

I allowed myself a moment, taking deep breaths and not assessing my situation until my heartbeat started to slow.

I released my grip on the blanket, feeling the soft bed along my fingertips. I was in a white room, with a window that was curtained up and a door that had a small window for someone to look in through.

I glanced around the room, taking note of my surroundings. Other than the bed in this room, it was almost completely devoid of furniture. There was a nightstand on the right side of the bed, a trunk at the foot of the bed, a wash basin and mirror close to the curtained window, and a large, wooden closet that was pushed next to the one door in the room.

Looking down at myself, I noticed the nightgown I wore… held little to the imagination. It was almost sheer, enough for someone to see the most sensitive parts of me. If I wasn't drowning in my own perspiration, I would have used the blanket to shield my body. But aside from that, there was no one in the room; not even Fenrir was around.

The only thing I could think about was that massive white wolf I met or the black wolf that was about to consume me.

Was it a dream or something more? She had once again called me "Daughter of the Wolf", something I was starting to get accustomed to hearing. I didn't know what it meant, but I was going to get answers from Kol whether he liked it or not.

A soft, almost tentative knock came from the door to the room. I stiffened, reaching for my leg where my dagger would be if I had been wearing clothes.

The door opened, and a slender, tall elf stood in the doorway. She was very pale, her hair as white as snow. She wore a dress that cinched at the waist, golden embellishments rimmed the wrist, neck, and lower dress portion. Her lashes were just as white as her hair, long and flecked with gold. Ears were elongated on either side of her head, pointed at the ends and almost hidden by the strands of her hair.

Everything about this elf was beautiful, save for her eyes. They were wide black orbs with a green rim around the iris, but her eyes were mostly dark.

"You're awake." The elf smiled. "Excellent."

Claws ranked over tile and before I could even blink, Fenrir was in my lap, tail wagging and tongue lolled out to the side as he licked me from head to toe, not once stopping to give me a moment to breathe.

"Fen!" I giggled, forcing him off of me. "It's nice to see you too, boy."

He circled, pulling more of the covers off of me as he laid down beside me, head in my lap. My hand instinctively went to him, running my fingers through his thick fur. My shoulders slumped, my coiled and stressed muscles responding to my wolf.

Touching him brought me so much comfort, and I was able to relax knowing he was around me.

"I was worried you would not awaken." The elf glided into the room, inspecting me carefully. "The God of Tricks will be back soon. Said he had some business to take care of."

I gave a slight shrug. "I don't care."

The elf's eyes narrowed. "And yet, just the mention of him seems to make your heart beat a little bit faster."

I frowned, running a hand through my hair. "I barely know him. We're acquaintances who have the same goal."

She wasn't necessarily wrong. There *was* something I felt towards Kol. He hasn't done anything to me that would warrant me not feeling safe around him. He's protected me, let me go realm jumping. Just thinking about those eyes sent a thrill through me, and I quickly stamped down the rising emotions.

Now was *not* the time for me to be falling in love with or even to be *thinking* about falling.

"Such as?" she prompted.

I fidgeted. "His goal is to steal something. Mine is to—"

"Not spoiling anything, are we?" Kol appeared in the doorway, leaning against the door jamb with his arms crossed over his chest and brow raised in question.

His hair was disheveled as though he'd been running his hands through the strands. His voice was cool and teasing, but I could sense the undertone within his words.

He added, "Because what fun is a secret if you spill it too soon?"

The elf's features soured at hearing his voice. "The God of Tricks," she greeted.

Kol's grin was wide, a slight twinkle in his eye. "Why hello again, Bodil. It's *such* a pleasure to see you."

The elf, Bodil, narrowed her eyes. "Pleasure is not the word I would use."

He clicked his tongue. "And yet," he said slowly, "you almost married me from the *pleasure* I brought you."

My mouth dropped at this conversation. Kol was engaged to an elf? I knew the gods took human wives and sired demigods, but I had never really thought about them hooking up with other races that weren't giants.

Bodil didn't even bat an eye. "I am thankful that I do not regret leaving you." She turned back to me. "Are you able to stand, Völva?"

I blinked, hearing that name for the first time for me. "Oh, no. I'm not a Völva."

Bodil glanced at my runes and then back at my face, searching for something.

I ran my hand over my other arm, feeling the slight heat that came from the runes. "I know magic, but I'm not a Seeress. I barely know anything about them."

"The only humans that can use Seiðr are the Völvas."

Kol peeled himself off the wall, walking over to where Bodil stood by the side of my bed. "Völvas have been extinguished, Bodil."

The elf blinked. "Since when has this happened?"

"I would like to think a couple hundred years ago, if not longer," he replied with a shrug.

She licked her lips. "Human lives are short, and there are many of them that walk this realm. We light elves have longer lifespans than most, but that does not mean we are not informed. I would have known if the Völvas were destroyed."

"I know your friends were the same—"

Bodil turned her head to me. "Who is your mother, child?"

"Astrid." My hand reached up, taking my necklace to hold on to for a moment. "Her name was Astrid."

"I know many with that name," Bodil sighed. "What was the name of your father?"

My brows knitted. I never knew hardly anything about my father. My mother made sure that I knew little about him, only talking about him whenever she felt the need to. That picture of them on their wedding day was the only picture I'd ever seen of them together.

Still, why would this elf want to know about my origins? Was it because she thought the Völvas were still alive?

It was impossible. Once Oeric killed them all, none of them remained in hiding or anywhere in the Nine Realms. To become a Völva, you need to have been born a third daughter. From my knowledge of my mother and her past before me, she had no children. So, me having this magic was merely a coincidence.

Kol's eyes flicked to mine. His eyes widened just a fraction, taking in my frame in this… almost see-through nightgown. I gripped the blankets beneath me, trying to get them out from underneath Fenrir's bulk to cover myself from Kol's heated gaze.

His stare started a fire in my belly, sending a slight shiver over my body. No man had ever affected me this way. At least, none that I ever dared to stay around long enough with.

This is just an arrangement, I scolded myself. *Nothing more.*

I cleared my throat, and Kol's eyes snapped up to meet mine. "I don't know. My mother never liked to talk about him."

Bodil seemed perplexed by my answer but didn't comment as she slowly walked over to me, placing a hand along my shoulder with her eyes closed. "You're mostly fine. I can sense the magic within you, but it's subtle. I gave you many treatments to help with your magical intake. It looks like it worked."

"I wasn't aware that jumping through realms caused so much of my magic to dwindle," I told her. "I'd never done it before except recently."

Bodil clicked her tongue, watching Kol out of the corner of her eye. "The God of Tricks should have told you the amount of magic used when jumping through realms. It's *not* recommended unless you are a god yourself or possess a lot of magic. From what I've seen, you don't have much to begin with."

"Which is why we came all this way," Kol cut in, watching the elf carefully. He reached into his pocket and withdrew the ring that he had made for me. "For you or another elf to put magic in this."

Bodil's eyes narrowed as she took in the ring in between her two fingers. "Dwarven made, I see." She glanced back at Kol before she placed it back in his hand. "You want me to place magic in this? It won't hold much."

"It will hold whatever I need it to," he replied. "Eitri and Brokkr made sure that it will hold plenty. I need it to do two things for me."

"Such as?" she prompted.

Kol's gaze bored into my own. "I need it to change Eira's appearance and to give her enough magic for us to get into Ásjá."

Bodil glanced over at me and then back at Kol, eyes narrowed in suspicion. "You are trying to get her into Ásjá? Why?"

"It's on a need-to-know basis," he said.

She rolled her eyes. "I hold no love for your 'All-Father' as you well know. He does nothing for anyone who does not reside in his realm. He means little to me."

"Either way, I'd rather not discuss the details."

Bodil squinted, looking as if she were pondering what to say. She sighed and held out her hand. "Fine, give it to me."

Kol placed the ring back in her hand. Bodil closed her eyes, her fingers clasping over it. Blue streaks curled from the elf's arms, circling around her forearm and into her fist. My eyes widened. I'd never seen another do magic in front of me before, save for Kol, so this was an entirely new experience for me.

All too quickly, the steaks that wrapped around Bodil's arms lessened until they were gone. She opened her eyes and walked over to me, her fingers still closed into a fist.

"Open your hand," she instructed me.

I did as I was told, holding out my hand for her. She placed the ring in the palm of my hand. It was slightly warm to the touch, the obsidian gem in the middle almost blinking with magical properties.

"Once you place this ring on your finger, you'll have a fraction of my magic and his. You'll be able to manipulate your shape and travel through the realms without tiring as you had before."

I picked up the ring and slipped it onto my finger. It fit perfectly, the warmth seeping into my skin. Almost instantly, I felt ten times better. I must have really been drained from my magic.

"Good." Kol walked over to the door. "I'll let you rest up for today. Tomorrow, we'll head for Ásjá."

TWENTY-SEVEN

I was not going to let Kol tell me what to do. Once he had left the room, I jumped out of bed. I felt so much better that I couldn't even describe this feeling. Elated? Hopeful? Perhaps even joyful? Whatever it was, I preferred this over lying in bed feeling sorry for myself and acting like I was dying from my lack of magic.

Bodil gestured to the closet. "I took the liberty of having your clothes washed. You should be able to change."

I gave her a smile and nodded my head. "Thank you."

"Do not thank me," she said. "It was that god you brought with you."

Fenrir bounded to his feet, jumping from the bed to follow as I opened the door to the closet. Bodil remained, almost like a ghost watching me.

It was a little unnerving, but I ignored her. I assumed she was the one who had undressed me, so me changing in front of her wouldn't bother her. It did irk me slightly, but since she had already seen me, it didn't really matter.

I closed the closet, leaving that sheer gown in there. I would *not* be needing that anytime soon. "Do you have anything to eat? I'm a little hungry."

Bodil raised a brow. "It's been so long since we housed a human. I almost forgot that they required something to eat and drink."

I frowned. "Do you not eat or drink?"

She shrugged and gestured for me to follow her. "Not necessarily. Light Elves thrive off the sunlight. We only consume food as it is customary to other races."

I was learning so much in such a short amount of time that it was making my head spiral out of control. I knew about the various different races in my world, but I never thought I would actually be seeing them, let alone *talk* to them.

Shuffling after Bodil, we left the comforts of the room and walked out into something otherworldly.

It was like I was standing in the treetops; the room itself was like a miniature home. Walking out onto the balcony, I could see Möl for what it truly was.

Trees as far as the eye could see, with mountains that rose into the sky and birds flying along the wind currents. A large river was set in the middle of the realm, homes dotting the outskirts of it. The sky was a lavender shade, a color I'd never imagined seeing in the clouds before. A large, almost crystal-like castle was built behind the lake, nestled in the mountains with spires made of glass and shimmering like a rainbow whenever the light caught on it just right.

At one time, I used to think Röskr was beautiful, but nothing will ever compare to Möl. This realm was something else, and I was eager to see what else this place held.

Bodil skirted around me and began walking down the staircase. Following behind her with Fenrir close at my heels, we began our long trek from the treetops to the forest below. We rounded around the stairwell, arriving at a silver elevator-like mechanism hung by... *nothing*. I put on the breaks, Fen hitting me in the back of my legs, huffing in annoyance.

Bodil didn't stop as she walked into the elevator and turned to look at me. "Coming?"

My mouth dropped open. Never in my entire life had I ever seen something like this. I'd seen elevators sure, but most used pulleys, rope, or gears. None of the ones I'd seen before ever held itself up by *nothing*.

Bodil seemed to sense my uncertainty because her sharp features softened, and she rested her hand along the railing of the elevator. "It's magic-oriented. It won't fall, I can assure you."

Warily, I stalked closer. Fen sensed my unease and stepped alongside me carefully, tail sweeping the floor behind him. Magic wasn't at all new to me, but new forms of it still left me feeling confused. However, Bodil seemed confident, and if Kol had just used it to leave, then it should be okay.

Stepping into the elevator, I went to the other end, my fingers wrapping tightly around the railing. Fenrir squeezed his head between the bars, ears perked forward with his tongue lolled out on the side. Bodil sniffed, and I turned to her to see a slight grin on her face.

The elevator began to move, and I gasped, holding onto the railing for dear life as we began our slow and steady descent to the ground. My eyes widened, but this time it wasn't from fear, it was from awe. We descended down from the treetops, allowing me a better view of the world below.

Elves were living *in* the massive trees. Several walked to and from the trunks, while wooden stalls held various food and drink and other trinkets. The other thing that intrigued me the most was the fact that I could feel the magic. It was *everywhere*. In the sky, the wind, even the air that I breathed.

There was no shortage of magic, and it was beautiful. Was this how my people lived back in Eiði before Oeric took control?

I glanced over at Bodil, who seemed interested in anything that wasn't me. "Hey, Bodil?"

"Yes?" She shifted to look at me, not appearing pleased at doing so.

I wrung my hands. What were the odds of her telling me the truth? She didn't know me; she was likely centuries old. Still, I had to know what it was like—to a place that might have been my home. "What was Eiði like?"

Bodil blinked, confused for a moment before she cleared her throat, her eyes taking in her realm. "It was a lot like it is here. The Völvas were a carefree people and spent most of their time using their magic to make creations."

"Creations?"

"I'm sure you know about the origins of the first Völva?"

I nodded. "She was one of Oeric's Valkyries, until he cast her to Eiði with the rest of the other lesser gods. But legends said that it was her third born daughter that became the first official Völva."

"Correct." Bodil seemed pleased by my answer. "They used their magic to create just about anything. Flowers, bugs, animals. They spent their days creating whatever they felt needed life in their realm. However, once Oeric decided that they no longer needed to live on this plane, he eradicated them, the magic lost with them."

Sadness clouded my vision with tears threatening to fall, mixed in with a little bit of rage.

Oeric had no reason to destroy an entire race of people for absolutely nothing. However, no one seemed to know the exact reason as to why the All-Father did what he did. I doubted Bodil would even know, as she only knew what she had seen and been told.

The elevator touched the ground, and I breathed a sigh of relief. I was alive, at least for the time being. Clearing my throat, I followed Bodil off the elevator and onto the dirt. It was covered in pine needles and leaves, but I could even feel the magic in the ground. The Light Elf waited for me to exit the elevator before she smiled and gestured to the realm around us.

"Ready to eat something now?"

I smacked my lips. "I've been ready."

TWENTY-EIGHT

After eating my fill, Fenrir and I decided to go for a walk in the forest. This wood reminded me of the one back in Röskr, and I felt comfortable enough to walk alone with my companion.

Bodil assured me that there wasn't anything in this forest that would warrant me being on edge or not thinking it was safe. So, with that in mind, I leapt at the chance to walk around.

The forest was my home as much as it was Fen's. We both thrived in this world, something we often found ourselves doing here lately. It wasn't that I didn't love hunting, but I felt that was the only time I ever was off into the forest, never appreciating the world around me.

Today, that would change.

Fen and I wandered for a little bit, but not too far that we wouldn't be able to find our way back to the main area. The forest was dense, far more than the forest I was used to back home. But that wasn't such a bad thing. In fact, I loved how dark this place was, but there was still light filtering through the treetops, giving me just enough to be able to see.

I found a nice tree with roots that circled around into what almost looked like a seat and took it for myself. I settled down, almost nestling into it like a bird would a nest and rested my back to the tree. Fenrir wandered around for a moment, nose to the ground as he sniffed.

Sometimes, I used to think he was more of a dog, but his attitude coupled with his massive bulk always reminded me of him being a full-blooded wolf.

I dug in my satchel, bringing out that journal I got from Eiði. I was still curious to see what all was written in this journal and who it came from. I knew for a fact that it couldn't have been my mother. Well, I hoped.

Finding out that she knew the two dwarves Brokkr and Eitri didn't settle well with me. They created the dagger and the necklace I kept with me. What else had my mother been up to before I was born? Just *who* was she?

Forcing my mother from my mind, I cracked open the journal and began to read from it.

Dear journal,

Today was supposed to be a special day. Ragnar and I were supposed to be wed in the morning. However, as I write down these words, I fear that it was all in vain.

He perished in battle. They're bringing his body back home to me to be burned, but I cannot seem to shake this feeling of loss and loneliness. Perhaps it is just me, but I don't think that. Ragnar's death affected everyone greatly, including myself.

What more can I say? What more can I do? He's gone and with him, my only chance to love, to grow, to become the mother that I'd always wanted to be. I was going to tell him that he was going to become a father, that I held a son in my belly ready to meet him and become just like him when he got older.

And now, both he and I will never get to know the father Ragnar could have become...

I sniffed, reading over this entry a second time. Whoever this girl was, she suffered greatly. Not only had she fallen in love with her sister's lover, but she was set to marry him. He died before they married, and she was pregnant with his child at the time.

The wind blew, ruffling my hair. I reached up to tuck a few strands behind my ear and the pages in the journal shuffled, landing on an entirely new page that was coated in runes I'd never seen before.

Dear journal,

Everyone thinks I'm crazy. They think that what I want to do is insane. Ragnar's body returned to me a few days ago, and his body is resting in the crypt below our city, waiting to be burned with the rest of his men who lost their lives in battle. I can't make myself go through this any longer and have decided that I will bring Ragnar back to life.

It is risky business, one that is deeply rooted in magic and riddles. I am no Völva; I could not bend magic to my will like my sister could and my mother before me. But I know someone, a woman who dabbles in the dark arts. She promised to help me bring my Ragnar back, but it would come at a price.

But I would pay anything bring him back. I didn't even ask her what it was that I would have to pay. Instead, I haggled a lot of coin and brought it with me to the woman's house into the forest. I'm thankful that she can bring him back, but once this is all said and done, we will need to leave this realm and start anew somewhere else.

I paused. Could this be my mother? This woman had not given herself a name, but she mentioned starting anew in a new realm. If this really was my mother, why on earth would she think to use the dark arts to bring back what possibly could have been my father?

There was only one way to find out, and that was to keep reading. Fen walked over and laid down beside me, resting his head on my thigh.

We met under the cover of darkness. I brought what I could with me, a hand on my belly that had yet to grow. Ragnar's body was uncovered, a cavity in his chest from where the axe had struck him in the chest. At least he wasn't covered in blood. His body was covered in runes of a nature I had never laid eyes on.

I'd only met this woman once and after today, I hoped to never see her again. She looked almost like a ghost, pale and lifeless. Her hair was braided, and her strands were as white as snow, something I'd never seen before. She went to work the moment I showed up, drawing over the runes in Ragnar's lifeless skin in her blood.

A few minutes ticked by, and I had begun to worry. The runes in Ragnar's body glowed a tinged blue, but other than that, nothing happened. The woman did not speak, did not blink, nor do I think she breathed. At least, not until Ragnar leapt up from where he layd, screaming in pain.

I went to him, elated to see him alive and well. The wound in his chest closed, becoming unmarked skin. The runes upon his skin remain, turning from blue to a crimson red. By the time I had reached him, I collapsed in pain, falling to the ground. Ragnar jumped from where he was to my side, the woman's soft cackles drifting over to us. "A life for a life."

I lost two things that day: my sanity and my child. I gained back my Ragnar, but he wasn't the same. He talked differently, thought differently, and the worst thing of all—he resented me for what I had done. I couldn't live without him and did what I thought was right, but in the end, it ended up costing me my entire life.

Closing the journal, I set it on my lap, contemplating what I had just read. This couldn't have been my mother, not even close. In fact, it felt like this woman's life ended in tragedy. There were far more pages left, but for now I would leave them and focus on the one thing I'd gathered from what little I'd read.

She brought back someone from the dead.

Reaching up to my necklace, I held it between my fingers, running my thumb along the vial, feeling the runes etched into it and the vines that wrapped around it.

If she had brought back someone from the dead using those exact runes... could I bring my mother back?

Sure I didn't have her body, but I had her ashes. It wasn't the same thing, but could it work? Would I be able to bring my mother back from the dead? She had all the answers to my questions. Why I was considered the "Daughter of the Wolf" and why she had these runes embedded into my skin.

It wasn't a realistic idea to be honest, but I would have given anything in this life just to see her again, to talk to her. She was everything and more to me, and just like my father, she was taken, stripping me of the only family I ever had.

Even if it did work and I brought her back, would she ever be the same? This journal mentioned Ragnar being different in everything he did, including hating the woman he loved.

The dead shall always be burned, Eira. No one should ever be forced to live a second time.

Those were the exact words my mother used a month or so before she died, almost like she knew that's what I wanted to do. I knew she was sick; the entire city knew she was sick, and yet no one came to the pyre I built for her.

Granted, I didn't like being around others as much, but at least it would have been a kind gesture for them to show up and respect my mother's memory.

But what did those words mean exactly? Did she know about this method and what would have happened?

As far as my knowledge was concerned my mother held no magic, just like the girl in this journal. It was still a possibility, however slim, that this was my mother's journal. They mentioned leaving their realm in favor of a new one to start over. Perhaps whoever this was met their true love and had me?

I shook my head. So many ifs and not enough knows. This was purely all speculation at this point.

Fenrir lifted his head, ears flat and his teeth bared. The stench of rot and decay hit my nose, and I recoiled in disgust from the foul odor. Bones rattled against bone. The clanking of metal rang through my ears, and I rose to my feet.

Fenrir was already standing, hackles raised as he took several steps towards the forest and the stench of rot.

I reached into my boot and grabbed my dagger. It was times like these that I was thankful for my weapon and the fact that I always kept it with me. It wasn't my bow and arrows, but it would be enough to defend myself from anything that came my way or Fen's.

Out in the darkness of the forest beyond, two blazing blue dots came into view. Fenrir lowered himself to the ground, growling and bounding forward to intimidate the intruder.

Within moments those two orbs grew, set inside a yellow and cracked skull. The skeleton was wearing armor, the metal and steel clanked from the bony frame.

Another creature shambled closer, this one more human-like. Flesh fell from bone, tendons and muscles still holding on for dear life. The stench grew with each scuttle, and I took a step back, nose wrinkling.

Draugr.

I'd heard of these monsters before. Undead creatures that wandered the realms, protecting their tomes and treasures. They were mostly human, brought back to life by nefarious means or possessed by a ghost that wanted to torment the living. The other downside to these Draugrs was that fact that they were immune to almost everything that wasn't fire.

Good thing I knew how to use fire. These monsters were bloodthirsty and would stop at nothing until their bloodlust was extinguished.

What bothered me the most was the fact that Bodil had told me that these woods were safe to travel in. Had that been a lie? Was she working for Oeric all this time? More Draugr emerged from within the forest, creating a circle around me and Fen.

TWENTY-NINE

Not once in my entire life did I ever think I would be fighting Draugr with Fenrir by my side. My life had never been this exciting, and it was all because I took that job to take back that ring that belonged to the god Kol. I never thought I would travel between the realms to meet dwarves, elves, and all other creatures that belonged to myth and lore. But every so often I would find us fighting a creature in a forest no less.

The Draugrs surrounded us on all sides, boxing us in. They held an assortment of weapons ranging from axes and swords to shields. An arrow whizzed by my cheek, the tip of it slicing into my skin.

I hissed, ducking down low as Fenrir howled and bounded forward. His canines dug into a Draugr's neck, knocking him to the ground.

The Draugrs made a noise that was in between a scream and a screech as they lunged for Fenrir. With my dagger in my grip, I ran forward, arching my arm and embedding the weapon into another Draugr's back. This one still had flesh, but it came away when I slid down my dagger through its back.

It slashed at me with its axe, narrowing missing me by a hair as I ducked and kicked out with my right leg, knocking over the Draugr.

Fenrir jumped from his attacker, going after another monster as I went for a second one as well. None of our blows fazed these creatures, and I knew that I would need to resort to my magic. I thought that since this dagger had been enhanced, it would have done some more good.

I was wrong.

"Fen!" I yelled at my companion. "Heel!"

Fenrir jumped off yet another Draugr, head turned back to me with uncertainty. After a moment, he bounded over to me, hiding behind my legs with his tail wrapped around me and his head on the other side, growling low and watching the monsters that shambled over to us.

I went to take off my gloves, confused for a moment when I realized that I never put them back on when we left the safety of Bodil's infirmary. I ignored that and stuffed my dagger back into my boot.

I held out my hands, palms outwards towards the zombies. "*Fiðri.*"

My runes blazed to life, red and scorching as fire erupted from the palms of my hands. The magic exploded from inside me, almost knocking me on my ass if Fenrir hadn't been behind me, holding my legs steady.

The Draugr's melted almost instantly, their screams piercing the sky, echoing throughout the forest. More zombies shambled hobbled into view, creaking as they came for us. Fenrir launched forward, chomping to scare them off.

A sound similar to a roar and jaw-popping came right to the right of us. Fenrir whimpered, ears flattened to his head as he pushed his bulk up into me, forcing me to take a step back. Even the Draugrs halted and turned to that new sound.

The ground rumbled, the trees shook, and my heart leapt into my throat when I recognized the bulk of fur that was barreling towards us.

Shit.

Jumping away from the oncoming grizzly, I let another volley of flames come tumbling forth from the palm of my hand. Fenrir leapt away from an oncoming Draugr, his claws digging in the dirt to stop himself from stumbling. The grizzly bear ran into the Draugrs, growling and slashing with his claws.

What on earth—the grizzly turned, and I held my hands up and ready to attack if need be. Except, this animal shifted back toward the Dragurs, fighting them off with sharp teeth and claws. Could it be—? No. It couldn't be Kol.

And yet... there was no other explanation. This grizzly wasn't attacking me or Fen, it was *protecting* us. It had to be Kol.

"Fenrir." I glanced down at my companion. "Stay."

He snorted but sat down as I barreled back into the fray. Kol's claws weren't doing much against the zombies, but it was enough to get them to slow down for me to hit them with more of my flames. The stench of burnt flesh and bone hit my nostrils, and it took everything in me not to gag. If I thought their smell was bad before, it was ten times worse now.

Slowly but surely, the number of Draugrs had begun to dwindle. Ashes and bones littered the ground, discarded weapons having been flung into trees or thrown down into the dirt. Sweat coated my brow, my shirt sticking to me in various places.

But somehow, I hadn't run out of stamina nor magic. Was this ring really giving me all this power and more?

The last Draugr fell beneath Kol's jaws, with him ripping the head clean off and tossing it out into the forest, never to be seen again. Even without the head, the zombie scuttled and jolted, like it was trying to think of where its head had gone in the first place before it finally stopped, lying lifeless in the dirt.

Resting my back against a nearby tree, I used it as leverage to keep me standing, until I decided that sitting down was the far better option. Fenrir hobbled over, panting, tired from the bouts of fighting we had done. He plopped down beside me, and I rested a hand along his back, comforting him.

The grizzly lumbered over, and each step he took elicited golden sparkles. By the time he had reached me, I was standing up and he was back in his full, handsome human form.

Kol rested a hand on the side of my head, dipping his head down low, his eyes filled with an emotion I'd never seen from him before.

Fear.

I swallowed, trying not to let his nearness get under my skin. I couldn't help but stare at his face, at the angles and planes. Of the snake's head that seemed to watch every move I made and had yet to make. But what unsettled me the most was the fact that I couldn't stop staring at his lips. Lips that were now twisted into a frown.

"Do you know what could have happened to you?" Kol hissed. "Why did you come to the forest by yourself when I told you to stay put?"

I rolled my eyes at him, brushing out of this interlocked embrace. "Why do you care? You made it abundantly clear that I'm only here to get Inkeri's Apple and that was it."

He pinched the bridge of his nose. "I don't have time for this."

I gestured to the fallen Draugrs, kicking a severed arm away from me. "Neither do I."

Kol gripped my wrist, turning me to face him. "Let's go."

"I'm not going anywhere with you." I yanked my arm free, taking a step back. I was beyond pissed off at him and how he felt the need to protect me at each and every turn when I could take care of myself. Fenrir came over to me, growling low in his throat at Kol's closeness.

Kol ranked a hand through his hair. "This isn't going to work if we're at each other's throats." He paused. "Why do you feel the need not to trust me? What have I done that's made you dislike me so much?"

"Never trust a god," I reiterated my mother's words. "They'd sooner put a blade through your heart than a grain of salt in your hand."

He blinked. "What?"

I flushed. "Nothing, it's just something my mother used to say."

His gaze softened. "Not all gods are bad, Eira."

"Yeah, well." I crossed my arms. "I'm not the one being hostile."

He groaned. "Is this the thanks I get for saving your ass? I could have let those Draugrs skin you alive and wouldn't have a second thought about any of this. But instead, I came to help you."

Wrinkling my nose, I eyed him warily. "I didn't ask to be saved. I could have handled them all on my own, you know."

He laughed dryly. "Yes, because you were doing so well against them with that dagger of yours."

I turned on my heel. "I'm leaving. Find someone else to help you steal this apple."

I started to walk away with Fen by my side until I heard Kol's voice, heard him say something that made me stop in my tracks. I wasn't sure I heard him right, and I turned my head, blinking at him. "What did you just say?"

"I'll give you whatever you want," Kol repeated. "All you have to do is name it."

"Can you really give me whatever it is I want?" I asked him.

Kol's expression was soft. "Yes."

What could I even ask for in return? The passage from the journal sprung to mind instantly.

Could he help me bring my mother back to life? It was a foolish request, one that I knew he would no doubt shoot down. If he didn't scoff at the mere idea, that is. And yet, it had happened before. Someone had died and was brought back to life using old runic symbols, the same ones that were etched into this journal.

Then again, Ragnar wasn't burned; his body whole and intact.

My mother was nothing more than ashes in the wind.

There was no way I could bring my mother back this easily. I would need to do more digging, more research before even making this rash of a decision.

For now, though, I would allow him to think I was on his side. At least until I got the apple. Perhaps I could barter with the All-Father. The apple for my mother. Would that even work? Doubtful, but it was worth a try.

"Why do you need this apple so badly, Kol?" I questioned.

He cocked his head, pondering my question. "Someone needs this apple."

"Who?" I pressed.

"I cannot say just yet," he replied. "But I will tell you that you don't want to be on his bade side."

I accepted that explanation for now. I would need to know sooner rather than later. Kol extending this slight olive branch was the push for my trust that I needed.

"What could you give me?" I asked, exploring my options.

Kol didn't skip a beat in his answer. "Eternal life."

I blinked. "In exchange for getting this apple, you'll give me eternal life?"

"Yes." He nodded. "And gold as well."

"Hm."

"It's my promise to you, Eira. If you help me get Inkeri's Apple, I will give you all that you desire. Eternal life and all the gold that will fit inside a pouch."

"Huh." I grinned. "A god's promise? How much is that worth in gold?"

"Plenty," he said.

"Fine," I lied. "I'll take the eternal life."

Kol held out his hand. "A deal then?"

I took his offered hand, shaking it. Slowly, my plan had begun to form. I would steal Inkeri's Apple all right, but it would not be handed over to Kol. No, I would steal the apple and then barter it for my mother's life.

Valhalla existed, the realm where the dead remain. I would get my mother back no matter the cost. Once she was back, I would get the answers I so desperately craved and maybe I wouldn't need to have Kol's help after all.

For now, though, it was best to keep my intentions hidden and play the part of a well-rounded thief.

THIRTY

The walk back to Bodil's home was longer than I expected. Kol and I remained silent for the duration of our walk, but I was bubbling with questions. The first being about those Draugrs. I'd heard countless tales about them, and each one was very consistent when they said that they thrived in tombs or close to them to protect their wares.

From what Bodil had said previously, she had assured me that nothing would harm me out in the forest.

I hadn't yet decided if that was a lie.

Perhaps she meant that nothing would bring me harm because I was skilled enough with my magic and blade, or because she knew that Kol would protect me.

Or perhaps she really was spinning falsehoods, attempting to get me killed. The idea made my stomach turn.

"You're awfully quiet," Kol commented.

My eyes narrowed. "Am I?"

"You are."

"Probably because the company I keep is rather… shitty, to say the least."

He huffed. "This shitty company saved your ass."

I shrugged. "I know. You don't need to remind me every thirty seconds."

Kol grinned. "It's not every thirty seconds. I like to think—"

"Perhaps you shouldn't?" I was growing more and more irritated by the minute with this banter.

Throughout this entire ordeal, he's not once been talkative or chatty until now. What changed? From the moment Kol left Bodil's home and came to rescue me and Fen, he'd been this way.

The forest opened back up into the main village, still teeming with all walks of life. I noticed Bodil easily, dressed in her white attire and standing by the same elevator that had taken us down below. Kol and I walked over, with Fenrir trailing behind.

Bodil noticed us and bowed her head respectively. "You've returned." Her eyes swept up and down my attire, her nose wrinkling. "Did you encounter some trouble?"

I gestured to the forest behind me. "Draugrs."

"*Draugrs?*" Bodil turned to the woods, scanning the vicinity, her expression twisting in fear. "Are you certain?"

"I think I know what they are," I replied, unable to help the bite to my words.

Kol cleared his throat, taking a step forward. "We'll be taking our leave now. Eira and I need to get to Ásjá as soon as possible."

Bodil's eyes narrowed. "What is the rush? You were just telling me—"

"Time is short, and I grow tired of waiting." He turned to me. "She has the ring, and her magic has welled up inside her like a raging storm. I need that item."

I frowned. "I don't see why we have to leave so quickly. You literally just said that we could rest before getting out and about."

"I did," he replied. "However, something has come up, and I—*we*—need to get to Ásjá as quickly as possible."

I watched Kol for a moment. He seemed on edge, his eyes never resting on anything that wasn't the forest or around us. Bodil noticed the change in him as well, but she didn't comment further on it.

What had happened in the time I had been gone for this new development? I hadn't been gone that long, and that shouldn't have been a problem. Unless...

"Are you worried about the All-Father?" I asked him.

Kol waved away my question. "No. But before we depart, you need to change your appearance."

I wrinkled my nose. "Change my appearance? What for?"

He gestured to my attire and body. "Since your little stunt back in Eiði, I'm sure Oeric knows what you look like."

"And he knows you're with me," I countered. "So, change *your* appearance."

"I can't," he said simply. "There aren't any other gods around that he would know."

I winced. "Yeah, that sounds right."

"Besides." He reached out, grabbed a lock of my hair, and twirled it around his finger. "All you really need to change is your hair and eyes."

I blinked at him, slapping his hand away from my hair. "No."

He crossed his arms. "If you don't, then all this will be for nothing."

Grumbling, I stomped away from him.

I hated to admit that he was right, but what other choice did I have? If I wanted to move forward with my plan, I would need to get into Ásjá. If I wanted to bring my mother back, I needed to cooperate and do what needs to be done.

Because one thing was certain, I wanted her back no matter the cost.

Sighing, I turned back around with my arms folded over my chest, shooting him a glare. "Fine. What shall I change to exactly?"

He shrugged. "I don't know. You just need to change your hair and eyes. Everything else is…" he paused, his eyes sweeping over my body. "Fine."

"*Fine?*" I didn't want to even further that conversation, so I turned my attention to Bodil. "How can I change my appearance?"

She gestured to the ring. "All you'll really need to do is think about how you want to change. Perhaps think of a hair color you've seen before and what eyes would correspond with it."

"Hm." Pacing, I tried to conjure up a hair color that I had seen quite often around Röskr. Not that it mattered, obviously. An image of my father's red hair sprang to mind, and I snapped my fingers. Perfect.

"Red?" Kol chuckled.

I froze, turning my head to look over at Bodil and Kol. I grabbed a lock of my hair and brought it over to inspect it.

Sure enough, it was just as red as when I had seen it on my father's picture all those years ago. My hair was also far longer than normal, almost reaching down to my waist. Cheeks flaming, I ran a hand over my new shade, glancing away from them.

Kol took a step forward. "It's... different. But it's not bad. I think it rather suits you."

Now my cheeks were flaming as I gazed into his eyes, waiting for him to come up with some sort of punch line or make fun of me or something of that nature.

"Although,"—he inclined his head—"I never took you for a red-haired beauty with green eyes."

"Can we not talk about my appearance?" I snapped, exasperated. "I did what you asked, now can we go?"

Kol's grin was wicked as he wrapped an arm around my waist and steered me over to Bodil. "What do you think, Light Elf? Does she look different?"

Bodil rolled her eyes and waved him away. "She's different, yes, but I don't think—"

"Excellent." He tried to steer me away, but I slid from underneath his arms.

"What has gotten into you?" I asked him.

He blinked. "What do you mean?"

I narrowed my eyes at him. "Don't play dumb. You know what I mean." I gestured to, well, *all* of him. "This playful, teasing way you have adopted out of the blue."

He sighed. "It's nothing. Realizing how close we are to our goal... it's changed me in a way. I'm eager to get this over with."

I rested my hands on my hips. "You know, you don't have to lie to me. You can't change in less than an hour."

Kol crossed his arms and turned to Bodil, seamlessly ignoring me. "You got a magic tree for us to skirt through?"

Bodil watched him for a moment, gauging his reaction and face before she sighed. "You can use just about anything around here. Just make sure when you create the rune, you destroy it once you jump through it. I don't want anything you're up to getting back to me or my people."

Sadness clouded my vision. I really wanted to stay longer in Möl and get a better lay of the land and step inside that amazing castle above the trees. Instead, it seemed like almost everything Kol and I did was cut short because he wanted to make haste on this apple mission.

Kol turned to me. "Ready to go then?"

I squatted down to wrap my arms around Fenrir's massive neck. "All I need is Fen. Everything else is irrelevant."

His eyes took in the length of me. "Well, we should get you something to change into first before setting out."

I rose. "What's wrong with my clothes?"

"They're dirty, and they don't—"

"I'm *not* changing."

He sighed and turned around. "Fair enough. Let's get going then."

I tapped my hip, and Fenrir rose to his paws, tail swaying back and forth as I turned to Kol. He waited for me for a second before began to walk away. Shifting so I could wave goodbye to Bodil, I followed Kol. Keeping stride with him was difficult, as his legs were far longer than my own, and he strode with a confidence that I hadn't seen before. I still didn't fully believe or trust Bodil after my encounter in the woods. However, there wasn't much I could do now.

The change in Kol unnerved me slightly, mainly because I don't know *what* happened to make him change this way. Perhaps it was something he dealt with earlier, his own demons, but I didn't know him well enough to gauge anything about it.

What I did know was that being around him was making my skin tingle and my breath catch. Being near him infuriated me because of how much we clashed with each other. I wanted to get this over with quickly before anything else happened or before I started to develop… feelings.

However, the way he looked at me after those zombies attacked us, that look of both relief and fear, stirred something within me. Only one other person in my entire life ever looked at me and *cared*: my mother.

While rare, I did like my men tall, brooding, and chiseled. Kol fit all those bills, save for his arrogance and his standoffish nature. Although, I hadn't taken him for anything other than a hothead. His change made me feel warm in all the wrong and right places, regardless of how much he annoyed the hell out of me.

Kol halted beside a massive tree, drawing out his dagger as he pricked his finger and began to draw on the bark of the tree. It was the same rune that was etched into my necklace and the same one that appeared everywhere. I guess it was safe to say that this rune was for traveling.

"*Nál.*"

The tree grew taller, the roots that held it in place twisting and groaning, creating a doorway that showed a water mirror and beyond that a beautiful, sparkling city in the clouds.

Fenrir brushed up beside me, offering me some semblance of comfort as Kol turned to me with an offered hand.

Reluctantly, I placed my hand in his, allowing him to lead me towards the portal. Without a moment's hesitation, we jumped through and straight into the new realm.

THIRTY-ONE

Á sjá. The Realm of the Gods. Never, in my entire life, did I think that I would be standing in a forest that was on the outskirts of the Eleven Gods' home.

But even now, standing before it, I couldn't believe my eyes.

The forest resembled the one in Eiði, with large and old trees of various ages. It was almost identical. Fenrir's ears perked up, his nose taking in all the scents and smells that came with this new place. He didn't leave my side, instead remaining closer to me, wrapping his tail around my legs in an effort to protect me. From what, I couldn't decide just yet.

I didn't wait for Kol or heed his intake of breath as I stepped out of the forest and into the new realm we had just jumped into. There was a bridge that connected this forest to the city beyond, water running through channels that connected into a lake that I could see in the distance.

Stepping onto the cobblestone bridge, I stalked towards the main city, but a hand grabbed mine and pulled me away, back into the safety of the forest. Kol spun me around, forcing me to rest with my back to a tree.

He hovered over me. Images from back in Jarl's longhouse sprang to mind, and I tried to stamp them down quickly.

"Are you insane?" Kol sounded more annoyed than angry. "You can't just waltz into Allrland like you own the bloody place."

"Allrland?"

His lips twisted. "Right, I forget. Humans don't know about this city."

I blinked at him, confused. "Is that the name of this city?"

He pushed himself off the tree, raking a hand through his hair as he sighed. "Allrland is the name of Ásjá's capital. All the other realms have their own capitals just like Röskr does."

"Huh," I said. "I didn't know that."

"Yes, well." He turned back to me. "Not many humans know about it."

"So we've established that I can't walk in there. Can you elaborate as to why?"

"Because you're not a god," he said simply. "We'll have to walk *together*."

I wrinkled my nose. "I don't think so."

He crossed his arms. "As you already know, humans can't use magic." He gestured to my arms. "And as such, no one who isn't a god can jump through realms. To see a human in Allrland is rare, unheard of even."

I raised my hands in exasperation. "Then what the hell was my changing appearance have to do with anything if a human being here is so unheard of?"

"Gods takes wives and husbands. They can be human, but they need to be *seen* with them," Kol told me.

"So then let's go." I began to walk forward but halted. Did... did he just say *wives* and *husbands*?

He smirked. "Judging by the look on your face, you just realized what I had said."

Pointing to him and then myself, my eyes bulged. "Did you just say *wives* and *husbands*? Does that mean—"

Kol held up his hands. "Don't worry. You're not married to me. You're my fiancé."

"*Fiancé*?" I squeaked. "I can't—no—there's no way."

He shrugged. "It's the only way, my little hellfire."

Stepping away from him, I pondered what this could mean. If I allowed myself to become his fiancé, that would gain me acceptance into Allrland without suspicion.

However, could I really play the part well enough to avoid detection? I had never experienced love that wasn't for my mother. How could I show these gods that I was playing the part of a woman madly in love with the God of Tricks? My appearance was different, sure, but what made Kol so certain that Oeric wouldn't recognize me? *Especially* with Fenrir around.

"Time's wasting," Kol remarked. "If you really want to gain eternal life and all that coin, I suggest you become my fiancé... *willingly.*"

Damn him. He was right. Pinching the bridge of my nose, I walked over to him. His smile was wide and warm, but seeing that look on his face just made mine all the more sour.

"Let's go then," I told him, lowering my hands to my pockets. "I want to get this over with."

Kol tsked at me, keeping stride as we began to leave the forest again. "Remember, we can't just waltz in and take Inkeri's Apple. We need to act the part of being in love and make them believe that we're not up to no good."

My cheeks heated. "I know. I remember."

"Good."

Fenrir followed us, nose in the air. His fur was standing on end, and his steps were light and careful, like he was trying to make sure he didn't make a sound.

What was it about this place that unsettled my wolf so much?

A throaty chuckle sounded overhead, followed by the beating of wings. Against my better judgment, I turned to the noise, seeing a single raven as it fluttered around the forest, head cocked to the side as it inspected us.

A golden rune blazed to life along its breast, and I instantly recognized him as one of the ravens I'd seen before.

Oeric's ravens.

Kol noticed the bird too and turned his head. Waving at the raven, his grin was spread wide. "Muninn, old friend! Care to let our father know I've returned?" He laced his hand through mine, holding our entangled hands up. "With a *fiancé*, no less."

I glowered at first before I forced a smile at the raven.

The raven—Muninn—literally coughed, ruffling up his feathers. "You? A fiancé?" He shook his head. "Pray tell, what did you pay this… girl to marry you?"

Kol drew me closer, wrapping an arm around my waist. "I can assure you that it was love at first sight."

"Hm." Muninn didn't seem like he believed Kol, but the raven took flight anyway, leaving us alone.

Kol turned to me, dropping his arm. "You didn't seem surprised that the raven could talk."

I raised a brow at him. "Just last month I didn't believe in the gods or anything else. It's not so hard for me to believe that a raven can talk. I'm human, not an idiot."

"I never took you for one," he retorted.

Rolling my eyes, I tore my gaze away from him and back to path out of the forest. We came across the bridge again and this time Kol didn't stop me as we walked across it.

Despite myself, I glanced over to see the river that cascaded through the channels. The water was crystal-clear with a few fish that swam through the waves.

Turning my attention to Allrland was something else altogether. I wasn't prepared for what I was about to see, nor did I think I would sense a feeling of... *unease* and déjà vu.

It was like looking in a mirror. All the buildings that were erected were similar to the ones in Röskr, right down to each and every brick. The streets were paved similarly, and even the vendor stands were exactly the same. The only difference between this city and Ellriheimr was the gleaming palace that rested high above the clouds, a vibrant rainbow that connected from the entrance to... I couldn't really tell where it ended.

Kol smirked at me, gesturing to the grandeur of Allrland. "Like what you see, my little hellfire?"

I swallowed, my eyes flicking towards his. "This is Ellriheimr."

"Not necessarily." Kol strode forward, beckoning me to follow. "You see, Ellriheimr was built to mirror *Allrland's* image."

My brows drew forward. "So everything I've ever seen in the city was a basic rendition of Allrland? How is that possible?"

"The All-Father chose Allrland as the model for Ellriheimr. He wanted the humans to live lavishly and well like we did, however small it may be. Contrary to what many think, Oeric actually cares about the humans. It's why he built Ellriheimr and made sure that no one could traverse the realms back to them."

I pointed at the rainbow high above our heads. "And what's that?"

His gaze turned to it. "That is the Bifrost bridge. It's connected to Röskr and Ásjá."

"But what does it *do*?" I questioned.

Kol tsked. "You really should have paid more attention to legends and lore."

My cheeks flushed. "It's hard for someone to believe in something that's never done them any good."

He shrugged. "The Bifrost connects Ásjá to Röskr. Meaning the gods can travel back and forth on that bridge rather than creating a portal to travel back and forth like we've done so far."

I turned to him. "So you mean to tell me that we've could've used the Bifrost this entire time?"

"No. Because the bridge isn't connected to any of the other realms, we would have had to travel using the portals anyway. If we had gone here first, then yes, we probably could have used the Bifrost."

"Hm."

"Done asking questions?" Kol asked me. "Because we really should—"

"Kol!"

Both Kol and I paused at the sound of the new voice. Fenrir's ears perked forward, and he growled but didn't move.

Turning my attention to whoever spoke, I noticed a rather young-looking man with blond hair, blue eyes, and a bright smile. He was wearing all white and had his arms wound around the waists of two voluptuous women.

Kol forced a smile, his arms spread wide as if he was going to hug this newcomer. "Eirik! How nice to see you again."

Eirik's smile was wicked as he turned his attention towards me. "And who might this woman be?"

I tried to shuffle backwards, but Kol was faster, his arm snaking forward to wrap around my waist and bring me forward. I wanted to smack him, draw my dagger, and slice off his manhood, but damn it his arm felt so... *electric* around me. That same, almost burning current I felt whenever he touched me sent a shiver down my spine.

"This is my fiancé," Kol replied.

My stomach tied itself in knots at that word. My heart even palpitated uncomfortably in my ribcage, almost like a caged bird trying to gain freedom.

"Oh?" Eirik's brows rose practically above his hairline. "You? A fiancé? You must be joking."

Kol huffed. "I'm capable of love just as much as you are."

"Says the man who's gone centuries without wanting to even *touch* a woman." Eirik ignored Kol's comment, instead allowing his eyes to roam over my body, and this time the shiver that raced down my back wasn't from warmth, but of disdain. "What's your name?"

Kol opened his mouth, but I interjected. "Astrid."

"Astrid." Eirik licked his lips. "It's a nice name. Reminds me of a girl that used to live here not long ago. Pretty thing she was."

My heart stilled. Surely he didn't mean my mother Astrid. From what I had gathered so far, my mother had dealings with the seven gods, the dwarves, and even the Vætt.

Other than that, there wasn't much else that I could find. There was the journal, sure, but that still held more questions than answers. Then there were the "Daughter of the Wolf" comments I'd received, whatever those meant. It seemed I was getting nowhere closer to the truth about my mother.

Eirik's eyes slid towards my wolf, and he stilled, looking slightly skeptical. "Is that a wolf?"

I wiggled out of Kol's grasp to squat down and wrap my arms around my companion's neck. "This is Fen. He's the gentlest beast you've ever meet."

Eirik sniffed. "I'm sure." He glanced at the two women on each arm and gave them a grin. "Shall we go then? Wouldn't want to miss the party tonight."

Kol blinked, and I rose to my feet as he said, "There's a party tonight?"

"Oh, that's right, you wouldn't know." Eirik rolled his eyes. "If you'd spend your time here in Allrland rather than gallivanting the Nine Realms, you'd know that today is Magnar's birthday."

Kol glowered. "Right, how can I forget dear Magnar's birthday, of all things?"

Eirik turned away from us, waving away Kol's words and glower. Instead, his attention shifted to me. "If you ever want a real man, Astrid, I won't be too far off. All you need to do is say my name, and I'll show you a *truly* good time."

"Back off." Kol's eyes glinted with malice, his arm wrapping around me in a protective embrace. "She's mine, Eirik."

Whoa, I thought to myself. That was rather possessive of Kol. Hearing him say those words sent a warmth through me, but it also terrified me slightly.

Eirik walked away, his cruel laughter carrying on the wind, making its way back to my ears.

Kol dropped his arm. "The bastard."

I turned to him, nose wrinkling. "*That's* the god of light and joy?"

Kol sniffed. "He's more like the god of lust and sexual preferences."

I frowned. "The legends never spoke of Eirik being this... this..." I struggled to find the words.

"It's because the legends would rather pick and choose whom they deem worthy of anything other than hatred."

Turning back to our path and crossing my arms, I said, "So what now?"

"*Now,*"—he steered me further into the city—"my beautiful little hellfire, we go and meet my family."

THIRTY-TWO

I wasn't exactly sure what I would see when I walked into the place of Allrland, but it certainly wasn't a feast. The inside of this palace was almost like a carbon copy of the longhouse that the Jarl lived in. The only difference was how massive this room was.

A table the length of the entire room was laid out in the middle of the foyer, with food already portioned out with wine, water, and other drinks. Women danced, men laughed and drank, and at the head of the table was Oeric himself.

Oh, fuck.

He was a tall and imposing man, with ash-grey hair that reached just past his shoulders, the right side of his head braided with jewels and beads. He had on a golden eyepatch, a runic symbol etched into the metal. His beard was just as long as his hair, the end of it tied to hold it in place.

He wore a suit of armor, with fur lining the shoulders. On each shoulder was a raven with those same golden runes embedded in their foreheads and breast.

This was the God of War, Magic, and Wisdom? This was the man—no, *god*—who had closed off all of the Nine Realms, had massacred all Vætt and who knew what else. This was also the god who would kill me if he knew who I was, what I could do.

Kol seemed unfazed when we entered the room, maintaining a calm façade as he led us over to the table. I tried my best to keep my expression neutral, but it was hard when this entire room was filled with every god imaginable and Valkyries stalked the room, watching for any sign of trouble.

"Stay calm," Kol urged me, voice quiet. "Don't show weakness."

"I am calm," I squeaked.

My entire life, I'd like to think that I was stronger than this, that I could defend myself and not fear anything. Today, however, I learned that I was not what I thought that I was. Never in my entire life did I think I would be walking into a room filled to the brim with beings that could snap me in half without a second thought.

The raven from earlier, Muninn, cocked his head to the side as we approached Oeric, who had yet to notice our arrival. I tried to quell my racing heartbeat t, but I couldn't do anything other than stare, wide-eyed, at the god of all gods.

The All-Father.

Muninn hopped over to Oeric's ear, whispering something that caused the god to turn his attention to Kol and me.

Kol bowed. "All-Father."

Oeric's gaze went from Kol towards me, his eyes narrowing in assessment. Something flickered across his features, but it was gone so quickly that I couldn't decipher what it was. He smiled warmly at me before he turned back to Kol.

"I was worried you wouldn't show." Oeric's voice was filled with authority, calm and collected, with a hint of accusation. "You've been gone for some time."

Kol grinned as he took my hand and ushered me forward. "I was busy courting this woman."

"I can see that," Oeric replied, turning to look at me once more. "She's quite beautiful. What's your name?"

I licked my lips. "Astrid." My face flushed, and I ducked my head. "Almighty All-Father."

Oeric chuckled, resting a hand on my shoulder. "Don't bow to me, child. I'm merely happy to see my son finally moving on."

Raising a brow, I glanced over at Kol, who had the audacity to look sheepishly away from the two of us. He coughed and shook his head. "I think I'll take Astrid to my—*our*—room and get her ready before eating."

"Of course." Oeric gestured to the table before him. "The festivities have just begun, so take your time."

Kol smiled and pulled me away from Oeric with Fenrir in tow. If the All-Father noticed Fenrir, he didn't comment on my companion or even bat an eye.

Fear seized me. Did he know who I was, even with this disguise? Glancing down at my arms, I sighed in relief when I didn't see my runes showing. Perhaps this disguise would work. I mean, he was the All-Father, the ruler of everyone and everything, so I was certain he'd see through this farce. However, this might buy me enough time to do what I came for before leaving.

One thing did register in my brain, and I frowned at Kol as we left the foyer and walked into a stairwell that led further up into the palace.

"Did you just say *our* room?" I asked him, narrowing my eyes.

Kol dropped my hand, climbing up the steps. "I did."

I crossed my arms. "I wasn't aware we'd be sharing a room."

He turned his head slightly, just enough to glance at me out of the corner of his eye. "We're engaged, Eira. It's customary to sleep in the same room."

"As long as you're sleeping on the floor," I snapped. "I don't care that we're sharing a room."

Kol's grin was wicked. "It gets rather cold in this palace. You'll be begging me to sleep with you before the night is over."

My face flushed. "I bet that I won't."

Kol's chuckle sent a warmth through me, and I had to mentally kick myself as we continued up the flight of steps and into a new corridor. Doors lined the hall, as well as vases of flowers, pictures of various scenery and gods and goddesses, and other intricate antiquities the gods had gathered over their many years.

"This way." Kol gestured for me to follow him.

I followed, my pace slow and my steps light. I wasn't sure if all the gods were down below, and I wasn't about to disturb anyone that they would come out of their rooms to see what was outside. He led me further down the corridor to the last door in the hall. After tracing a rune over the wood, a lock from inside clicked, and the door opened.

He took a step back and held out his arm. "Welcome to my humble abode."

I stepped through the door and across the threshold. A light flicked on, and the room was awash in light.

It was a nice room, far more impressive than what I would have expected of Kol. There was a large four-poster bed with four metal rods that connected on top, with red satin curtains that hung on all sides, providing shelter and warmth.

There was a large fireplace in the back of the room with a fire that was already crackling, the scent of burnt pine wafting into my nose. At least now I knew where that scent came from now, since Kol smelt like that. A couch was placed over a nice fur carpet before the fire, a few blankets strewn over the couch. A window was curtained, but judging by how high up we were, the view would be incredible in the morning.

Next came a few chairs and a table, with papers placed on top with a quill and ink that rested beside them. The only other things in this room were a nightstand on either side of the bed and a closet that was left open.

Kol noticed me taking in everything about this room. "What?"

I blinked. "What?"

"Why are you looking around like you thought I wouldn't have something nice to sleep in?"

I grinned. "I don't know, because you're far too busy courting a mere commoner."

He rolled his eyes, gesturing at the closet. "I'll need to change." He jabbed his thumb behind him to the other door in the room. "You can use the bathroom if you need to. It's just through that door."

"I'll take you up on that offer." I wandered over to the bathroom, opening the door.

Once again, I never thought I would see something so lavish from Kol. His bathroom was just as massive as his living space, complete with both a tub, toilet, *and* a shower. I would shower later, but I had to wash my face.

Turning on the water in the sink, I splashed water on my cheeks and forehead before taking a towel to wash off the excess droplets.

Striding out of the bathroom, I halted in the doorway, mouth agape. Kol was standing by his closet, shirtless, his arms crossed with his right arm on his chin, running his fingers through his mustache and beard. Upon hearing me enter the room, he turned, and my eyes immediately went to his chest.

I'd only see Kol with his shirt on, and I hadn't imagined that he would look this... muscular. I knew that he had changed his appearance in front of me before, but I hadn't realized that this was actually what he looked like.

Kol was completely ripped.

He raised a brow, a smile playing on his lips. "See something you like, Eira?"

Face heating, I slammed the door closed and walked over to the fireplace, my gaze boring into the flaming pit instead of the handsome god behind me.

Kol chuckled and then shuffled around behind me.

Fenrir was lying in front of the fire, his head almost lost in the sea of fur that lined the carpet he rested on. I got down on my knees, running my hands through his fur and up to his head where the earring Kol had given him remained.

Without this earring, Fen wouldn't be with me now, and I smiled at how thoughtful Kol had been, even if it was only for me to follow him to the All-Father's home.

Boots thudded behind me, followed by an intake of breath. "Ready?"

Rising to my feet, I gestured for Fen to follow, but Kol held out his hand, stopping me. "We shouldn't bring him along," he warned. "It's not wise."

"Why?" I asked.

"Because it will be easier being just the two of us. I should have told you to leave Fenrir home instead of tagging along."

"Is it because we don't know if Oeric knows that Fenrir is tied to me?"

He nodded. "Preciously."

I sighed and dropped down, digging my hands into Fenrir's fur. "I'm sorry boy, but you need to stay behind."

Fen whimpered, but understanding flicked in his eyes, and I kissed his head. This wasn't the first time that my companion had acknowledged my words. We did have an understanding of each other, but it went mainly so far as gestures. This time, however, it seemed like he was agreeing with Kol.

Rising to my feet, I noticed that Kol was already by the door, waiting for me. Running a hand through my hair, I followed Kol out the door and back into the corridor.

He took my elbow, making me halt. "I'll protect you no matter what."

My heart warmed at his words, a flush creeping into my cheeks. "Hopefully it won't come to that."

He released me. "I hope so, too. Let's go."

THIRTY-THREE

The party was in full swing by the time we made it back to the main foyer. Oeric hadn't moved, but the room was now filled with more women, men, and gods. I tried my best to recognize each and every one of them, but since I hadn't really paid any attention to my mother's stories, I was as lost as a child in a busy street.

"Come." Kol took my hand. "I want you to meet someone."

I wrinkled my nose but didn't argue with him as he led me into the throng of dancing bodies. Drums beat, women sang, and men howled into the night as everyone moved to the rhythm of the music.

Wings flapping overhead made me look up into Muninn's beady black eyes as he pruned his feathers.

The bodies swallowed us whole before spitting us back out at the end of the foyer and far enough away from Oeric and his prying raven's eyes.

A middle-aged man was seated on a wooden throne, a hollowed-out horn in his hand while the other rested on the knee of a beautiful woman with golden hair. The woman moved, and tendrils of her hair shifted from the floor. The man had long reddish-brown hair, his beard long and slightly unruly despite the beads and bands that attempted to hold the strands in place.

His blue eyes were lit with mischief, his fingers thrumming on the blonde woman's knee. A short, metal hammer rested at his side, runes etched into it. I knew who this was almost instantly just by the hammer alone.

Magnar, the God of Thunder.

The woman beside him was probably one of his concubines if not wives. However, judging by the unearthly beauty she held and that long hair, she had to be one of the many goddesses that thrived in Ásjá.

Magnar noticed us first, standing up and pulling Kol into a bone-shattering hug. I stepped back, wide-eyed at the gesture. Kol made a rude noise, cursing, and I couldn't hold in my snicker as Magnar placed Kol back on the floor, smiling from ear to ear.

"It's so nice of you to finally show up!" Magnar chuckled, turning to the woman who now stood, bowing her head slightly at Kol. "Who's this woman with you?"

"Astrid." I held out my hand.

"Fearless." Magnar took my offered hand in his own, squeezing my fingers more than I would have liked. "I like that."

"Yes, well." Kol tore his gaze away from mine to Magnar's. "I just had to come and say a hearty congratulations for your birthday."

Magnar released my hand, placing his arm around the woman beside him. "How rude of me. This is my wife, Sigrid."

I smiled at her, offering a small wave. "Hello."

Sigrid inclined her head. "It is nice to meet you, Astrid. The All-Father spoke about a beautiful mortal girl who managed to take the heart of Kol. It's been quite some time since the last one."

I turned to Kol, brows knitted in confusion. A pang of jealousy coursed through me, but I stamped it down quickly. "The last one?"

He waved me off. "It's nothing."

"Have you talked to Roar and Njal yet?" Magnar asked Kol.

"No, I have not. Why?"

The God of Thunder shrugged. "I don't know. They just asked me not too long ago if you'd come back home."

Kol frowned. "Then I'll go find them. Come, Astrid."

He took my wrist and led me back into the throng of bodies. This is the second time that someone had mentioned a "last one", and I couldn't decipher what it meant.

I wasn't dumb; I knew the gods lived long lives, so I was sure that at one point or another he had fallen in love or at least cared for someone. It shouldn't bother me, but I couldn't help the twinge of jealously that tore through me knowing someone else had loved him once.

What was I even thinking? I knew for a fact that I didn't love Kol, but I couldn't deny this spark, this attraction, for much longer. His touch sent excitement through me, something I hadn't ever felt before with any of the previous men I'd ever been with.

I didn't love Kol, but I did in fact care for him.

Slightly.

The bodies spit us back out into the opposite side of the foyer, this one more calm than the other section of the room. I turned, catching the gaze of Oeric before I snapped my attention back to what Kol was saying, or rather, who he was talking to.

"Magnar said you wanted to say something to me?" Kol's tone hinted at annoyance, and a vein in his right temple flared. "I've got a few things to do, so make it quick."

The god we stood before was slightly taller than Kol, with brown hair that was tied back in braids, the sides of his head shaved with the sigil of a raven's head buzzed into the right side of his skull. His green eyes crinkled at the corners, his brown beard just as long as Oeric's, if not slightly longer.

"It's about time you came back. I've been planning this ruse for the last several weeks." the other god frowned. "You've been gone far longer than you said you would."

Kol scratched the back of his head. "I know, Roar. It wasn't my intention to be gone that long. But do you have everything in place?"

Roar, The God of Vengeance.

Roar smiled. "The All-Father won't know it's us. I'm sure if—"

229

"Plotting something?"

My heart stopped as a raven settled on my shoulder, head tilted to the side so he had good view of the three of us.

Neither Roar nor Kol seemed fazed by the raven's appearance, but I nearly screamed, too startled to speak. I wasn't exactly sure what Roar and Kol were plotting, but I hoped it had nothing to do with the fact that I was here.

"Huginn," Roar greeted. "How nice of you to join us."

The raven huffed and hopped to my other shoulder, taking in Roar's features. "You forget that I am always around. I may not care much for what Muninn does, but I like to make stakes and have fun just like the lot of you."

"Pesky creature," Kol chuckled. "What are you plotting?"

"Nothing as of late," Huginn assured us. "However, I am most interested in learning what it is you are plotting this time. Do you intent to steal Sigrid's locks once more?"

I narrowed my eyes and turned my attention to Kol. "You *stole* Sigrid's hair?"

Kol waved me away. "It was merely a joke, nothing more. No one was harmed."

"I wouldn't say that," Magnar said from behind me, approaching to stand within our circle. "My wife was devastated."

"By the grace of the gods!" I jumped away, scattering Huginn from my shoulders. I placed my hand over my heart, eyes wide. "You scared the shit out of me."

Magnar held up his hands. "It wasn't my intention. I'm sorry."

Kol laughed, clapping both Magnar and Roar on the shoulder. I warmed, seeing Kol appear so carefree and happy to be back among his friends and family.

Which, once again, begged the question as to why we were stealing something so precious anyway. I didn't know what Inkeri's Apple even did other than the small snippet that Kol had given me, but was this what Kol was plotting with Roar?

Oeric's booming voice took over the thrumming of the drums, the voices of everyone going silent as all eyes turned towards the All-Father seated at the head of the table, holding up a horn in his hand.

"Áræði!" Oeric glanced around the room. "Mortals and other creatures from across the Nine Realms, I thank you for coming to my son, Magnar's birthday. While today was only to be celebrated for my son's new age, I've come to find out that another one of my sons, Kol, has found himself a fiancé."

All eyes in the room turned from Oeric to mine and Kol's. I wasn't always the shy type, but I slid behind Kol slightly, not liking this unwanted attention. Kol took it in stride, bobbing his head and cracking a grin to the others.

"This whole week shall be a celebration, one that will end in these two finally bonding and marrying each other," Oeric continued.

I balked, coughing. Did he just say that by the end of the week I'd be married to Kol? *Hell no.* I turned to him, his gaze telling me to not say anything or cause a scene.

"Now, why don't we eat? I'm sure we're all famished. Kol, Astrid, why don't you come sit down beside me?" Oeric held up his horn, smiling at me and Kol.

It was a question, one that we could not say no to. This was the All-Father, and I'd be damned if I told him no. Instead, I smiled, took Kol's hand, and led him towards Oeric, acting like this wasn't sending off any warning bells.

Everyone around the room took their seats, already digging into the food that was laid out. I sat beside Kol, who was on Oeric's right, with Magnar on the left.

The God of Thunder kissed his wife's brow before he grabbed a turkey leg and began to devour it. Silence filled the room save for the clinks of glasses, the scrapes of silverware, and the chuckles and hushed tones from other conversations.

I picked up my fork, spearing a few vegetables and some pork and deer before I began to eat slowly. Women walked around pouring more wine and mead and filling empty plates. Oeric was on his third plate long before I was even finished with my first.

"So, Astrid," Oeric said slowly, "how did you come to meet Kol?"

I took a sip of mead, setting my fork to the side. "It's a long story full of peril."

Oeric raised a brow. "Is that so? I would love to hear it."

Kol clamped a hand on my knee, a warning.

I smiled. "We met at a Jarl's party. I couldn't find the bathroom, and he was kind enough to help me."

"That's not very perilous," the All-Father commented.

"I saved her at least three times from the Jarl's advances." The lie flowed from Kol's tongue rather quickly, his smile slow and steady. "We went outside, talked some, and ultimately, I decided that I rather liked her. But,"—he took my hand, sending a shiver down my spine—"I didn't know I was in love with her until fairly recently."

"Oh?" Oeric sat forward, brow raised in question. "Do tell."

I swallowed. "Yes, Kol. Do tell us this story."

"Well…" Kol's thumb ran across my knuckles, almost like he was lost in thought. "We were taking a slight detour before coming here. Seeing her in her natural element was rather alluring. She can handle herself pretty well, and it was like a light had gone off when I realized that I could have potentially lost her."

He didn't skip a beat, and I admired just how quickly he was able to spin the tale. Although, was he possibly telling the truth? I forced that thought away. There was no way he could love me; I was nothing more than a means to an end.

Oeric chuckled. "Sounds perilous indeed."

I continued to eat, keeping my gaze on my food. I could sense a pair of eyes on me but didn't dare look around to see who could have been watching.

Kol wiped the side of his mouth. "It's getting rather late." He turned to me. "We should be getting to bed."

I smiled at him. "I'm quite tired. Perhaps we should get some rest."

He took my hand and helped me up. "We'll see you in the morning, All-Father?"

Oeric nodded, his eyes zeroing in on mine before he turned away. "Yes. After all, we have plenty of things to discuss."

Kol led us away from the table, where many of the other patrons had already finished, talking amongst themselves and drinking silly.

The look the All-Father had given me unsettled me, but I couldn't imagine why at the moment as I noticed Eirik in the corner with his two women from earlier, his mouth feasting on— I turned away, face flushing. If Kol noticed my unease, he didn't show it as he led us out of the foyer and back into the corridor to his room.

THIRTY-FOUR

he moment we walked through Kol's door and into his
room, I dropped his hand, crossed my arms, and shot
him the coldest, hardest glare of my life.

"What?" Kol began to slip off his clothes, not
seeming to care that I would rather him *not* be shirtless.

I gestured to the door. "We're getting married in a week's
time? Are you serious? Hell no."

He sat on the bed, taking off his socks. "Eira, we're not getting married. This is a rouse, remember? We need to act the part
of being together."

"That doesn't mean marriage," I countered hotly.

"We're engaged. Obviously that means we're going to get
married. It would seem, however, that the All-Father would rather speed that up."

"Why?"

Kol stood. "Oeric has many grandchildren. I'm one of the
last remaining ones to bear him one."

I froze. The idea of spending intimate time with Kol, of kissing and feeling that body—I shook my head. I should not be

thinking about this. Face flaming from my unwanted thoughts, I turned away from him.

"I'm going to take a shower."

I didn't wait for his answer as I stomped into the bathroom. I heard him mumble something under his breath but ignored him and closed the door. The shower had a marble floor with glass all the way around it. It wasn't ideal, as I liked my privacy, and those glass walls offered none, but a shower was something I so desperately craved.

I discarded my clothes quickly, slipping into the shower and turning the handle. Hot, almost scalding water hit my head and back, and I almost moaned at the pleasure it brought me.

Gods, how long had it been since I last showered? I wrinkled my nose. Had I smelled this whole time?

The door to the shower opened, and Kol stepped into the shower, wearing nothing but his pants as he strode towards me. I squeaked, jumping away to cover myself as my back hit one of the many glass walls.

"Kol what the *fuck* are you doing in here?" I almost screamed at him.

He placed a finger over his lips. "Ssssh."

"*Ssssh?*" I screeched. "You want me to sssssh?"

Kol got closer, so close that his bare chest was almost touching mine, my knees quaking at how close he was to me. "I needed to tell you something, but I couldn't do it out there."

"*Why?*"

"The All-Father has his eyes and ears everywhere. I can't trust that no one would listen in on us and report back to him."

"Can't I just put on some clothes and we talk *outside* the shower when I'm *dressed?*"

"There's no time," Kol said, voice urgent. "It's important."

"*Fine.*" I kept my arms folded over my chest, glaring at him. "Make it quick."

"Inkeri wasn't at the celebration tonight."

I raised a brow. "Okay, and?"

He rolled his eyes. "Eira, if Inkeri wasn't at the celebration, then that is going to make it harder for us to find her and get that apple."

I frowned, dropping my arms slightly. "So, you think that just because she wasn't at Magnar's birthday bash, she's going to be hard to find this entire mission? Doubtful."

Kol's gaze dropped to my chest, then lips, and then rose to my eyes, his expression earnest. "If she wasn't there, that means something's up with the orchard where the apples are kept."

"What could be wrong with the orchard?"

"I don't know," he said. "But if it does pertain to the orchard, then this whole thing would be for nothing."

I lifted my hands in exasperation. "So you mean to tell me that we came all this way for nothing if something happens to Inkeri's orchard? That's a far cry to make, Kol."

He drew closer, face mere inches from my own, and I tried to take a step back only to realize that I was already flush with the glass wall behind me. "There was something else I wanted to say."

"What?" I glowered. "Spit it out."

"I meant it earlier when I said that you were beautiful," he whispered.

My face flushed. "I wasn't thinking about that at all."

"No?" He raised a brow.

"Nope." I turned my head. "Not at all."

In a flash, Kol's hands snaked out, taking my wrists and holding them above my head, his lips on mine.

I froze, not comprehending what was going on in this moment. Kol's lips were soft, almost featherlike. A fire I hadn't ever felt before ignited, burning me from the inside out as I closed my eyes, kissing him back.

Kol dropped one of his hands from my wrist to explore my body. It began at my face, his fingers tracing the planes and angles, tucking a wet strand behind my ear before his hand strayed to my collarbone and lower still.

Kol bit my bottom lip, and I opened my mouth wider, meeting his tongue with mine. Heat pooled in my navel, my legs quaking, my entire body electrified by Kol's simple yet seductive touches and caresses. His hand found one of my breasts, cupping it.

I gasped at the new sensation it brought, giving him more entrance into my mouth as his tongue and teeth grazed me.

He grabbed a nipple between his fingertips, toying with my supple flesh. It was then that he finally released my hands, and I wrapped my arms around his neck, burying my fingers into his long locks as he grabbed my ass and hoisted me up. My legs wrapped around his waist as his mouth descended on my breast. I brought my head back, moaning as his teeth nipped and sucked at me.

Warning bells chimed in my mind, telling me to stop this before it got any hotter. But I couldn't deny this attraction I'd felt towards Kol the moment we had met back at the Jarl's longhouse.

I shouldn't crave his touch, shouldn't want more than just a few caresses and kisses, but I did. I wanted *more*. I wanted to know what it would be like to have Kol, to be wanted by someone that wasn't out to hurt me.

But in the end, this was just a job.

My hands found Kol's shoulders, and I used what strength I could muster to shift him back slightly. His lips dropped from my nipple, but I was still in his arms, his hands pressed firmly to my ass.

"We can't," I panted. "We *shouldn't*."

Kol's chest rose and fell with mine, his gaze boring into my own. "Why?"

"Because." I closed my eyes. "This is just a job. Once this is done, I'll go back to Röskr. We won't see each other again."

"That doesn't mean we can't enjoy enough other's company," he grinned mischievously. "I know you feel what I do."

"I *do*," I told him. "That's the problem."

Kol set me down, and I covered up my chest and body, my mind screaming at me to rescind what I had just said, to let him touch me and do things to me. I *craved* Kol—more than I'd ever craved a person in my entire twenty-one years of life.

Hurt flickered across his features for a moment before it was replaced with an emotionless mask, and he took a careful step away from me. "I see."

"Kol—"

"I'll let you finish up your shower," he said. "In the meantime, I'll try to figure out why Inkeri hadn't shown up to the party and go from there."

He turned on his heel and left the shower, leaving me alone and hating myself for what I had just done.

THIRTY-FIVE

I changed quickly back into my clothes and left the safety of the bathroom. Kol was dressed in different clothes, and he was sitting at his table shifting through some papers.

My entire body quaked when I laid eyes upon him, and I had to bite my lower lip to calm myself down as I shuffled closer, intrigued by what he was reading and doing.

"Sigrid brought you some clothes." He turned to me, all business. "If they don't fit, we can get them fixed for you."

I glanced around the room. "Where are they?"

He gestured to the bed. "Right there."

"Thanks." I gripped my shirt, pondering what to say next. What *could* I say? That I was sorry I—we—were getting all hot and bothered?

What happened for him to elicit that type of reaction? This entire time, he was nothing but a flirt and kept his distance. I hadn't been aware that he felt what I was feeling, however small. I did feel a spark with him, but that wasn't enough for us to do what we almost did.

Once you went down that route, it would be hard to get back. Submitting myself to him wasn't an option. Shaking my head, I walked around the table, pulling out the other seat and sitting down across from him.

Placing my elbows on the table, my face in my hands, I watched him read and shift through more papers. "What are you doing?"

He sighed, sitting back in his seat. "Nothing in these letters tell me what I need to know."

I dropped my arms. "About Inkeri's Orchard? Perhaps—"

"Astrid," Kol used my fake name. He gestured to his ear and eyes before I got the gist of what he was trying to tell me.

Right. I winced. How could I forget?

He cleared his throat. "Honestly, it doesn't make sense. Everyone should have been there today."

I didn't know what else I could say to ease his mind. I didn't know enough about the seven main gods to really say much of anything. I didn't know them, and I'd met Kol a few weeks prior. I sighed, rising to my feet and heading over to the bed.

"I think I'm going to go to sleep," I told him.

He turned to me. "I'll sleep on the couch."

I turned my head before he could see the redness in my cheeks, my mind instantly going back to those lips over my mouth, neck and—I shook my head. "Night."

"Night."

I clambered under the covers, feeling Fenrir's familiar bulk as I tucked us both in, wrapping my arm around him. I buried my face in his fur, letting his warmth shroud me in comfort.

I didn't need Kol to make me warm when I had Fenrir. He was my companion, and he wouldn't ever leave my side. He huffed, his wet nose in the crook of my neck as he began to snore. I giggled, hugging him tighter as I forced myself to get some sleep.

I awoke the next morning with a crick in my neck and a massive migraine. Stretching, I reached out to rest my hand along Fen, but his massive bulk was not next to me.

Shooting up, my eyes glanced around the bed, seeing it devoid of my companion. The curtains on this bed were pulled closed to block out the sun and a pesky god that I would rather not see just yet.

"Down, Fenrir." Kol's chuckle broke through my thoughts.

Crawling towards his voice, I heard Fen's unmistakable huff of annoyance followed by the eager thumping of his tail. Peeling back one of the curtains, I popped my head out of safety of my—Kol's—bed to see what was going on.

Kol was sitting at his desk like he was last night. He held a plate in one hand with a slab of bacon in the other, holding it over Fenrir's head.

"Speak," Kol ordered.

Fenrir regarded the god before he licked his lips and made a small grumble. Kol tossed the bacon, and Fen did not hesitate before devouring the slab. He immediately sat down, watching Kol as the god lifted up another piece.

I cleared my throat. "Sorry to intrude on this little… hangout, but what are you doing to my wolf?"

Kol placed the plate on the desk and gave Fenrir the bacon before he stood, arms crossed over his chest. "Teaching him some tricks. He's rather smart."

"He's a *wolf*," I reminded Kol. "Not a *dog*."

Kol waved away my comment. "Dogs are descended from wolves, Ei—*Astrid*."

Clambering out of bed, I stood before Kol. When our eyes met, the scene from our shower sent a thrill through me. If Kol felt the same or was thinking about last night, he didn't show it.

"I'm going to see Magnar here in a minute. Do you think you'll be fine by yourself until I return?" Kol asked.

My eyes narrowed. "Why do I have to remain behind?"

"Because, my little hellfire, I don't trust you enough to not keep your composure without me."

I gaped at him. "*Trust?*"

He shrugged a shoulder. "You almost lost your concentration last night being around Oeric. If you were to let loose your real identity, we won't be able to continue this."

I opened my mouth to say some choice words but thought better of it. The journal called to me, and I'd been hiding it from him since the moment I took it from that home back in Eiði. I hadn't had time to myself to read from those pages and discover what else lay beyond, so perhaps this would provide an opportunity to read without Kol's prying eyes.

Still, I wouldn't let him go without giving him some harsh words.

I glowered. "Seems like *you* were the one who almost lost his composure last night."

Kol tilted his head to the side, watching me carefully before he shook his head. "I'll be back."

He stepped out the room, closing the door with a thud as he went. Fenrir glanced from the door to the plate of food on the table, and then to me. He did that twice before I rolled my eyes and sat down, eating the leftovers and handing my wolf pieces here and there.

Thankfully, my satchel was in the seat across from the table, so I didn't have to go far to grab the journal. Placing the plate on the floor, I cracked open the journal, trying to find the contents I had already read. Shifting through, I noticed that a piece of paper had been stuffed between the pages. It was folded neatly in a square. Plucking it with ease, I unraveled what was inside it.

Those same runes from before, the same ones that were used to bring back this person's lover from the dead. Not only were the runes etched into this paper, but also there were some instructions about what she had witnessed during the resurrection of her Ragnar.

Throughout the years, I had enlisted the help of many Seeresses, including one similar to the woman who had conned me years before. However, I knew the ins and outs of this old spell, and it seemed to me that if administered properly, it wouldn't have any adverse effects on a human or animal.

Specimen One: A dead deer that had been mauled by a predator. Mostly bone, with very little flesh. After etching the runes and following what was written, the animal came back as a zombie.

Specimen Two: A woman that was found by the icy riverbanks. After a few days of preparation, she too came back like Ragnar—unscathed, but filled with hatred and malice, as she killed herself willingly.

Specimen Three: Deceased for good.

Specimen Four: Deceased after a few hours of mobility.

Specimen Five: Killed by nearby villagers for being a Draugr.

Specimen Six: Successful.

After three years and many experiments, Specimen Six survived. A grain of ash that was left over from a long-forgotten pyre, a woman who had died from an unknown illness, brought back to life by a single grain of ash. She claimed she didn't remember anything, only that she wished she could remember her life before being resurrected.

From what I gathered, bringing back someone from merely nothing was more successful, as they weren't freshly dead. Their spirit had crossed but returned without remorse or hatred. Instead, they were grateful. I will need to experiment more, but if this is the case, then perhaps we won't have a child mourn the loss of their parent, sibling, or other loved one in the future.

I put the paper down, my head in my hands. Whoever this woman was had spent her entire life trying to figure out how to use this runic spell. She didn't want someone to suffer like she had when her husband perished. Taking my necklace off and placing it along the paper, my finger tracing the runes and vines, I began to think.

Could this actually work? I wasn't great with my magic; I only knew the simple magic that my mother had taught me from a young age, or rather had me read the magical runes from long-forgotten tomes she had "lying around" the house.

It had taken me almost a decade to learn the most basic ones, so who was to say how long it would take for me to learn this runic spell, the one that could resurrect the dead?

I wasn't equipped with this knowledge, but there was someone out there that could do this for me instead.

If I continued on this path and retrieved Inkeri's Apple, I could barter with Oeric into finding someone who could bring my mother back. A small thought crossed my mind of asking Kol if he would be able to, but I knew that it was impossible. Kol wasn't the All-Father; he wasn't the God of All Nine Realms.

I needed more to read, and this journal wouldn't provide me with anymore answers that I had questions to.

This was Ásjá, The Realm of the Gods. There was no doubt vast knowledge within these walls, a library that held many myths, legends, and various other things. Folding the paper back into its square shape, I stuffed it back within the pages, grabbed my satchel, and tapped my hip for Fenrir to follow.

"Fen." I ran my hand down his massive head, scratching him behind his left ear. "It's time we go out into the world of the gods."

Fenrir yelped excitedly, scampering over to the door. Making sure my disguise was pulled up fully, we walked out of the room and into the hall, on our way to cause trouble.

THIRTY-SIX

I honestly had no idea what I was looking for. This palace was massive, far more roomy than the Jarl's longhouse I had been in before.

There were many doors, many stairs, and many, many human servants that wandered about.

There were a few hushed whispers and some scowls, but I had chalked that up to me being engaged to Kol rather than anything else. Or it could be because I had a massive wolf with me.

I rounded my fourth hallway, finding myself back where I had started to begin with. Why was it so hard to find something that you were truly looking for?

I bet if I wasn't looking for the library, I would have run right into it by now. Stamping my foot in frustration, I stole a glance over at Fenrir, who was scratching himself and licking his toes. Dropping down to one knee, I grabbed his chin and forced him away from his toes to look at me.

"Do you think you can sniff out a library?" I asked him.

He tilted his head in confusion, his eyes narrowing as if he was trying to think about what it was that I had just told him. I sighed; how stupid was I to ask him? There wasn't anything—

Fenrir wrangled from my grasp, turned on his heel, and walked in the other direction. I watched him for a moment before I got up to follow him.

Finally, Fenrir halted by a door, sitting down in front of it and turning his head to look at me with his tail swinging back and forth. There was a rune etched into the wood, but it was an older rune, one I never laid eyes on. I knew the basics and some of the Old Tongue, but I didn't know *all* of them.

Despite myself, I glanced at my arms, sighing in both relief and reservation when I couldn't see my runes. At least I knew my glamour was still in place. I patted Fenrir on the head, reaching out for the knob.

"Out and about I see?" Eirik's voice sounded pleased from behind me.

I paused. When had he snuck up on me? I groaned inwardly. Just how bad of a hunter was I to allow this to happen?

I turned with a smile on my face. "Of course. Kol left for the day, and I decided to seek out the library since I love reading so much."

"You know." Eirik walked over, and I took a few steps away from him until my back hit the wall behind me. He placed his arm near my head, dropping his face closer to mine. Fenrir's hackles raised, and a low growl emanated from his throat, his fangs bared for all to see. "I meant what I said before. If you're seeking a good time—"

The sound of light footfalls from down the hall echoed, coming closer. After a moment, a new voice entered the conversation. "And I'm sure your many whores would appreciate another woman added to the mix, but what's the point of adding another if you can't please the ones you already have?"

Eirik turned as I craned my neck to see who had just spoken. The woman had long golden hair that fell down her back in various braids. Her blue eyes were bright and vibrant, full of life and youth. Her face was quite innocent, with a button nose and full lips.

She wore a long white dress with a slit on the side that exposed one of her toned legs. A leather satchel was slung over her shoulders, with one of her hands resting on it protectively.

"Inkeri." Eirik pulled away from me, glowering at her. "It's nice to see you."

This girl was Inkeri? I don't know what I expected honestly, but it wasn't this. The way Kol made it out to sound was like she was shy or that she tended to her garden so much to avoid any and all contact.

Inkeri clicked her tongue, ignoring him as her eyes turned to mine and then back to his, boring into him. "If you're done harassing her, you can leave now. I'm sure your father would love to know what you're up to."

Eirik's expression soured, and he mumbled something I couldn't quite hear under his breath before walking away slowly in defeat. Fenrir lowered himself, hackles still raised as he followed the god, making sure that he wouldn't return just yet.

I turned to Inkeri. "Thank you. I'm—"

"Astrid," she said kindly. "I know who you are."

I blinked. "You do?"

She raised a brow. "Why, of course. The All-Father tells me a lot of things. He told me of you years ago."

Years ago? Fear seized my throat, choking me. If he knew of me years ago, could that mean that he knew exactly who I was and that this Astrid was a disguise. And if that was the case, why hadn't he acted upon it the moment I walked into his palace with Kol?

Inkeri giggled. "The All-Father has premonitions. He told me about a red-headed girl coming to Ásjá with Kol years ago."

I nearly fainted. "Oh."

She gestured to the door behind me. "Were you visiting the library as well? We can go in together."

I nodded, stepping away from it. "Please."

Inkeri placed her hand over the door, speaking the word that was etched into the wood. "*Vé.*"

The rune on the door turned a bright midnight blue. Then a mechanism inside clicked, and the door swung open. Inkeri smacked her hands together as if to clear them of debris and stepped to the side, holding out her arm for me to enter first.

I turned to tell her that I was going to wait for Fenrir when he hurriedly walked in before me, his ears perked forward and his nose sniffing the air.

I followed him inside, marveling at the scene. I had thought the library back in Ellriheimr was magnificent, but compared to this, I was so wrong. This place was like it was out of a story-book my mother used to read to me when I was a child.

Rows upon rows of shelves lined the walls, filled with books and some displaying unique curios and relics. Tables were rounded in the middle, a few scattered out and about, with one set next to a large window-like-wall holding a view of the vast forest beyond. There was a second floor with a balcony, more books, and artifacts like broken weapons, watches, necklaces, and vases with various runic symbols. A tree rose from the middle of the room, branches wide and tall and full of leaves.

Inkeri giggled. "Magnificent, isn't it?"

I turned to her, eyes wide. "I've never seen anything like this place before."

"And you wouldn't," she told me. "Although, from what I've been told, your city of Ellriheimr was modeled after Allrland. I would like to think that even the library is similar in some way, but I am not certain."

"It's identical," I admitted. "In certain aspects, I mean. It's not exactly the same."

She nodded her head towards the window and table. "Why don't we sit there? It's my favorite place to read."

She didn't wait for me to respond as she began to walk over to the table. I began to follow, but *something* compelled me. Was that… a voice?

"*Eira.*"

I turned, scanning the room. The last time I had heard that voice, it had been one of Oeric's ravens speaking. If that was the case, then perhaps they were messing with me, or they definitely knew who I was.

My eyes caught on a mural on the wall next to the door displaying two wolves, one white and one black. The white wolf had a blue crescent moon on its head, with the stars and moon on its back. The black wolf had a red sun on its head but nothing on its back. The white wolf was chasing the moon, and the black wolf was chasing the sun.

I felt a hand touch my arm, and then Inkeri was standing beside me, staring at the same mural I was. "Sköll and Hati," she informed me. "The Wolves of Darkness."

I reached out, tracing the white wolf. That wolf… was she the same one I had seen in my dreams? Was she the one trying to talk to me?

Turning to Inkeri, I said, "What are the Wolves of Darkness?"

She made a face. "They are the wolves that are said to help bring the gods to their knees."

THIRTY-SEVEN

I frowned. "These wolves are evil? What makes them that way?"

Inkeri watched me carefully, almost as if she was deciding whether to tell me or not before she tapped my wrist. "Follow me. Perhaps it would be easier for you to read about them rather than have me tell you."

She didn't wait for my answer as she began to walk away. Stealing another glance at the white wolf, I followed her. My eyes kept wandering the library, but I always noticed the way Inkeri held her satchel close, like she was afraid someone would take it from her. Perhaps she was hiding something, like the apples?

I turned my focus away, back to the mural. There was a reason I was so drawn to the wolves. I needed answers, and Kol's apples could wait for now.

Inkeri led me deeper into the library, underneath the second floor. The further in we walked, the more I could smell the dust and decay. These books were ancient, and some smelled as if they were long gone or about to be.

"Here." Inkeri stopped just shy of halfway in this section. She walked down the aisle. I heard shuffling, a few muttered words I couldn't make out, and a minute later Inkeri walked out of the aisle holding three books in her hands.

They were old tomes, just like the ones I had gathered from the library back home. I held out my hands, ready to receive them.

"This is everything we have on them," she told me, passing them to me. "It's not much, but the All-Father likes for us to remember everything from the past."

"Thank you," I told her.

She smiled at me. "Now that you have some reading material, how about we go and actually read?"

I frowned. "But where are your books?"

She tapped her satchel. "I keep everything in here."

Inkeri and I walked back to the table by the window. I set my books on the floor, picking up one of them. The title read *The Wolves of Darkness*. Running my hand over the cover of it, I noticed that there were two wolves running in a circle, just like the mural, each one going after the moon and the sun.

Out of the corner of my eye I noticed Inkeri shifting through her satchel, pulling out a medium-sized ash box on the table before she grabbed her book and then put the box back in her bag. Shaking my head, I opened the book to the first page.

There are many wolves in myths and legends. None of them compare to the major three: Fenrir the great wolf and his two children, Sköll and Hati. Sköll was a black wolf with red eyes and a red sun on his forehead to match. He was chosen to chase the sun while his sister, Hati, was chosen to chase the moon. She was a white wolf with blue eyes and had the moon on her forehead. She was also the only one to have the stars on her back.

Named the Wolves of Darkness, these two siblings would help their father bring forth the age of Ragnarök and destroy the world with it.

To stop the impeding storm, Oeric imprisoned their father, Fenrir, in chains deep below Ásjá. He believed that holding the father of the siblings would be enough to halt Ragnarök from coming forth. Unfortunately, both Sköll and Hati devised a plan to break their father free from his chains.

Oeric knew of this plan and thus devised a plan of his own. He would allow the siblings entrance into the Realm of the Gods, but in doing so, would ultimately change them in ways they could never defy.

The moment Sköll and Hati entered Ásjá, they were trans-formed into humans and be cast into Röskr, the Realm of the Humans.

I stopped reading, reaching down to run my hand through Fenrir's fur. What were the odds that my wolf was named after the same wolf in these legends? Mother had told me that Fen's namesake came from our mythology, but she never elaborated, and I never delved any deeper into it. Closing the book, I shoved it away from me to glance out the window.

The forest of Ásjá stretched as far as the eye could see, with mountains that dotted the landscape, snowscapes at the tips. There was a large river that channeled into a lake, a few boats settling and sailing to and from. Birds flitted on by, deer grazed in the fields, and I could see the bridge from where Kol and I had entered into Allrland.

"It's beautiful." Inkeri's voice broke through my thoughts, mirroring exactly what I was thinking. "I've lived here my entire life, and it still amazes me."

I nodded. "I don't think I would ever get over the sight of this."

She giggled. "It's one of the main reasons why I come here so often. Everyone thinks that I'm shy, but it's quite the opposite in fact. I love company, but no one shares my love for reading."

My smile this time was genuine. "I never cared too much for reading, honestly. But I've found it comforts me."

Inkeri nodded. "I'm glad you're here, Astrid. It's nice to make a friend in a place like this."

My brows drew together. "What do you mean?"

She gestured around us. "No one shares my love for reading and gardening, so most everyone leaves me alone. Save for the All-Father. He's always coming to see me when I'm in my orchard. It's also because of the All-Father that no one wants to be friends with me."

"Because they think you'd rat them out to him," I said.

She nodded. "Precisely."

I opened my mouth to comment further when I heard a voice outside the library. Both Inkeri and I turned to it, with Fenrir's head lifted from where he lay by the tree.

"You said she was in here?" Kol's voice rose just loud enough for me to hear.

"I did," Eirik replied. "She's with the Apple Keeper."

Out of the corner of my eye, I saw Inkeri bristle when Eirik said the words "Apple Keeper." My heart went out to her. I didn't know exactly what her apples did, but it was enough for her to keep to herself and avoid gods such as Eirik.

The door to the library opened, and Kol strode in. At first, his expression was tight and filled with anger, but when he noticed me, it softened, and his shoulders slumped as he walked over, stopping to pat Fenrir on the head before he stood by the table, hands on his hips.

He nodded in Inkeri's direction. "Inkeri."

She repeated the gesture. "Kol."

He turned to me, brows raised when he noticed the book on the table that I was reading. "Having fun?"

I shrugged my shoulder, settling into my chair with my arms folded. "I *was* until you ruined it."

Inkeri giggled. "I like this one, Kol."

He rolled his eyes. "So I've been told."

My smile faded. Why did everyone have to say that towards me? I'd already gathered that Kol was centuries old; he was a god, so I assumed he would have cared for another person in his many years of living. What I didn't count on was how jealous it made me.

Kol turned to Inkeri. "May I take my fiancé back? We've got to get her ready for dinner."

"Not at all," Inkeri replied.

Sighing, I picked up the books Inkeri had helped me gather before I gave her a smile and a goodbye as I followed Kol outside the library and back into the hall.

Neither of us said a word as we walked back to our—his—room. Once we entered, Kol's entire demeanor changed.

He whirled on me, a frown on his face. "I thought I told you to stay here until I came back."

Placing the books on the table, I narrowed my eyes at him. "I don't answer to you, Kol."

"You should," he seethed.

Rolling my eyes, I walked over to the table, pulling out a chair to sit in as I began to unlace my boots. "Because you have a need to control things?"

"Because we can't be reckless," he replied.

Boots unlaced, I kicked them off. "Reckless? I'm the one who found Inkeri. I talked to her, Kol."

"I'm aware," he said. "I saw you two together, obviously."

"And I'm sure I know where she keeps her apples."

He rolled his eyes. "Yes, in her orchard."

Shaking my head, I stood. "No, Kol, she keeps them with her."

He raised a brow. "What do you mean *with* her?"

"I noticed an ash box she keeps in her satchel. She was oddly protective of it. I saw her always touching her satchel and then saw the box before she hid it back in her bag."

He frowned. "That's merely speculation. You don't know for certain."

"Maybe," I said. "But that could be where she's hiding her apples."

He pinched the bridge of his nose. "I don't think so."

"You don't believe me." I tried my best to keep my hurt at bay, but it bled through.

Kol and I hadn't known each other long enough to form some sort of friendship. We merely needed one another for a purpose. We did trust each other slightly, but it wasn't enough apparently for him to believe me.

"I would be more inclined to believe you if I didn't already know where she kept her apples," he told me softly. "Apples grow on trees, and Inkeri tends to her orchard daily."

"Then why don't we just go to her orchard?" I retorted. "Why do we need to do this whole thing in the first place?"

"Because the only people who can gain access to the orchard are Inkeri herself and Oeric."

I blinked. "You—no one can enter it but those two?"

Kol nodded. "Yes. It's why I brought you along. You need to gain Inkeri's trust to the point where she'll let you go to the orchard with her. From there, you can steal her apple."

"I mean, I can just steal an apple," I said.

He shook his head. "You can't just steal *an* apple. You need to steal the one that's special."

I placed a hand on my hip. "But it's an orchard, Kol. There are probably *thousands* of apples. How am I going to find the right one?"

He shrugged. "That's why I said you needed to gain her trust. What we're doing now is headed in the right direction. Although," he said slowly, "I would have preferred it if I had been around to protect you."

My eyes narrowed. "I don't need your protection. I can handle myself."

"I'm aware," Kol said. "But you've never needed protection from another god."

"I've fought plenty of my fair share of powerful beings," I told him. "I've spent my whole life wanted for the runes on my skin that all I've *ever* done was protect myself."

"Gods are different," Kol sighed as he glanced at the time. "There are some clothes in the bathroom for you to change into. I'll wait out here."

Huffing in annoyance, I walked over to the bathroom, placing my hand on the knob. "Are you *sure* you're going to wait out here this time? The last time you said that, you ended up in the shower with me."

He grinned. "I promise I'll stay put."

Rolling my eyes, I opened the door and went into the bathroom. Kol was right, there were clothes in here for me. At least a dozen of them sat bundled up in a basket that was weaved from vines and branches.

The dresses were fairly simple, primarily made of linen. Delicate fur lined the shoulders. Sighing, I stripped and dressed quickly just in case Kol didn't hold up to his end of the bargain and stay in the room rather than breaking into the bathroom.

Once I was dressed, I left the confines of the bathroom to see Kol shifting through the pages of the three books that I brought back from the library. His eyes went from the page he was reading to where I stood, his gaze roving over me for a moment before he met my eyes with his.

"You really are beautiful, my little hellfire," he murmured.

Face flaming, I turned my face away from his to hug Fenrir. Kissing his forehead, I stood and walked over to Kol.

"Ready?" I asked him.

He nodded. "Let's go."

THIRTY-EIGHT

L eaving Fen behind was always difficult, but I didn't
have the mental capacity to take him with me. I didn't
trust Oeric to not mention my wolf seeing as the gods
hated the wolves because of Sköll and Hati.

I was surprised that Kol hadn't acted differently towards Fenrir, considering he was a wolf that was named after the deadliest
wolf of them all. I made a mental note to ask him that later, along
with what else he knew about the Wolves of Darkness.

Just like last night, the party had already begun by the time
Kol and I made it to the room. Oeric sat at his usual spot, his two
ravens perched on each shoulder, watching the patrons expectantly. Running a hand along my arms, I tried to see if I could feel
my runes. Thankfully, I couldn't feel anything, which meant that
they were still glamoured.

Kol wrapped an arm around my waist, drawing me closer to
him. "Shall we dance?"

I wrinkled my nose. "I don't think so."

"We need to act the part," he reminded me.

Frowning, I allowed him to take one of my hands, resting my other on his shoulder as his remaining hand went to my waist. His touch sent a shiver down my spine, my heart thudding in my chest. Everything in me screamed to tell him to let me go, that I didn't *want* to dance with him.

This is all just a façade Eira, I told myself. *This isn't real.*

And yet I couldn't deny this feeling that coursed through my veins. Kol brought the thrill of excitement, adventure, knowledge, and so much more.

As much as I tried to tell myself that this would all end the moment I gave him the apple, I couldn't help but hope that, deep down, Kol felt the same way towards me as I felt for him.

The image of me being naked in the shower, of his lips pressed against my own, the skillful hands he had—I shook my head. That couldn't have been more than a simple act of weakness on his part.

Kol lowered his head, his breath stirring my hair and tickling my neck. "You're blushing, Astrid. Thinking about that shower again?"

Damnit, why did he have to say that? It was easier for me to forget when it wasn't mentioned, but when he brought it up, it seemed to bring back more clarity, like I was actually back in that shower rather than just thinking about it.

I swallowed. "I wasn't."

Kol chuckled. "And yet I can feel your heart beating rapidly."

Biting my lower lip, I decided that it was best to ignore him completely, trying to focus on the movement of my feet. If I didn't focus, then I would indeed step on his toes—if I hadn't already done so.

The feeling of being watched made my skin crawl, and no matter how much I tried to think of Kol's touch or something else, I was brought back to that same feeling.

Oeric was in this room, and so were his two ravens, which meant that they were no doubt watching me. I knew Oeric wouldn't move from his seat, so that meant his ravens were watching me from above, but I couldn't exactly pinpoint where.

Kol twirled me, forcing me back to him with an oof as my chest collided with his, both his arms encircling my lower back, dangerously close to my ass.

"Do you think this will all end before the week is up?" I whispered quietly.

"Why?" he chuckled. "Worried about marrying me?"

I scoffed. "Hardly. I just want to get home."

"Well, just in case we don't get this done in a week," he replied slowly. "Just know that I am a *very* generous lover."

My heart almost leapt out of my chest as the image of Kol naked and hovering over me, those hands and lips covering every inch of my body.

I forced myself out his arms, running a hand along my hair as I mumbled, "I'll be back."

Kol didn't try to stop me as I slipped into the crowed. I needed a bathroom—*something* to wash my face and calm my racing heart. A part of me wanted this done and over with before the weeks ended because I didn't want to get married to Kol, but another part of me craved knowing what it would be like to lay with a man like him. A god like him. .

I don't know how I managed to find the women's restroom, but I did. Forcing open the door and making a beeline for the sink, I splashed cold water over my face and neck, letting the water run from my nose down the tip of my chin. But it did little to help the heat flaming my cheeks.

The creaking of the door, followed by a gasp of surprise, made me turn off the water and grab a towel to clean my face off. Perhaps I should have locked the door on my way in, but I was far too occupied with thoughts of Kol's naked body to think about much else.

The woman was tall, just slightly taller than me. Her skin was the color of caramel, with black hair woven into intricate braids held together with metal hoops and clamps. Her green eyes were wide and bright, but her lips were turned into a smirk when she noticed me.

"I'm sorry," she said. "I should have knocked first."

"Don't be." I placed the towel back on the counter. "I was just leaving."

I made a motion to leave, but she stepped in front of me, blocking me from the door that led back into the party. Turning my head up, I noticed that her smirk had changed into a wicked grin, her lips pulled so thin that I could almost see her white teeth.

"You're Astrid, aren't you?" she drawled. "Kol's fiancé."

I nodded, narrowing my eyes. "I am."

"It's nice to meet you then." She smiled.

I tried to force my own smile, but there was something about this girl that unsettled me. "I'm sorry, I don't think we've had the pleasure to be introduced before. What's your name?"

The woman's expression darkened. "I'm a little hurt that he wouldn't tell you about me."

Anger rippled through me for a second before I stamped it down. Just who was this woman? Was she meaning Oeric or Kol? Maybe another god entirely? "Who?"

"Kol," she replied matter-of-factly.

I shook my head. "I'm sorry, but no, he has not mentioned you to me."

"Shame." She turned away from me to the door. "I guess it stood to reason that he didn't want the *new* fiancé to meet or get to know the *old* one."

I blinked. "Did you say *old* one? Were you Kol's fiancé before?"

I don't know why, but a flare of jealously raced through me again, this time stronger than before. Was this what everyone meant by the "other one?" Was this woman, goddess, the one that held Kol's heart before? If so, I didn't blame him in the slightest for leaving; this woman seemed like a snake.

"I was," she sneered. "But it doesn't matter now, does it?"

I went to respond, but she was quicker as she left the bathroom, leaving me alone.

THIRTY-NINE

I wasn't sure how long I stood in the bathroom before Kol decided to come looking for me. I hadn't locked the door still, so it wasn't a surprise when Kol simply waltzed into the bathroom, looking both angry and upset at the same time. But when he noticed my expression, he crept closer to inspect me.

Kol reached out, running his hand along my face, cupping my chin so that I could gaze into his eyes. "What's wrong? What happened?"

Wrangling free from his grasp, I watched him carefully. "Kol, who was your fiancé before me?"

I shouldn't have sounded hurt, but there wasn't anything I could do to stop myself from asking that question to him. I knew what this arrangement was, I knew what it entailed, and yet I couldn't stop myself from caring or feeling, regardless of how much I tried to stop it.

Kol's expression darkened. "She's no one."

"Kol," I warned.

He sighed, running a hand through his hair. "She's… no one. Not anymore at least."

I narrowed my eyes. "She's someone."

"I'll tell you everything later," he promised me. "But first, we should get back to the party before someone suspects something."

"Like what?" I asked him. "We're engaged, remember? I'm sure they wouldn't care if we'd gone missing. They'd no doubt think we were fooling around or got up to no good."

"Eir—*Astrid*," he corrected himself quickly. "Now isn't the time for this."

"If I'm going to continue helping you," I warned, "you need to trust me."

His brows raised. "What does my former love life have to do with trust then?"

Kol was right, his prior love affairs had nothing to do with trust, not really. I was just being petty because my feelings were hurt, and the jealously was tearing me apart. I couldn't stop myself from feeling this way, but something told me that it would be okay to let myself feel something for once. It took me weeks—*years* to mourn the loss of my mother.

The moment she died, I couldn't let myself feel anymore. I still held no control over my magic, and to feel meant that I wouldn't be able to control my magic. If I couldn't control it, then Oeric would have found me sooner, and then where would I be now? Dead, more likely.

Even now, with so much control, I was feeling my magic within me shattering, wanting to let loose, to feel. I needed to make a choice: either recognize my feelings for Kol, or risk being discovered by Oeric.

I sighed. "No, you're right. It has nothing to do with it."

Kol appeared to weigh his options for a moment before he spoke, voice soft. "Let's head back to the party to tell the All-Father that we're leaving to our room for the night. I'll tell you everything once we're there, okay?"

Kol reached out, taking my hand to lead me back. I allowed him to lead me from the bathroom, my mind spiraling.

There was no reason for me to act this way because this was nothing more than a job. I began to worry that this was beginning to become more than just a job. How long would it be before I couldn't even trust myself? Kol was my employer, and he was giving me what I wanted most—in a way.

My heart twisted at the betrayal I was using against him. I was going to steal Inkeri's Apple, but I didn't plan on handing it over to him.

I was going to hand it over to Oeric in exchange for my mother's life.

Oeric was powerful, the most powerful of the gods and goddesses. If anyone could help me bring my mother back, it would be him and for me to gain an audience with him was to steal the apple right from underneath Inkeri and Kol's own noses.

We soon reached the foyer, where Oeric held out a block of cheese for his ravens to eat from. We walked up the small steps to stand before him, and he turned, eyeing us carefully, his gaze lingering on me before returning to Kol.

"All-Father." Kol inclined his head respectively, tugging me closer. "My fiancé is feeling a little under the weather. I think we'll—"

"Nonsense." Oeric waved away the rest of Kol's words. He glanced at me. "Why don't you chill with Inkeri? I'm sure she'd enjoy the company."

Forcing a smile I said, "Absolutely. I may just need to rest my feet for a moment."

Worry clouded Kol' features before he masked it . "I don't think—"

"Excellent." Oeric clapped his hands together. "I have been meaning to talk with you anyway, Kol. It's rather important."

Kol released my hand, and I slipped through the crowd. I wasn't exactly sure where Inkeri was, but it didn't take me long to find her. She was sitting alone by the window, head turned to the pane of glass, watching the night sky.

I walked over, seeing a glimmer of Eirik's face as he watched me from where he stood, almost like he was waiting for me to say or do something to him.

"You really do like to be alone." I stood beside the table, brows raised when I noticed that Inkeri was holding the same box from before in her lap.

She startled, covering the box with her dress as she offered me a small smile. "Astrid. It's good to see you. Are you having a good evening?"

My smile faded as I sat down across from her. "I want to say yes, but I'm rather tired and don't feel so well. The All-Father suggested that I sit with you for a while."

"Odd." Inkeri's lips turned down into a frown. "Why wouldn't he allow you to go to your room?"

I shrugged. "Probably because he needed to talk with Kol about something important."

Out of the corner of my eye, I noticed someone watching me and turned my head, heart freezing in my chest when I saw the woman from the bathroom.

I leaned in closer, my gaze going towards where Kol and Oeric stood, almost hidden from prying eyes.

"Hey, Inkeri?" I said.

She turned her head from the window at hearing the tone in my voice, her brows pinched in concern. "Yes?"

Biting my lip, I asked her the question that unsettled my stomach. "Who was Kol engaged to before me?"

Inkeri frowned. "To Annelisse. Why?"

I tried to hide my rage and sadness, but judging by the look of sympathy from Inkeri's features I could tell that I wasn't doing much good in that aspect.

Annelisse. What a pretty name.

That same pang of jealousy tore through me, almost making me fall to the floor.

Why on earth was I allowing myself to get so worked up over this? I didn't have any feelings towards Kol.

And yet, I told myself. *You think of him often.*

I think of the way he talks, of the way he walks. I see myself cradled in his arms back when we were in the Realm of the Giants and how he cared for me back with the elves and dwarves. Of his soft words and gentle touches.

I stood, my chair scrapping the floorboards. "I'm sorry," I stammered. "I shouldn't have pried. I should—"

"Nonsense." Inkeri reached out, gripping my fingers in her own. "Don't be upset. It was a very long time ago. He has you now."

Except I'm not really his fiancé, I thought to myself bitterly. *This is nothing more than a farce.*

"You're right," I sighed, forcing a smile. "He has me now."

I once thought I was a shitty liar, but being a thief meant that I had to trade identities daily and quickly on the fly. They were usually names and nothing more, maybe an occupation difference, but nothing like what I was doing now.

This job was really testing my limits, and I wasn't sure how much longer I would be able to do this before someone, namely Oeric, realized that my name really wasn't Astrid.

"Astrid." Inkeri's eyes narrowed as she hauled me forward, blinking.

"What?"

She shook her head, releasing me. "Nothing. For a second there I thought I saw your hair was a silver-grey instead of red."

Shit.

My hand flew to my hair, running my fingers through my strands in an effort to show that I was playing with my hair rather than inspecting it for my natural hair. I could see my reflection in the windowpane, seeing the same fiery red that I came in with.

I almost sighed in relief, but instead I fixed the chair back in place, my heart hammering in my chest. "I'm growing tired," I told Inkeri. "Perhaps I should get some rest."

She shook her head, eying my arms for a brief second. "I think I will do the same. I thought you had tattoos on your arms as well. These shadows must really be toying with me tonight."

Now I was beginning to worry. If Inkeri noticed that slight change in my appearance, then so would Oeric and the rest of the gods that were in this room.

Inkeri stood. "You should come by the library tomorrow. I do enjoy some company."

"I'd love to," I said, forcing a smile.

I stepped to the side to allow Inkeri to leave before me. Dancing on the balls of my feet, I scanned the length of the room, not seeing Kol or Oeric.

What I did see, however, was one of his ravens watching me from a distance in the ramparts, black eyes glistening.

An arm suddenly encircled my elbow, drawing me closer into the darkness. On instinct, I kicked my assailant in the leg, hearing him curse under his breath, but he didn't let me go.

Frustrated that my kick didn't work, I drew back my head, connecting with their nose and hearing a crack. His hold on my arm slackened enough for me to twirl around, dagger in hand and poised at... Kol's throat.

"Fuck, Eira." Kol held up both his hands, blood pouring from his nose. "That hurt."

"Kol!" My anger immediately dissipated, and my dagger dropped to the ground with a clatter. Realization at what I had just done hit me like a tidal wave, but it was also the fact that Kol had uttered my *true* name rather than my alias. "You should have known better than to sneak up on me."

"Yeah." He grabbed his nose, setting it back in place before he swore a second time. "I noticed."

Biting my lower lip, I pressed my hand to the side of his face, closing my eyes so that I could use my magic to heal him when he gripped my hand, drawing me closer, my eyes flying open.

"Don't," he warned. "We're being watched."

"What should we do then?" I whispered, afraid of who it was that could be watching us.

Kol's eyes scanned the room for a moment before his gaze bored into mine. "Kiss me."

"I don't think—"

"Astrid." Kol's voice had lowered, his lips dangerously close to mine. The look in his eyes was different, boring into my soul and sending a fire through my veins.

Was he looking at me, Eira, or this version of me that went by Astrid?

"For fuck's sake."

Grabbing his face, I brought his lips the last few inches, that electricity circling around us, starting from my heart all the way down to my toes.

I didn't care that I could taste the coppery tang of his blood, or that his tongue demanded entrance, or the fact that one of his hands was fisted into my hair while the other was resting along my ass, his thumb grazing through the fabric.

All I cared about was having more of this man, going further than I should actually want.

The kiss between us deepened, shifting from slow and gentle to hot and inviting. Our tongues danced, my breasts pressed against his chest, one of his legs spreading my legs apart.

I couldn't breathe, couldn't think. All that mattered was this kiss, of the way it—Kol—made me feel.

He broke the kiss, resting his forehead against mine, breathing heavily. My chest rose and fell with each deep breath, my heart fluttering and my legs quaking, begging for more.

"I think they've stopped watching." Kol glanced around, not letting me go.

"Does… does that meant you'll let me go now?" I whispered, hoping that he wouldn't.

He blinked, letting me go slowly, his hand taking my own. "Let's head back to the room."

FORTY

Kol opened the door to his room, ushering me inside before he closed it behind him, locking it. Fenrir greeted me the moment I stepped inside, rising up on his hind legs to lick me on the cheek.

Giggling, I grabbed his massive head and wrestled him to the ground, rolling on the floor with him like we used to do when we were both small.

"You and that wolf have a deep bond." Kol walked around us, almost stepping directly on Fen's tail. He sat down on the bed, unlacing his boots and taking off his shirt, tossing them aside. "It's quite remarkable."

My eyes drifted to his chest, and I swallowed before I stood with my arms crossed. "Fenrir and I have been together since the beginning. He's always been around."

He ran a hand through his hair. "He's still an animal. One day he'll—"

"And until that day," I cut him off, "I'll act like nothing is wrong."

I never dwelled too much on the fact that Fenrir was getting on in age. Honestly, he was still just as light and limber as the first time we met.

We saw each other as equals, Fen and I. As long as nothing bad happened to him, I would be fine, but I tried and did my best not to think about it too often. I'd seen my fair share of death, and I was not going to ruin Fenrir's life by acting like he was an egg that was going to crack any second. Hopefully, I had many, many more years before he passed.

"Right." Kol stood, cracking his knuckles before he yawned. "I'm going to shower."

I watched him leave the room, the door closing with a click. A minute or two after, the sound of running water came.

Last night tumbled forth in my mind, and I had to close my eyes, fists buried in my lids to try and keep those images at bay. After a moment, once my heart had stopped beating out of my chest, I walked over to the table that still held the books Inkeri gave me.

I grabbed the one title: *Becoming Human: The Life of Sköll and Hati.* I turned it over in my hands a few times, wondering just what this entire book held.

From what I had read previously, both wolves were turned human because Oeric didn't want them to let their father roam free. After that, they were thrown into Röskr, my homeland, where they lived for who knew how long.

Tucking the book under my arm, I changed into something more comfortable and took my place in the bed, flipping to the first page of the book, with Fenrir right at my feet.

The day Sköll and Hati found their father, Fenrir, was the day they became human. Oeric had placed a powerful curse made by one of his Valkyries that anyone who entered the room where Fenrir dwelled, they would become human.

The siblings knew nothing about this curse, nor what it would do to them. When they set foot inside the room, they had changed from massive wolves to humans. Try as they might, they could do nothing to sever the chains that bound their father to the rock and were forced to seek out outside help.

However, no one wanted to go against the gods—Oeric especially. The All-Father was the most powerful of them all, and even if they did try, he would already know thanks to the fact that he could see the future.

Oeric later came down to where Fenrir was imprisoned, finding the two siblings as they tried to gain their father's freedom. Oeric used his magic and sent the siblings down to Röskr in their human forms, lost to time and scriptures as they became mortal—

"You've been doing a lot of reading here lately, my little hellfire." Kol's voice cut into my focus, and I set the book on the table beside me, scrunching my nose at his bare, glistening chest and dazzling grin.

Rolling my eyes, I patted Fenrir on the head, scratching him behind the ears. "No one else seems to want to tell me things," I commented. "So, I need to read to get my knowledge."

Kol settled on the bed, running a hand through his damp locks. "Ask me your questions, and I'll answer them."

I eyed him carefully. "Tell me who Sköll and Hati were."

He raised a brow. "The Wolves of Darkness."

I chucked the book at his head, not the least bit surprised that he caught it with ease, flipping it open to read through a caption before he closed it and handed it back to me with a smile. "I know that's not what you meant."

"Indeed," I grumbled.

Kol stretched, fluffing up the pillow behind him before he laid down beside me. I should have stopped him, told him to go back to the couch, but I couldn't make my voice come out. It was like it wanted Kol in this bed with me.

Despite how much he irritated me, I liked the way he challenged me and made me feel. His presence gave me comfort. My heart tugged, and my knees quavered for a moment before I crossed them at the ankle, running my hand along my right arm, watching the skin go from unblemished to back to the old runes.

"I know you think those runes are a curse," Kol said gently. "But they're special, like you."

I snorted. "Right, because I'm nothing but special."

"You know why you have those runes, Eira," he said. "You don't need to keep wondering why or acting like you don't already know the answer."

I remained quiet, listening to what he had to say. He was right—partially. I hadn't given it much thought since coming here because my mind had been so focused on finding Inkeri and stealing her apple while trying to not get caught by the All-Father.

Although, it never left my mind. Instead, I was plagued with more questions as to why I had seen Hati in my dream, why I could hear her voice, like my mother's, calling to me.

Deep down, I knew what I was, I just never wanted to express it. Everything led right back to the Völvas. The only thing that still made me doubt what I am was the fact that I wasn't my mother's third-born daughter. I was her first, which meant something more. Maybe I was a Völva, but not a genuine one.

Kol sighed as he wiggled underneath the covers, rolling on his side so he was looking at me. "Your wheels are turning."

I gave him the side-eye but didn't respond. Frowning, I turned around so that my back was to him, my head pillowed on my fists as I stared at the wall, mind racing and heart hammering in my chest at how close Kol was to me—in a bed, no less.

I really should have told him to fuck off. Kol's chuckle made the hair on my skin raise, and I forced back the shiver that ran through me as I focused on one single thought:

I was a human girl, and I possessed the most powerful form of magic—Seiðr.

FORTY-ONE

There was an endless forest around me. Darkness blanketed the area, the sound of cicadas, croaking frogs, and finally, the howl of a wolf made me stop in my tracks. The leaves in the trees were full, the branches filled with low-hanging fruit. The foliage above me held off what little light came from the moon. It was hard for me to see, but I could glimpse the sliver of it, however slight it was.

The breeze was cool against my skin, ruffling up my hair. The grass beneath my feet was soft, but the further I walked into the forest, the more the scenery began to change.

It was subtle at first. The sounds had grown in intensity, almost like they were right in front of me rather than scattered throughout the forest. The grass had changed to rock and gravel, and the familiar clambering of rocks falling confirmed my earlier suspicion. The trees had begun to thin out considerably, the leaves all but dead and gone, the fruit rotten. The sky had changed from midnight blue to a fiery red, the moon now gone.

I swallowed as I continued on. Every muscle and bone in my body told me to turn around, to run in the opposite direction, but my feet acted of their own accord. It was like they were being controlled by someone other than myself.

I tried to turn around, to make myself go back, but I couldn't do much more than breathe. It was like I was watching myself through another lens, outside of my body.

There was a tug at my navel, the wind coming from behind me, propelling me forward. It was like I was being drawn to something. as Another howl tore through the sky just as I broke through the brush, standing in a small clearing. A high-pitched sound hit my ears, followed by the trickling of water as it washed through a stream and across a bed of rocks.

A boulder rested in the middle of the clearing surrounded by three rocks. A branch broke in the distance, a white ball of something walking towards me from the tree line. I didn't have to wait long to see who it was that was coming.

A massive head emerged from the trees first. White fur, long and unkempt covered her face, almost hiding the midnight-blue moon that was tattooed on her forehead, her eyes the same exact color. Her massive shoulders came next, and then her hindquarters.

Stars raced along her back, dotting the fur like the night sky. She didn't pay me any mind as she walked through the clearing, jumping on the boulder to stare down at me.

Hati.

"You've returned." Hati didn't seem surprised.

I shuffled my feet, running a hand through my hair in an effort to distract myself as I figured out what to say.

"You seem distracted." Hati licked her nose, lowering her head so that she could see me properly.

"How am I here?" My voice finally came, sounding more like a squeak.

She tilted her head. "You called me here, little wolf."

"I called you?" I gasped. Clearing my throat, I tried again. "I called you? What do you mean?"

"You asked me here," Hati said simply. "I assumed it was important."

I shook my head. "I didn't call you. You must have the wrong—"

"Eira," Hati snapped, the wolf standing on all fours.

I paled. "How do you know my name?"

Hati huffed. "I see you still haven't figured it out yet, little wolf."

My brows furrowed. "Figured what out yet?"

Hati jumped from the boulder, stalking towards me. Glancing around me, I noticed the forest seemed to have grown darker. The trees were barely visible, shadows overwhelming me as I took several steps back, hitting the tree behind me that I hadn't seen originally.

"Do not play dumb." Hati's voice was gruff, her eyes glistening with emotion that I instantly recognized. It was an emotion that my mother had given me often.

Love.

Hati's form shimmered for a moment, revealing a woman dressed in white, her shimmering purple-silver hair flowing around her face, but it was enough for me to recognize before the form of Hati took over once more.

I swallowed. "M-Mother?"

I reached out, hoping to touch the wolf, but she moved her massive head away from me, her eyes clouded with sadness, remorse, and fear.

The name that raven had said before came crashing into me. "Daughter of the Wolf," the raven had called me. Was—no. I couldn't be. There was no way.

The day Sköll and Hati found their father, Fenrir, was the day they became human.

I fell to my knees, wrapping my arms around my shoulders, staring off at nothing. My mother, the women I'd known my entire life, wasn't a Völva after all. She was Hati, one of the Wolves of Darkness. A harbinger of death and destruction. A beast that would cause the end of days by capturing the moon in her clutches.

"Eira." Hati lowered her head, her nose touching my forehead.

I reeled back. "No."

White-hot fire exploded behind my eyes, making me cry out in pain as I toppled forward, almost face-first in the dirt. The reve-

lation slapped me in the face, made my chest hurt as I tried to process this new information.

I felt warmth trickle down my forehead to my nose, dripping off the tip of it and into the dirt in between my hands.

I was Hati's daughter.

I was the daughter of one of the Wolves of Darkness.

I lifted my hands from the ground, dirt and blood mixed into my palms. "Who-who am I?" I whispered.

Hati—Mother—strode over to me slowly, pressing her nose into my right palm, her tongue rolling out to lick my skin, clearing away the grime and my blood. "You are darkness, Eira."

My head rose, tears brimming out of the corner of my eyes. My entire life had been nothing but a lie. I was living a nightmare, being someone I wasn't.

"Eira!"

Kol's voice erupted around me, almost like he was standing behind me, grabbing my shoulders as he shook me.

I couldn't move, couldn't breathe. All I could think was the fact that I wasn't human, not really. I had no idea what this all meant, but I had a feeling that the only person who would know something would be the very same man I was trying to manipulate into bringing my mother back.

Oeric.

"Eira!"

My head snapped behind me at hearing Kol yelling my name, but I couldn't see him. The hands on my shoulders morphed from *ethereal beings into real human hands, one that I recognized as Kol's.*

Hati bobbed her head at me, backing up until she was by her boulder that she jumped on, resting her massive head on her paws, watching me with those eyes that changed from that blue to a brilliant green and then back again.

Kol's hands grew insistent, grasping my clothes, hair, shoulders as he attempted to draw me back into the world of the living. I cried out, reaching for my mother, but it wasn't enough. I was swallowed by darkness and despair.

FORTY-TWO

M y eyes snapped open, the world around me cold and distant. The sound of my mother's breathing and her voice slowly ebbed from my mind.

The forest changed into Kol's room, the sound of insects and birds long forgotten. Fenrir's howl snapped me from my trance, eyes wide as I felt an unknown pressure on my body, hands grasping my wrists, holding me steady.

My vision swam for a moment, a dark figure hovering above me. Blinking a few times, my eyes took in the sight before me. There was a throbbing on my forehead, right where my mother had touched me.

"Eira." Kol's voice was strained, his hair spilling around his face, creating a halo. His grip on my wrists was firm yet gentle. One of his legs wedged in between my legs, keeping me from moving any further.

"Kol?" I exclaimed, bewildered.

"Are you alright?" he asked me before he turned in the direction of Fenrir's howl. "Can you tell him to be quiet please? I don't want anyone to come in here."

I blinked. "Fen. Heel."

Fenrir's gave a last howl before he went silent, his head popping up from the side of the bed to stare at me expectantly. I turned my head back to Kol, his gaze boring into mine.

I tried to move my arms with no success. "Can I have my arms back?"

Kol's lips were set in a firm line. "Only after you tell me what the hell happened just now."

My eyes slid down Kol's body, admiring his toned chest before I realized that I was in a position that gave me enough room to raise my leg. The thought of hitting him square in the balls was tempting, but I knew that wouldn't do me good in the long run.

But what did he mean when he just asked me that just now? What had happened while I was asleep?

Kol's expression softened. "You screamed. I tried to wake you up, but you wouldn't." His gaze strayed from my face to my forehead, resting there. "And then a crescent moon appeared over your forehead, and you began to chant in old runic."

My eyes widened. A crescent moon appeared over my forehead? Trepidation dripped down to pool in my stomach. A mark, similar to Hati's no doubt. I tried to gain my freedom back, but Kol's grip was firm.

"Kol," I whispered, "what do you know about the two Wolves of Darkness?"

Kol watched me carefully. It took him several long seconds before he finally sighed, releasing my wrists and sitting up, swinging his legs over the side of the bed. "I know enough."

"Kol," I warned.

He ran an uneasy hand through his hair. "What do you want to know?"

Crawling over to where he was, I sat beside him, looking up at him through my lashes. "Did they have children?"

Kol closed his eyes. "As far as I'm aware, only Hati did."

"What child was born?" I pressed, heart hammering in my chest like a caged bird wanting to be set free.

"One. A daughter."

I drew back. "You *knew*."

Kol didn't move, but his eyes followed me. "All the gods knew."

I backpaddled. "They-they know about me?"

Fear gripped me, icy tendrils wrapping around my throat, choking me at this revelation. If they already knew I was the daughter of Hati, then why was I even here to begin with?

"They know of *Eira*," Kol corrected himself. "They don't know *Astrid*."

Shaking my head, I slid from the bed, not even thinking as I grabbed my boots, sitting at the table to lace them up. Kol remained silent for a moment, watching me.

Fenrir whimpered, his nose pressed into my thigh, his tail dragging behind him. As soon as my boots were laced and my dagger was sheathed, I went for the door, my hand on the knob as I heard Kol's voice, stopping me in my tracks.

"You shouldn't go out this late," he said to me. "It's dangerous."

I didn't turn to him, but I summed as much venom in my voice as I could muster. "They know Eira," I reminded him. "They don't know Astrid."

The hall was quiet and cold. Good, I would need this. I was a thief; I thrived in the darkness. As I walked alone down the corridor, all I could think about was what my mother—Hati—had said to me before I woke up.

You are darkness, Eira.

I frowned. What did she mean by that? Was I destined to shroud the Nine Realms in nothing but shadows? And even if that *was* my purpose, who's to say that I couldn't change my fate?

I rounded a corner, finding a flight of stairs that went downwards. I had no idea where I was going, but I didn't care, and it didn't matter. I needed to be alone, to gather my thoughts after everything that had just happened.

Despite my mind churning, I remembered that I was supposed to be disguised. Ducking into the shadows of a nearby hall, I made sure that my silver-grey hair and other distinguishable features were hidden behind the mask that was known as Astrid. It was a careless mistake, one that I hoped wouldn't end in my demise later. But for now, I would need to be more careful. Once that was done, I continued on my merry way.

After a few agonizing minutes, I managed to find the main hall where all the partying had gone on earlier in the night. It was empty thankfully, but the sound of beating wings high in the ramparts made me grow still. I should have known that both of Oeric's ravens were around.

Subtly holding my arms out, I inspected my skin. My eyes roved over my flesh, not seeing my runic tattoos or anything else that would give away my true identity.

I forced myself to walk out of my hiding spot and into the foyer. The movement near the ceiling intensified, followed by a dark chuckle and then nothing at all.

My ears strained, trying to pick up any signs that someone was following me, and when I still heard silence, my shoulders sank with relief as I made it to the front door, throwing it open and walking through it with ease.

Part of me thought someone would stop me or that those pesky ravens would descend from the ramparts to question me and then tell Oeric what I was doing out in the middle of the night.

I sighed in relief as the breeze cooled my skin, the gust sending a few strands of my red hair in my face. Swiping them away irritably, I followed the winding path around the palace and straight towards the river and the forest that we came from in the beginning. But then I paused. Going so far this late was bound to invite trouble. Instead, I turned and strolled behind the palace, seeing a small forest like area.

As I walked all I could think about was that the woman I'd known my entire life was a wolf. Not just any wolf, but one of the two wolves that would destroy the world if they caught their respected sun and moon.

Why hadn't she told me what she was? Who she was the entire time?

I reached up, taking the necklace with her ashes in my hand. Glancing down, the bottle rolled along my palm, my mother's ashes going with the motion. The vines wrapped around the glass ceased to wilt and decay. They held firm, holding everything together with the clasp and cork.

Gripping the necklace tightly in my hand, I broke the chain, throwing the necklace with my mother's ashes into the dark forest. I heard it fall to the ground but couldn't pinpoint where, and I truly didn't care in that moment as I fell to my knees in the grass.

Tears sprang in my eyes, the weight of everything coming over me in a tidal wave of emotions—emotions that I had tried to conceal for the last several years.

Despair for never grieving when I should have, rage at her for never telling me who and what she was, hatred at myself for holding everything in, loss for being alone, love that I held for her still, and lastly forgiveness. What else could I do but forgive her?

For all I knew, she had done this to protect me from the All-Father. Perhaps it was also because she didn't want to relive a time where she was seen as the villain. Didn't want to bring me into that life. Expose me to that darkness.

Rising to my feet, I took a step towards where I had thrown the necklace, pausing when I heard footsteps from behind me and the last voice I wanted to hear right now.

"Astrid." Eirik's voice was lazy, almost uninterested as I turned, seeing him leaning up against a tree with his arms folded over his chest and grinning from ear to ear. "It's quite late, isn't it?"

"Really?" I replied sarcastically. "I didn't notice."

I turned to leave, but he caught my wrist, stopping me in my tracks. Heart thudding, I didn't move as he spoke. "Where are you going?"

"For a nightly stroll."

Eirik's grip on my wrist tightened. "Who are you?"

My chest tightened, fear searing through to my bones as I tried to form a coherent thought. Had I lost my glamour during my emotional tirade?

I cleared my throat, turning my head slightly so that I could see him out of the corner of my eye. "I don't know what you're—"

"I *saw* you change." Eirik tugged me closer. "I won't ask again. Tell me who you are."

A thousand different scenarios raced through my mind. I could deny Eirik all I wanted, but the truth remained that he had seen me without the glamour. I could try and talk my way out of this, *or* I could kick his ass and be done with it.

"I said—"

"I *heard* you," I replied bitterly.

Eirik tugged me closer, and that was all that I needed. I twirled, slinging my wrist out of his hold with a jerk, my dagger already in my hand as I slammed my fist into his stomach. I kicked him in the balls for good measure before I forced him against a tree, my weapon poised and ready at his neck.

"*What the fuck!*" Eirik's voice was strained. One of his hands cupped his manhood while the other rested along his stomach. A slight cut along his brow had begun to bleed, the crimson droplets descending from his stupid, perfect face.

"Touch me again," I sneered, face inches from his, "and this dagger will cut off something you value above all else."

"I suppose I have missed all the fun?"

Kol's voice interrupted my thoughts, and it took everything in me not to turn around to shoot him a glare and do the same thing to him as I had just done to Eirik—again.

"Kol," Eirik spat. "What are you up to?"

A hand rested on my shoulder, another gently touching my wrist, pulling my dagger away from Eirik's throat.

"I'm not up to anything," Kol replied firmly. "In fact, the next time you harass my girl will be the last time you ever breathe."

Eirik's smile was cruel. "I can't die, remember? Do your worst to me. I can take it."

"All gods can die," Kol said. "I will just have to find a way. Leave us."

With Kol's hands, he made me release Eirik, the golden-haired Adonis running his hand along his throat, staring at me with rage and hatred.

"I don't know who you are," he said to me, "but don't worry, I'll figure it out."

With those last words, he turned around and began to stalk away, back towards the palace. Kol and I watched him leave, kicking up dirt and rocks as he went. We didn't say a word to each other, the silence stretching between us.

All I could think about now was how the way Kol had said "my girl" sent a thrill through me. I tried to force down my emotions because of the information he had withheld from me, but it rose to the surface, making me feel warm and slightly offended that he wouldn't let me kick Eirik's ass for being where he shouldn't be—where *I* shouldn't be either.

I grated out, "Kol—"

"Lose something?" he cut me off, holding up my mother's necklace in the moonlight.

My eyes went wide. "But how…"

He rolled his eyes, gesturing for me to turn around. "Did you really think that I would have allowed you to wander around here without someone watching over you?"

I stiffened. "Maybe."

Kol placed the necklace around my neck, the chain cold against my skin, but it wasn't that that gave me chills. No, it was the way his fingers touched my skin, remaining there for a little longer than normal. The way his breath stirred my hair.

I closed my eyes, trying to think about anything that wasn't Kol. His hands slid to my shoulders, spinning me around and forcing my back to a tree.

"I'm sorry for lying to you." Kol's gaze met mine, holding me captive in those blue depths. "It wasn't my intention for that to happen."

"You've known all along," I replied. "This whole time."

Kol lowered his head, his forehead touching mine. "I know. I shouldn't have lied."

I bit my lip trying to quell the way my heart was racing. This close proximity wasn't doing me any favors, not to mention the fact that in three days' time I would be married to him if we didn't find Inkeri's Apple before then.

Forgiveness wasn't my forte. Kol didn't deserve my forgiveness just yet for lying to me for this long. However, this job required me to steal the apple while also playing the part of a lovesick woman. If I continued to keep my distance and my anger towards him, it wouldn't work.

I needed to forgive him, at least for now. Once this was over and we parted ways, I could continue to be angry at him.

This was why I didn't trust, and while Kol had carefully made my walls crumble, he still wasn't able to get to my core.

I swallowed reaching up to run my fingers along his chest, right where his white shirt was left opened, exposing some of his skin for me to see.

"Kol," I whispered, drawing closer.

He cupped my cheek in his hand, his thumb running over my lower lip, his features unreadable in this wain light. I ached to know what he was thinking, what he felt. He brought his head down, his lips soft and featherlike over my own. It was brief, a simple peck.

He went to draw away, but I wrapped my arms around his neck, crushing my mouth to his. Kol didn't hesitate as he pressed my back to the tree, his tongue sliding in my mouth to meet my own. His teeth grazed my lower lip, tugging on it gently as I greedily accepted more of him.

His hands went from my shoulders to my waist and lower still, his hands cupping my rear as he hoisted me up. My legs wrapped around his waist to hold myself steady as he braced us against the tree.

I gasped, my entire body thrumming with electricity as Kol's kisses grew sensual, slower as he pulled away, trailing his lips along my cheek to my neck, nibbling at my skin before giving it a kiss. His mouth went lower, pressing into my collarbone where the buttons to my shirt were still very much on and holding the rest of my burning flesh.

Kol gripped the first button of my shirt with his teeth, tearing it free and exposing the top portion of my breasts. He didn't hesitate to run his tongue along them, sending a ripple through me as he gently bit down on my right breast, making me cry out.

He grabbed another button and then another, my chest now fully exposed. Kol's gaze turned hungry. His head tipped back to kiss me, his right hand moving from my butt to my right breast. His thumb skimmed along my nipple, sending a thrill through me as I kissed him back hungrily, begging—no *wanting* more of this man and his sinful touches.

His merlot, frost, and pine scent enveloped me, almost as intoxicating as his touches and those lips. He kissed my neck again, nipping and sucking as he went lower to my chest. My breath hitched in my throat as I felt his breath touching one of the most intimate parts of me when a shrill caw broke through our silence, making both Kol and I jump.

Kol released me, trance broken as I gripped the sides of my shirt, doing my best to bring them forward and hide my exposed chest from the raven's gaze and ultimately Oeric's.

"We should head back." Kol ran a hand through his hair, his face strained. "Before anyone else notices we're missing."

"Kol—" I reached out to him, wanting to grab his hand, but he was already striding away.

Taking a look around the forest, I tried to get my eyes to adjust the area around me, but I couldn't see the raven. *Fucking bird*, I thought to myself bitterly. *When I find you—*

"Astrid?" Kol called. "Are you coming?"

"Mischievous god," I grumbled as I began to follow him, holding my shirt together to the sound of the raven laughing at me as we left the forest and our passion behind.

FORTY-THREE

The next morning, I awoke alone and hollow inside. Kol walked me to his room and then told me he was going to be right back, but never came returned after that.

I had spent the remainder of my night cuddled up with Fenrir, holding onto both my companion and the vial of my mother's ashes. If only Mother could see me now, almost lying with a god.

A part of me wanted to consider changing my ways towards Kol so that the memory of my mother wasn't in vain from everything she'd told me about the gods. However, she lied to me my entire life, cursed me with these runes, and then died before she could even explain to me what was going on.

I would need to decide my own fate now, one that didn't rely on a dead mother and a trickster god.

In truth, my idea had been to bring him back to bed and continue where we had left off in the forest, but he had other plans. If I was honest with myself, that raven had done me a solid. As much as I wanted to jump Kol's bones, I couldn't get distracted.

I had exactly three days to get Inkeri's Apple. And that was another thing that bothered me.

My judgment was clouded. I felt something with Kol, that was undeniable. It wasn't love, but it was enough for me to re-think my whole plan once more regarding this apple.

What mattered to me more, my mother or the god that I had met just a few short weeks ago? Groaning, I hid beneath the blankets, using Fen as my pillow and teddy bear as I held him closer, burying my face in his fur.

A knock at the door made me jump. Fenrir tried to adjust himself, attempting to pull his head from underneath the blanket to sniff the air, but I wouldn't let him.

If it was Kol, he could let himself in, and I wouldn't have to get out of bed. Maybe I could—

"Astrid?" Inkeri's voice carried over her second knock. "Are you awake?"

I popped my head out from the blankets. "Barely."

"Do you still want to spend time together, today?" Inkeri's voice was hopeful, but I could hear the uncertainty hidden with-in.

I never had many friends growing up. Mother always tried to get me to spend time with children my own age, but I preferred her and Fen's company over anyone else's. Inkeri was the closest thing I had to a friend in a way. She cared for me, talked to me like an equal, and above all, she chose to be there for me when no one else ever had before.

I sighed as I threw the covers off, running a hand through my hair and along my face.

"Yeah," I called, rolling my head back and forth, kneading my muscle with my fist. "Can you give me ten minutes? I need to shower really quick and compose myself."

"Okay!" Inkeri's voice was cheerful. Her footsteps echoed through the corridor as she walked away to go do whatever it was she normally did.

Standing, I stretched, grabbed some clothes, and raced into the shower. I was still amazed at how hot the water ran here, and it almost made me sad to think about going home to that freezing-cold landscape and lukewarm water.

I hated to admit that I would miss being in this place even though I'd only been here two whole days.

Turning the shower on, I let the water pound into my skin, rolling off me in scorching waves. Steam rose into the air, fogging up the glass and the area around me. Self-consciously, I glanced around me as I washed my hair, wondering if Kol was going to show up and talk to me. Part of me quavered in excitement while the other part shriveled in on itself.

The events of last night washed over me as I scrubbed my body clean. Kol's hand along my breast, his mouth on mine, those teeth that grazed and nibbled my flesh sending both a shiver and a slight flash of pain that morphed into pleasure.

If my face was red, surely it was from this hot water and not because of Kol.

Turning off the water, I grabbed the towel and wrapped it around myself as I stepped out of the shower. It was still steamy in here, but I relished it like I would if I had chosen to be in a sauna. I brushed out my hair, braided it in my favorite style, changed, and stepped out of the bathroom.

My heart plummeted in my boots. Kol still hadn't returned, but Fenrir was sitting by the door watching me with those massive eyes that I loved.

I sighed and grabbed the books Inkeri had given me about the Wolves of Darkness and stuffed them in my satchel. Today I would try and convince Inkeri to take me to her orchard and then work my way up until I would steal that apple she hid so carefully from prying eyes. I crossed my fingers that I would be able to do this in three days, but a small part of me knew better.

Fully dressed and ready for the day, I opened the door to see Inkeri behind it, arm raised and ready to knock on my door once more. She smiled brightly at me before she bent down, scratching Fenrir behind the ears like I always did.

It warmed my heart knowing that someone else loved my companion as much as me, regardless of how little she knew him.

"Ready?" Inkeri asked me.

I smiled as I stepped into the hall with Fenrir right behind me, closing the door. "Absolutely."

Inkeri and I spent a better part of two hours holed up in the library talking and chatting about things we liked and disliked.

I tried my best to listen to her ramblings, but my mind wandered to last night in the forest behind the palace. Had Eirik gone back to Oeric and told him what he had seen? If so, what was the All-Father planning for me?

"Astrid?" Inkeri's brows furrowed, and she set down her book. "Are you okay?"

"Hm?" I glanced at her, confused. "What do you mean?"

"You seem... distant. You've been on that same page for the last thirty minutes, and you haven't stopped staring out the window the entire time either."

"Oh." I settled back in the chair, closing my book about the birth of Röskr to cross my arms. "I guess I'm a little distracted today."

The door to the library opened, and I glanced over, heart in my throat as I hoped for the man who sent an electrical current through my system.

Instead, it was a god that I didn't fully recognize, and I turned away from him. Another part of me hoped that Eirik wouldn't appear. Had he already gone to the All-Father since last night? It stood to reason he would tell Oeric of his suspicions. It was only a matter of time until he connected the dots leading him to me.

But I still couldn't help but wonder why, if he'd known all this time that I was Hati's daughter, he hadn't come for me. What was stopping him?

"Astrid?" Inkeri reached out, waving her hand in front of my face. "Earth to Astrid!"

"Huh?" I shook my head, focusing on Inkeri.

She frowned. "I asked if you wanted to go out in the gardens with me today since it was such a nice day out. But you looked distracted again."

"I just have a lot on my mind," I told her honestly.

Inkeri rose, gathering up her books. "I would too. You have three days until you're marrying Kol. It's easy to feel nervous about it."

Shrugging a shoulder, I stood, glancing out the window again. The forest spanned out as far as the eye could see. But there was something different about it that I couldn't quite put my finger on. I scanned the area, taking in everything I'd noticed over the last several days.

A low, shimmering golden hue penetrated through the middle of the forest, almost hard for me to see if the clouds hadn't been overcast.

Inkeri tapped my hand, snapping me out of my thoughts. "Ready?"

I nodded, shouldering my satchel and whistling for Fenrir to follow. "Let's go."

FORTY-FOUR

I t was times like these that I wished I could be myself. I hardly knew Inkeri, but I felt like I could trust her in a sense—which scared the shit out of me.

Trust wasn't something that came naturally to me, but with Inkeri, I couldn't help but trust. The reason being was the fact that she was a shy and sheltered person. She preferred the company of books and nature rather than those of the rival gods who lived here.

She wouldn't talk to anyone because she didn't want to, and even if she did, what would she gain from it?

That didn't mean I would tell her who I was.

From what Kol had mentioned last night, everyone knew who I was, or rather who *Eira* was.

To them, Astrid was just another girl who hailed from Röskr. She wasn't the daughter of a most powerful and deadly wolf, and she certainly wasn't afraid of the gods. However, I suspected that Oeric had an inkling of who I was considering the fact that he acted so friendly towards me. He was the All-Father, a man who could *see* premonitions.

Surely, he knew that the identity I held was nothing more than a glamour or farce. Instincts told me to run, but the logical part of me made me realize that staying was the best option. Running would make me look vulnerable, weak, and most of all, guilty.

"It's rather nice out despite the chill and the clouds." Inkeri's voice drew me from my thoughts, making me glance over at her. "It would be so much better if the sun was out."

I nodded. "I agree."

I took in our surroundings. We had been walking for quite some time now, almost hidden beneath the copes of trees right outside the library's window. I hadn't spotted that same golden glow since the moment we stepped outside, but that could be because we were almost in the forest rather than staring at it from a distance.

A rabbit hopped onto the path, rubbing its small paws over its face before it turned, noticing us for the first time.

The creature watched us carefully, beady black eyes glistening and never leaving my wolf's form. Fen took a step towards the other animal, the rabbit tucking tail and hopping away. Fenrir bounded away from us to give chase, his bark of excitement sending a smile to my face as he crested the hill, disappearing before our very eyes.

"He's quite well-mannered. For a wolf," Inkeri commented.

"He is," I agreed. "My mother taught him well."

Inkeri gave me a sympathetic look. "How long has she been gone?"

I reached up, running my fingers along the vial of her ashes, thinking about the way I treated her last night in the forest. If Kol hadn't found it and handed it back to me, I probably would have searched all day and night or worse, left it behind.

I swallowed. "Long enough."

She held out her hand, offering me a small smile. "May I?"

Hesitating, I gripped the vial tighter. If I wanted to gain more information and learn the whereabouts of her apples, I would need to show her that I trusted her.

She had no reason to trust me, just like I had no real reason to trust her. And yet, Inkeri was the closest person to a friend that I'd ever had in my life. She accepted me, laughed with me, joked and talked with me.

But that was only for Astrid. What would she think or say if she knew who I really was?

Slowly, I removed my necklace and set the vial in the center of her palm, feeling cold and alone without it touching my skin. Inkeri held it gently, tracing the runes and craftmanship with her delicate touch.

"It's dwarven made," she observed.

"Yes," I said with a small nod.

She frowned, handing it back to me. "This seems pretty old. How did she acquire something made from the dwarves? It wasn't fairly recently that the realms were closed off."

Think, Eira, I told myself. *Think.*

Shrugging, I slid my necklace back on, tugging it beneath my shirt. "It's an heirloom. I never asked her, and when I wanted to—"

"She was already gone," Inkeri finished for me. "I'm sorry."

I turned to the forest, trying to think of something to say but coming up short. "It's okay."

"No amount of time will lessen the sting of losing a loved one." Inkeri's words were wise and filled with affection. "All we can do is learn to cope without them around."

I forced a smile. "You'd think after so many years I would have had this grief thing figured out, but I really don't."

Inkeri giggled. "I've lived several centuries, and I still haven't figured anything out yet."

"And they say those who live longer are wise," I teased.

Inkeri looped her arm through mine with a snort, beaming at me. "Shall we continue on? There's a rather nice spot where we can—"

The flapping of wings followed by a throaty chuckle made us stop as one of Oeric's ravens rested on a rock next to us. The raven cocked his head to the side, inspecting us for a moment before he spread his wings and made a caw. That same golden rune was etched into its chest.

My heart stopped. Was… was he here for me? Was Oeric finally seeking me out for my treachery?

"Hugunin," Inkeri said distastefully. "What brings you here?"

Oeric's Shadow chuckled, hopping closer. "I bring news, of course."

Inkeri dropped her arm from mine, crossing her arms. "What news?"

"All-Father has requested one of your…" Hugunin paused for a moment, his black eyes assessing me. "Precious items."

Inkeri rolled her eyes, gesturing to me. "You mean one of my apples? You don't have to beat around the bush around Astrid. She's my friend."

My heart lifted at hearing that word. *Friend.* For the first time ever, I had a friend. My heart deflated almost as quickly. I finally had a real friend and, in the end, I was going to betray her.

What price was I willing to pay to bring my mother back?

Hugunin didn't look pleased, but he didn't comment further on that. He ruffled his feathers. "Whatever the case, All-Father needs one of your apples."

Inkeri frowned. "Can't it wait until this afternoon? I gave him one a few days ago."

"I'm afraid that isn't possible."

Inkeri pondered this for a moment. Silence stretched on for a few heartbeats before she spoke, anger lacing her tone as she sighed. "Alright. Tell him I'll be over there as soon as I can. I don't have any on hand, so I need to harvest them."

Hugunin inclined his head. "I shall relay the message."

The raven took flight, but not before shooting me another meaningful glance. Inkeri and I watched him leave before she turned around towards the forest.

"You might want to call back Fenrir," she told me. "We won't be gone long, but I'd hate for him to think we've left him behind."

Cupping my hands over my mouth, I yelled, "*Fenrir!*"

Silence came, and just when I was about to call for him a second time, I heard his howl of acknowledgment and then saw him crest the hill, racing to me with as much speed as he could muster.

His black coat was covered in dried blood, and he reeked of mud and some other stench I couldn't identify.

By the time I had turned back around, Inkeri had already walked forward slightly, glancing in several directions before she inclined her head, giving me a sidelong look.

"Ready?" she asked me.

I nodded. "Let's go."

FORTY-FIVE

The trail Inkeri led us down was hard to follow. This path led deeper into the woods, but it seemed that no matter how far we walked, I still was able to see the palace as plain as day.

We should have been in the heart of the forest by now, so why was I able to see the palace so clearly?

"*Seiðr*," Inkeri told me without turning around.

I startled. "What?"

"This forest." She paused, gesturing around the area. "It's laced with *Seiðr*."

My brows furrowed. "Magic?"

Inkeri nodded. "*Seiðr* is what holds this place together. This forest is teaming with it just like the rest of the realms are."

I jabbed my thumb behind us. "Is that why I can see the palace?"

"Yes. It's a protective mechanism to make other people believe that they haven't even reached the middle of the forest yet. It's a nice deterrent, honestly. Most give up after the first hour."

I turned around in a circle, brows raised. "So where are we then?"

"Right where we need to be," she assured me.

Way to be vague, I thought to myself.

Inkeri walked over to a tree, placing her hand over the bark. I'm not sure exactly why she chose this tree, as it looked exactly the same as all the others.

She placed her forehead to the bark, her two hands on either side of her head. I saddled closer, ears straining to catch what it was that she was saying. "*Mǫrk.*"

Mark? I wasn't that well versed in old runic, but I had heard my mother say that word a few times and had found it to be "mark" or something similar. I made a mental note to ask Kol later—if he came back.

The ground beneath us began to quake, the trees in the clearing growing taller, their roots jutting out of the earth to twist and rise, branches and leaves weaving and threading together.

Then, all at once, the trees *moved*. They began to entangle with each other, morphing and growing into one singular tree that arched itself into an archway. Beyond that, a glimmering veil displayed a brightly lit area with a single, massive apple tree.

Inkeri stepped away from the tree, wiping her brow with the back of her hand. She clutched her bag close, nodding towards the open doorway. "You jump through first."

I hesitated for a moment, glancing down at Fenrir, then at the veil, Inkeri, and back again.

Uncertainty tugged at my bones, but there was no going back. I needed to find the apple and retrieve it, and this is exactly what I needed to know for later. So why did I hold back suddenly?

Reaching down, I tapped Fen on the head, and he jumped through the veil without hesitation. After a second, I hopped through myself, landing in the clearing.

The area was wide open, the trees that encircled it forming a protective embrace, but not even near the apple tree. Sunlight streamed down onto the tree. Leaves of reds, browns, and orange were gathered around the base of the trunk, roots wrapped around a stone bench that rested just beneath it.

This area was far more magical than I thought possible. It was serene, almost like it was hidden just so that no one else would experience its beauty.

Inkeri breezed right by me, opening up her satchel. She sat on the bench, the roots leaving enough room for her to sit as she pulled out that same ash box I saw the other day in the library. I inched closer, watching the scene unfold before me.

She turned to me, eyes glistening. "We made it just in time."

I had no words because I didn't know what to say or expect. A single red apple grew before my very eyes, the skin of the fruit flecked with gold as it grew to ten times the size of a normal apple, the branch that held it tilting slightly towards Inkeri.

She reached out, cupping the apple in her right hand, her left going back to her satchel, rifling through its contents.

She swore, turning to me. "Do you have a dagger I can use to cut it free?"

I blinked, reaching into my boot. Flipping the dagger so that I was holding the steel, I offered it to her, my eyes never leaving the fruit that finally stopped growing. Fenrir was right beside me, his ears perked froward and his head cocked to the side as he probably didn't understand what it was that we were both seeing.

Inkeri grabbed my blade, slicing through the branch that held the apple with ease before she handed it back to me. Placing the ash box in her lap, she opened it to reveal its empty contents.

She ran her fingers along the apple, giving it a kiss and placing it in the cavity. The large fruit minimized, shrinking to the same size of a regular apple before she closed the box and stuffed it in her bag, closing it and rising to her feet. The tree groaned, roots covering up the spot where she had just rested.

Inkeri giggled at me. "You should close your mouth, Astrid. You'll catch flies."

I clamped my mouth shut, still never taking my eyes off the tree that had just born a grown ass apple easily ten times the size of normal before shrinking into an *actual* apple.

Fen sniffed Inkeri's satchel, snorting before he walked around the tree, sniffing and scratching.

"How—"

"*Seiðr*," she said simply.

My brows furrowed. "But Kol said that you had an orchard."

She frowned. "No one knows the truth about this place, save for the All-Father. In fact, it was he who told me to tell everyone that I had an orchard hidden in the woods."

"*Why?*"

She bit her lower lip, glancing around the area before she lowered her head. "Because no one can know about this place. If they knew, they would surely take it for themselves."

"But what do your apples *do*?" I never really got the full story on why these apples were so important. All I knew was that they were well sought after, and I kicked myself mentally now for never listening to my mother's stories and for not even attempting to read what they actually did.

She raised a brow. "You don't know? I thought Kol would have told you."

I crossed my arms. "You'd think."

Inkeri rolled her eyes. "Leave it to him to leave out important information. I thought that since he was marrying you, he would have at *least* informed you about everything that went on around here."

I shrugged a shoulder. "Kol's not known for his... trustworthy information."

"And yet you're marrying him."

My cheeks flushed. "He's got some rather unique qualities to him."

Inkeri giggled. "I would imagine."

I gestured to her satchel. "So, the apples do what exactly?"

"Oh, right." Her cheeks tinged pink in embarrassment for a second before she composed herself. "These apples give those who eat it eternal life."

My eyes went wide. Did—did I hear her just right? Those apples gave people eternal life? If these apples indeed granted everlasting life, why would the gods need them? Weren't they already immortal to begin with?

I blinked. "But don't you all have immortality? You're gods."

Inkeri shook her head. "We're mortal, just like you, Astrid. We live these last centuries because of these apples. A single apple grows every two days."

"So, how do you all share it?" I asked her. "Do you need to only eat a piece of it?"

"No. The apple needs to be consumed in its entirety for it to work. Normally, a different god gets the apple every two days since we can thrive a month without it before we start to age. Unfortunately, the older we get, the more we need to eat the apples to regain our youth."

"Is that why he needs another apple?"

She nodded. "Yes. The All-Father is far older than any of us, and as such he needs it more than anyone else."

I frowned. "I'm sorry. That sounds terrible."

"It's the price we must pay to live," Inkeri told me simply. "Without these apples, we wouldn't be able to survive."

I began to follow Inkeri out of the clearing, jumping through the veil and back into the dark forest, waiting for her to pop out. I noticed Inkeri turn back to the tree, walking back to where Fenrir had dug a small hole. She bent down, covering up the hole.

I would scold him later, but first I needed to mark something around this area so that I would know how to get here the next time I needed to come and get this apple.

Making sure that Inkeri was still preoccupied with the tree, I flipped my dagger out of my boot and carved a small X onto the bark of the tree. I took several steps back, admiring my work. From a distance, it wasn't noticeable, but up close you could tell what it was easily. Hopefully, Inkeri wouldn't notice.

She hopped through the veil, the trees unwinding and going back to normal almost instantly the moment her feet touched the dirt. She dusted off her skirts, looped her arm through mine, and together we walked away from the clearing and away from the target that I had come to steal.

FORTY-SIX

B y the time Inkeri and I returned to the palace, it was nearly dusk. It was strange to see how much time had flown by since this afternoon. It only seemed like less than an hour ago I was in the library with her, reading and chatting. Then we popped out of her magical clearing for it to be dark out.

We parted at the front door as she left to go and attend to Oeric.

As I walked back to Kol's room, all I could think about was what Inkeri had told me.

The gods weren't immortal; they were just like me. *Mortal*. It was strange to think that these people had such magical properties among other things and could die from old age like anyone else.

The fact that they could only live a month without ingesting an apple left a bad taste in my mouth.

Just what exactly did Kol need them for then?

Fenrir barked, but I ignored whatever it was, lost in thought until I slammed right into a very, very familiar figure. A deep rumble made his chest vibrate and damn was I filled with that heavenly scent of him.

"Someone's thinking pretty hard," Kol chuckled. "I can almost smell the gears grinding."

Stepping back, I turned my head up to meet his gaze and that crooked grin. My heart palpitated, and my legs quivered. If I wasn't so mad at him for last night, I would have literally fallen from the loss of my legs.

I crossed my arms. "Where have you been?" I tried to keep the accusation from my voice, but it bled through like blood through a tightly wrapped bandage. In truth, I was beyond upset that he had left me high and dry and not come back or say anything to me. It was downright disrespectful.

His smile faded, his eyes scanning the corridor we were in. He opened his mouth to say something but stopped short, eyes wide as he reached out and took my arm. "We need to go. *Now*."

I wrinkled my nose. "What? Why are you—"

Kol forced me forward, tugging me down the corridor. I tried to wrangle my arm free, but his grip was firm and unrelenting as he propelled us forward, not stopping for a single second.

Fenrir gave a low growl in warning, but Kol didn't bat an eye as we reached the hall where his room was. He opened his door, tossing me inside and slamming the door shut behind us. If it wasn't for my steady footing, I probably would have fallen.

I whirled on him. "What the hell was that for?"

Kol placed his hand over the door, murmuring something before he turned. "In the bathroom."

My face heated. "I don't think—"

"Don't argue with me."

My brows furrowed at his candor. What had gotten him so wound up all of a sudden? He went from playful to stone-cold in a matter of seconds.

I planted my feet firmly in the ground, crossed my arms, and jutted my chin. I was *not* going to let him speak to me this way, as someone that needed to be protected. My mother didn't raise me to care for the whims of men, and I was not going to sully her memory with listening to a god who didn't tell me everything, regardless of how his smile gave me butterflies.

"No."

He ran a frustrated hand through his hair. "Normally, I would find your hard-headedness attractive, but we need to speak in private." He glanced around the room uncertainly. "*Without* prying eyes and ears."

I frowned but relented. If it wasn't for the change in his tone, I wouldn't have succumbed too quickly.

Turning around, I walked into the bathroom. He followed behind me closely, but not enough that he could touch me. Once we were inside, he closed the door, walked into the shower, turned it on, and came back out.

Kol held out his hand. "I need to see your ring."

My brows rose. "My ring? What for?"

He sighed, gesturing to the mirror in the room. "Look for yourself."

Doing as he said, I glanced at myself in the mirror. I gasped at my reflection. My bright, crimson curls were replaced with my natural silver-grey and black roots, the runic tattoos spiraling around my arms like they normally did.

The only difference about me now was that I had gained a new facial tattoo. The ones on my lip, nose, and underneath my eyes were done by myself and my mother. This new tattoo was of a black crescent moon with two dots, one on top and the other on the bottom.

Reaching up, I rested two fingers along the moon, biting my lower lip from the slight sting that elicited from it. I turned to Kol, sliding the ring off my finger to place in his palm.

"What happened? Do you think the magic Bodil placed in it wore off?" I asked.

He lifted the ring in the air, glancing at it in the light. "I don't think so. Bodil's magic is pretty powerful, so unless you went somewhere you weren't permitted or used up all the magic, then it would make sense."

Threading my hands together, I lowered my head. "Would... would going to Inkeri's Orchard count as somewhere I wasn't permitted to enter?"

Kol was silent for a moment, and I thought he hadn't heard me. I opened my mouth to repeat what I said, but he replied before I could even utter a word. "It's possible that Oeric has that place heavily fortified with magical barriers. That would have triggered any possible magical counters into nonexistence. However, since Bodil's magic is just as powerful—"

"It held firm until afterwards," I finished for him.

He nodded. "Yes, that is what I think too."

This was a problem. If going through that portal into Inkeri's Orchard meant losing my glamour, it would make it nearly impossible for me to steal the apple and not get caught. I could tell Kol where the entrance was, but he likely might not be able to find it or the X that I marked on the tree. How will this work now?

Leaning against the wall, I watched the water from the shower dripping down the glass walls, trickling down the drain. "So, what do we do?"

Kol closed his hand into a fist. A light magical blue glow emanated from his fingers before he opened up his hand, holding out the ring to me. "This should offer enough magic to get you through the night. Tomorrow morning, I'll head straight to Mol and have Bodil add more of her magic inside the gem."

I nodded, peeling myself from the wall to take the ring, placing it back on my finger. "How early are we leaving?"

"We aren't," he said. "I am. You're staying here."

"The hell I am," I snarled. "You can't just leave me here."

"Listen to me, Eira." Kol grabbed my hand and brought me forward, our faces inches from each other. "I can't risk taking you with me without the both of us getting caught."

"Why? Because I'm a woman?"

He chuckled. "No, you're far more formidable than most men I know. I can't take you with me because if I do, they—especially Oeric—will wonder where we'd gone off to in such a hurry together. And without that disguise, we'll surely get caught. Now, for me, I'm almost never around, so it's not uncommon for me to not hang around for less than a few hours."

"So what?" I spat, wrenching my arm free from his grasp. "I'm just supposed to sit here and wait until you return?"

"Yes."

"Kol—"

"Trust me, Eira." His voice had grown soft, his fingers trailing along my newly formed tattoo, his thumb grazing my lower lip. "When I come back, we can get the apple and finally be done with this whole situation."

I wanted to trust Kol. I ached to trust him, to want him to want me in a different way than what this was.

I wasn't exactly sure what was happening between us, but it scared the living hell out of me. The thought of finally leaving this place, of leaving Kol behind, made my heart shatter.

His fingers took my chin, forcing my face up as he planted a light kiss to my lips. "Get dressed. We have two more parties to deal with."

Numb, I followed him out of the bathroom. Like normal, I changed into a dress and other garments before we were ready to go. As we walked down to the foyer, all I could think about was what I was going to do once this was all over. I still had plans on taking the apple for myself to give back to Oeric in exchange for my mother's life.

Could I even go through with it if I did that? Even now, my stomach knotted thinking about having to betray Inkeri and take her apple while another part of me regretted wanting to betray Kol as well. Either way, I was betraying two people I had come to grow and care for.

Sure, I hadn't known Inkeri but a few days, but it was enough for me to feel remorseful for what we were about to do.

Two days, that's how long it would take for another apple to regenerate. Two whole days before I was set to marry Kol in this fake arrangement.

Would we actually go through with it? Would we have to if things went awry? All these questions and more swirled in my head, but there wasn't much I go do or think about in this moment as Kol opened the door to the party.

The atmosphere was different.

Around this time, the party would usually be in full swing. Women would be dancing, men would be brawling and drinking, drums would be sounded, and everyone would be in general hysterics of happiness.

No, tonight everyone seemed gloomy. The table was filled with food and drink, but no one ate, no one even spoke. A few women wandered around, but other than that it seemed devoid of any life. My eyes trailed over to the throne where Oeric normally sat, finding it empty of the man in question.

Instead, a woman was seated at his throne. Her hair was long and red, plaited in several braids that were adorned with beads, gems, and metal hooks. She wore a crimson-colored dress with fur that lined the shoulders.

I turned to Kol to ask who she was when a door opened and everyone in the room turned to the sound. Oeric walked in, glancing around the room at the occupants within before he went to his throne.

The woman inclined her head as she stood. "Husband."

So, *this* was Oeric's wife. I hadn't seen her since I'd arrived in this palace a few days prior. I thought it was because these types of things weren't for her, but ultimately that wasn't true at all as I gazed at her in the flesh.

Ansa, Queen of Ásjá.

The All-Father stood before his throne, arms held out wide. I watched, right before my very eyes, as his hair began to change. The first time I had seen him, his hair had been an ashy grey. Now, I was watching as his hair changed into a vibrant red. He rose to his full height, smiling down at everyone as the wrinkles in his face disappeared and became smooth once more.

"Why are we acting like it's a funeral?" Oeric chuckled. "It's a party! Let's celebrate!"

No one else needed any encouragement as they jumped from their seats and began to dance. The men drank, the women danced, and the sound of the beating drums mirrored my own racing heartbeat. I hadn't spotted Inkeri in the crowd, and a little part of me grew sad at not seeing her.

Instead, it was Eirik who caught my eye. He was sitting at a table in the far back with two other gods, a man and a woman. Both had long blond hair, but other than that I didn't know who they were. Eirik's eyes never left me as Kol took it upon himself to lead me over to them.

Kol stopped us by the side of the table, not paying attention to Eirik, his cheeks red and eyes that glinted with malice. If the other two gods noticed Eirik's change, they didn't mention it as they turned to Kol and me.

The woman had a slightly rounded face with blue eyes that were soft and warm. Her blond hair was tied back in a single braid down her back. She wore a cloak of feathers and a leather circlet around her forehead. The man was almost a spitting image of the woman, save for his chiseled features and five o'clock shadow.

"Carin." Kol smiled at the woman, who offered her own smile in turn. "Ivar," he said to the other.

The Goddess of Love, Sex, Magic and War and her brother the God of Peace and Fertility.

Carin stood, enveloping me with warm arms. "It's so good to see that someone has finally warmed this god's heart."

Ivar laughed. "Dear sister, I don't think even she could do such a thing. She's only there to warm his bed and then some."

She tsked, smacking her brother before she turned back to me. "Ignore him."

I smiled. "None taken."

"It's been some time, Ivar," Kol acknowledged. "You two done pillaging the giants to finally come back?"

Ivar downed his flask. "Hardly. We only came back because we heard the great news about your wedding. The others should be returning either tonight or tomorrow."

No one acknowledged Eirik, who was sitting there in his seat fuming from being ignored. After a few more words were exchanged between Ivar and Kol, Eirik stood and left the table without another word.

"What's gotten into him? Carin asked.

Ivar shrugged. "Who knows, dear sister. Who knows."

Kol took my hand. "I believe my fiancé and I would like to dance for a little while. What do you say?"

Could I refuse? Probably. Did I want to? No.

Grinning, I allowed him to lead me to the dance floor where he took both my hips, and my hands wrapped around his neck. The drums grew louder, the brawling deadlier, and the feeling of eyes on me was everywhere.

I lowered my head. "Kol?"

"Hm?" He twirled me, bringing me back with an oof.

"You don't seem concerned about Eirik."

"Ah." His brows raised. "That's easy. He won't say or do anything."

I blinked. "How so?"

"Because as much as he's a daddy's boy, he's not stupid. He talks a big game, but if there's one thing I know, he won't just mention something to his father on a mere whim. He doesn't know what he saw, and even if he did, he would need evidence. Since he has none, he won't say anything.

"However, I'm sure he's thinking about how he can expose the both of us as we speak. There's not much to go on. The only way would be for him to go to Röskr and speak to the city folk about a red-haired woman by the name of Astrid with a wolf as her companion. Eirik hates humans almost as much as he hates dwarves, so there's little risk he would do that anyway."

I frowned. "But those women we see him with are—"

"Human," he finished for me. "Correction. He hates *male* humans. He prefers the company of the women."

I snorted, rolling my eyes as he twirled me a second time. "Did you notice the All-Father?"

He nodded. "I did. He's regained some of his youth. Which means Inkeri has given him an apple."

The drums began to beat slower. Everyone around us chose a partner and started to dance. The crescendo was low and slow, almost mirroring a song I once heard back when I was a child.

Kol's grip on my waist tightened, his forehead falling forward to rest alongside mine. "You have no idea how badly I want to tear that dress off and have my way with you," he whispered.

I shivered, my lips turning up into a grin. "And what would you say if I wanted that to happen?"

I shouldn't have teased him, shouldn't have even entertained the idea of it. But it was too late, my course was set and finally, for once, I wanted to be in control of something instead.

Kol's smile was wicked as he took my hands, kissing my nose.

"Is that an offer?" he teased.

In response, I pressed his hands to my collarbone, gazing up at him through my lashes. "I believe it's an invitation."

Kol was quick, wrapping his arms around me as we dipped, his lips capturing mine in a spellbinding kiss that made my toes curl and my heart flutter.

"Ahem."

Shit.

Kol brought us back up slowly, breaking the kiss as we turned to see Annelisse standing behind us. My face flushed, but he didn't look the least bit ashamed as he stared at his old fiancé.

"What do you want Annelisse?" he asked her, voice flat.

She smiled, not the least bit put-off by his tone of voice with her. "It's not what I want per se. It's what the All-Father wants. He's requested your fiancé come sit with him for a few moments."

"That's fine." He laced our fingers together. "We'll go—"

Annelisse had the gall to place her hand on his chest, stopping him in his tracks. That *bitch*. "He said just Astrid. He said nothing about you."

Kol took her hand, peeling it off him before he ran his hand over his chest like he was trying to clear it of dirt or grime. "In that case, I'll make myself scarce." He turned to me. "I won't be far."

Annelisse watched him disappear into the throng of people before she turned to me. Her eyes narrowed, and she glared at me for a long moment before she turning on her heel to leave. I didn't really care about Annelisse's ire towards me, but it was downright annoying to say the least, and this was only my second interaction with her.

I walked over to Oeric and Ansa. The queen didn't spare me a glance as she eyed the dancing bodies, searching for someone else.

Oeric, however, was watching me as I came over, his eyes never leaving mine as I stood before them. Oeric remained still, almost like a statue as he sized me up from head to toe.

He gestured to the seat empty beside him. "My son has decided to go off and do some... investigating. Why don't you sit here instead? I'm sure he wouldn't mind."

I took the seat, not saying anything as a servant came over to push me further towards the table before she departed to the whims of the other gods and goddesses.

"*So.*" He let the word draw out as he reached for his horn, drinking its contents. "I hear you and Inkeri have gotten rather close these last two days."

I raised my chin. "We have. She's really nice. I quite like her."

"Hm." Resting his elbow on the table, he swirled the rest of what he held in his horn. "My raven tells me that Inkeri took you to see her orchard."

My skin crawled. Those pesky birds would be the death of me. I would need to find a way to get rid of them before too long. With them hanging around, I was sure to get caught.

Running a hand along my right arm, I stared at my flesh out of the corner of my eye, hoping that it was unblemished by my runic tattoos. Sighing with relief, my attention turned back to Oeric as he waited for me to respond.

"She did." Reaching out to take my own horn, I licked my lips the moment the fragrant wine permeated the air. *Gods,* I thought. *They sure do know how to choose the best of wines in the entire Nine Realms.* "It was a nice place."

"It is." The All-Father glanced around the room, lowering his head so that he was right next to my ear. "I know you and my son are having a little quarrel. I'm not sure what it is you and Kol are up to, but let it be known that I am *always* watching."

He suspected something. It wasn't hard for me to hear that dangerous tone in his voice.

He was warning me in his own way, letting me know that he didn't know exactly it was that I was doing but that he knew *something* was going on.

Oeric sat back. "I hear that you've been doing a lot of research. More specifically on those two dangerous wolves."

My heart skipped a beat, and I tried my best to hide the look of shock on my face, but judging by the gleam in his eye, he knew that he had struck a nerve with what he had said. Try as I might, there was no use in hiding my despair. I would only have to keep up my façade and hope he would take it.

Shrugging a shoulder, I lazily scanned the area. "I only began to read about it because of that mural you have painted in the library by the door. It was then that Inkeri told me about it and found me those books since I had no knowledge of it."

"Tread carefully," Oeric warned me. "You may discover something you don't want to know."

I leaned forward. "I'll take my chances then."

"I believe you are sitting in my seat." Eirik's voice was cold and hard, his glare searing right through me as I turned to face him.

"Eirik!" Ansa rushed over to him, running her hands along his body. "Are you okay? You aren't hurt, are you? Perhaps I should—"

He grabbed her hand, holding it away from him as he rolled his eyes. "I'm fine. You know nothing can kill me."

She stamped her foot. "That doesn't mean someone won't try to harm you."

"Well." I pushed the chair back, the legs scraping along the floor as I rose. "I should get back. Kol's expecting me."

Ansa ignored me as she wandered around her son, inspecting him for any sort of injury. Eirik shot daggers at me but said nothing. The All-Father and I exchanged knowing looks, but he didn't say anything as I disappeared through the crowd, searching for Kol.

A hand touched my shoulder gently, and I turned to see him hidden in the shadows. "I'm surprised you didn't whoop my ass for touching you."

"I thought about it," I teased.

Peeling himself off the wall, he gestured for the door. "Let's get out of here. I'm sure we have a lot to discuss."

I couldn't agree more.

FORTY-SEVEN

B ack in the safety of the room, I released the glamour, sighing as my true face came back to me. Glancing in the mirror, my gaze instantly went to that new crescent moon tattoo on my forehead, a symbol that resembled my mother's on her own. I wore the face of Astrid so often that I was starting to have a hard time distinguishing which face was truly my own.

"That moon makes you even more beautiful," Kol said from the bed, taking his shirt off.

Biting my lower lip, I ignored his comment as I went to my usual place on the bed. Slipping underneath the covers, I ran my hand along my skin on my tattoos, drawing comfort in them. I wished more than anything that I could use my magic. Snorting, I ran a hand through my hair, mulling over what Eirik had said earlier.

"What did Oeric want?" Kol asked me, finally easing in beside me, turning over and resting his cheek on his hand so he was propped up on his elbow.

"He knows we're up to something," I told him.

Kol nodded. "I gathered as much. It's not often that I stay more than a couple of hours to a day here, and for me to spend so much time here... it's probably off-putting. Not to mention he *is* the All-Father. He hasn't lasted this long without being careful."

"He also knows that I've been looking into the Wolves of Darkness."

Kol's eyebrows shot up. "He knows Hati had a child, but he probably doesn't think it's you—yet."

"Yet?" I frowned. "What do you mean?"

He clicked his tongue. "You have a connection with wolves. You *have* a wolf as a companion. It's not hard to believe that you could be the daughter of the Wolf of Destruction."

"And then there's Eirik."

Kol sighed, rolling over so that he was on his back, arms behind his head. "And then there is Eirik."

"Ansa asked him if he was hurt, and he said that nothing could harm him." I bit my lower lip. "Is that true?"

Kol yawned. "For the most part."

I blinked. "What do you mean 'for the most part?'"

"He's a god, Eira. We can be killed. For him, however, it would be harder to do."

"How?"

Kol didn't answer me for a moment, his eyes closed like he was sleeping. Snorting in frustration, I crawled over to him, placing my hands on his chest to apply pressure to it. He grunted, opening an eye.

"*How?*" I asked again.

He sighed. "Mistletoe."

"Huh?"

"If you keep standing over me, I'll be forced to do something about it. You're showing quite a bit of skin, and I don't think I can force myself to sleep from this sight."

Fuming from both frustration and his comment, I flopped back down, my back to him. After a moment, the bed dipped and an arm wrapped around my waist, drawing me closer to him. His bare chest touched my back, warm and inviting. I shivered, getting my senses back and tried to wiggle out of his grasp.

"If you keep doing that," he whispered in my ear, "I won't be able to stop myself from what's about to happen next."

I swallowed, falling silent.

I was acutely aware of the heat that radiated off Kol in waves, and I wasn't a stranger to sex. However, as much as I wanted to allow him to do all those wicked things to me, something stopped me from allowing this to go further.

I had a job to do, and if I was going to betray both Inkeri and Kol, I would need to keep my distance.

Kol buried his face in my neck, his breath stirring my hair as he began to snore lightly. I drew comfort in that noise for a moment, thinking about my plan. Stealing one of Inkeri's apples would be easy, but what would one single apple do if more grew back every two days?

Oeric wouldn't accept my offer of the apple when he could easily get more. No, for this to work, I would need to cut down the tree and take an apple with me. From there, I could barter.

Restart your orchard with this apple and give me someone who can help me resurrect my mother. Another part of me didn't want to follow through with this plan because if these gods needed these apples to survive, I would inadvertently hurt Kol and Inkeri in more ways than one. The thought of Kol getting hurt— by me specifically, left a bad taste in my mouth.

Reaching up, my fingers wrapped around my necklace, drawing comfort from the only remnants I had of my mother. "What should I do?" I whispered. "I need you."

Stupid. She's dead, she won't answer you.

Dropping the necklace, I settled deeper into Kol's chest and closed my eyes.

Cold seeped into my bones, forcing me awake. Shivering, my eyes cracked open to see a familiar foggy forest. A howl came in the distance, followed by the beating of wings.

Siting up, I took in my surroundings, not the least bit surprised that I was back in the same forest I had seen Hati, my mother, twice in.

Hati appeared from the darkness of the thicket, taking her usual seat on the massive boulder, ears perked forward and tail swishing from side to side. Her massive eyes trailed the length of me before stopping right at my forehead where that new crescent mood rested.

I pointed at it. "What is this?"

"The Mark of the Wolf," my mother said simply. "It's because you're my daughter that you will now bear it."

Stepping forward, I held out my arms. "And these? Where did these come from?"

"Runic Seiðr," she replied. "I carved them into your skin when you were but a baby. Too young to remember both the pain and the memory."

"*Why*?" Anger laced my tone, but I didn't care. I needed to know these answers, needed to know that there was a reason that I was going to bring her back and betray the two people that I cared about. "Does that make me a Völva then?"

Hati shook her head. "Not necessarily. To be a full-fledged Völva, you would have had to been born the third-daughter of my children. These,"—she jutted her nose in my direction—"are artificial. Created with ancient Seiðr to mimic the same magic."

"But why? Why would you go through all this trouble?" I asked her.

She jumped from her boulder, walking over to me. "Because my duty to this world is not done. You need to end what I started centuries ago."

I whirled on her. "Ragnarök? You want me to change into a wolf and devour the moon the same way you were supposed to?

The same way Sköll was going to before you both got caught trying to free Fenrir?"

"No." She shook her head. "The age of the gods has gone on long enough. Oeric rules cruelly and killed many just for looking in his direction. Don't be fooled by his one-eyed appearance. He's as cunning as he is handsome. He's trying to prevent Ragnarök, but in turn, he's starting it without knowing."

I blinked. "What?"

"Oeric carved out his eye so that he could see vast knowledge of the Nine Realms. In doing so, he inevitably could see the future. He knows the day he will die, the day Ragnarök happens, and the day the world will fall with it."

I frowned. "How could he be bringing forth the age of Ragnarök if he can see how to stop it before it happens?"

"Oeric's actions are what start the age of darkness," my mother replied. "He thinks he's trying to prevent it, but he's inevitably starting it."

"But Ragnarök can't start unless the moon and the sun get devoured by you and Sköll. If you're gone and Sköll is dead, then it can't come to pass."

Hati shook her head. "The prophecy is already coming full circle. It is only a matter of time before it begins."

I took a step forward. "It won't. I'll stop it."

"You can't undo centuries worth of darkness, Eira." My mother glanced at my necklace, sadness pooling in her eyes. "You're still wearing it."

I took the necklace in my hands, running my thumb along the glass vial. When I answered, the lie flowed through easily. "I never took it off."

"Good." She nodded, walking back to her boulder to rest upon it, watching me. "It was created for a purpose. The glass was made from the hands of the gods, the runes made from the elves, and the vines were branches from the Yggdrasil so that you could pass freely between the Nine Realms."

I dropped the necklace. "And yet I still feel as if you're withholding the truth."

"I've answered all your questions."

"Why?" I pressed. "Why would you choose to become a wolf a second time? You were human, you were married, you had me and Fenrir. You died, leaving me without a word of what to do."

Hati's gaze softened. "That illness I died from was the work of Seiðr. It was no normal disease that claimed my life, but I'm sure you can gather who gave it to me."

"Oeric."

She nodded. "It was not my wish to leave you, but Fate has other means for those who pass on from one life to the next." She lifted her snout, sniffing the air, her ears perked forward. "I'm afraid it's time for me to go."

Tears filled my eyes as I ran over to her, wrapping my arms around her neck, face deep into her fur.

No matter how much I wanted to hate her, I couldn't. She was my mother; she had been the only constant in my entire life from the moment I could remember. With her gone, I felt lost and alone. I needed my mother back.

"I know what you plan to do," Hati said sadly. "It's not wise. I'm happy where I am."

I drew back. "You're happy being dead?"

"No," she chuckled. "I love you with every fiber of my being. I thank the gods that I was able to become human and have you. I regret nothing. My life was full."

Wiping my eyes, I clung to her with more force as she tried to back away. The strength left my body, and try as I might to hold on any longer, I couldn't, and I fell to the ground as she continued to back up towards the forest behind her.

"Remember what I said, Eira."

"*Mother!*" I reached for her, but she was gone, replaced with darkness.

FORTY-EIGHT

Tomorrow was the day I would be able to steal the apple from Inkeri. Tomorrow, I would be walking down that aisle to marry Kol, the God of Tricks.

If I wasn't quick enough to steal that apple before the ceremony for tomorrow, I would become the bride of a god.

I snorted. It seemed like only yesterday I was back at home preparing to go on hunting trips with Fenrir. I would be thinking about how we would need coin to pay the rent and food to fill our bellies. Now, I would give anything to stay here in Ásjá. It was warm, inviting, and I was beginning to feel remorse for what I was about to do.

Try as I might, it was hard for me to breathe with the clock ticking.

I should be spending time with Inkeri, should keep getting to know her as Astrid even though I so desperately wanted her to know Eira. The real me, not the fabricated version that was only here to take her most prized possession rather than her friendship.

Today felt like a waste of time.

Kol was in Möl with my ring to fuel it with more magic from Bodil. I would need it if we were going to go back into that forest and into the veil that crossed into Inkeri's Orchard. While it was only a single tree, I didn't know what else to call it, as orchard sounded appropriate for it seeing as how everyone else called it that.

Being forced to stay indoors was torture for Fen and me. We should be out in those fields, frolicking and basking in this warmth because the moment we stepped back into Röskr, it would be nothing but endless cold and dreary weather.

However, if my plan actually worked and I managed to finally get my mother back, then staying in that cold home wouldn't be so bad.

Sitting on the ledge, I stared out the window at the bright and sunny day. Birds flitted on by, children of the gods played down below, and animals roamed the area in peace. The mountains in the distance were far larger than the ones back home, and I would miss this sight with every fiber of my being.

Ásjá was almost like a paradise and I ached to stay.

But I couldn't.

The only good thing about staying indoors was the fact that Kol had gone to the library and picked out some books for me to read in his absence.

He assured me that he wouldn't be gone long and that he would return before the party tonight. I wasn't exactly sure if I wanted to go and mingle. The gods had done nothing to me, had been nothing but nice, and here I was about to take something that they needed to live just so I could get my mother back.

Would it be worth it in the end? Would she come back like the rest had before her?

The thing is, if I could convince Oeric to bring my mother back, then maybe she wouldn't be like the others. It was a foolish hope, but one that I clung to with as much strength as I could muster.

"Fen." Turning my head, I noticed that he had taken up residence on Kol's side of the bed, his tail thumping along the surface of it. I pointed to the mound of books. "Fetch."

Fenrir rose on all fours as he went over the stack. He gently grabbed the first one, but I stopped him with a raised hand. "Not that one," I told him. "The third one."

He cocked his head to the side like he didn't understand at first, but after a moment, he did as I asked. He used his nose to push the second book off the stack to reveal the third one, using his teeth to take it over to me.

"Thanks, boy." Kissing his forehead, he huffed in response before he jumped back on the bed to close his eyes.

I studied him for a moment. Could my wolf truly be the father of Hati and Sköll? Was that why he could understand me so easily like he spoke my language?

There was no way for me to know, not unless I spoke with my mother again, and from the way she said goodbye to me last night, it sounded as if she would no longer be able to communicate with me. How she could in the first place was beyond me, but there were a whole lot of things that I had yet to understand.

Looking down at the book in my hands, I reeled back in amazement. The book was titled: *Ragnarök. The End of an Era.*

I shivered, placing the book down for a second to collect myself. What were the odds? I just wanted a random book and got one that pertained to the end of times.

I knew little about the events that would occur to bring forth the age of darkness. What I did know was that it was comprised of several different events that would all lead back full circle to the greatest battle the world would ever see.

No one knew what events would lead up to this happening, but the gods also gave little hints throughout the years.

One of which were the Wolves of Darkness. They were one of the many events that would take place to being the war. Then there was Fimbulvetr, otherwise known as "endless winter."

Mother spoke of this one a few times about the winter that would span for years, a winter that was said to wipe out nations and the rest of humanity. There were more events, but no one really knew them.

Setting aside the book, I walked over to the bed to see what all was left behind by Kol. Most of the remaining books were myths and lore about the Nine Realms, and others were about the origins of the gods. One in particular caught my eye almost immediately.

Shoving the other books aside, I looked over the one I had seen.

The Birth of the All-Father.

Settling back against the cushions, I cracked open the book to read. Skimming a few chapters that didn't interest me, I found one chapter that popped out on the page to me. It was a myth, one more specifically trained to how Oeric lost one eye and gained his sight for premonition.

Interesting.

I began to read when the door to my room flung open and Kol waltzed in like he owned the place—which he actually did. Startled, I jumped, the book falling from my lap to the bed, a hand over my heart.

"For the love of the gods—"

He rolled his eyes. "You act as if you were busy."

I picked up the book, chunking it at him. "I was."

He caught it with ease, not even skipping a beat as he cracked it open with one hand to see what it was that I was going to begin reading. He made a face, tossing it aside as he closed the door. "I can tell you that story easily."

"Oh?" I raised a brow, crawling over to him. "I'd like to know."

He snorted, setting down a wooden box on the table. "It's quite a dull story."

Shooting him a glare, I sat back, arms crossed over my chest. "Almost as dull as your personality?"

He grinned. "If only that were so, my little hellfire."

I shivered at the use of the nickname he had given me.

Before, I would have scolded him, maybe even gave him a swift kick in the shins. Now? Now it was different. It sent a thrill through me, made my heart skip a beat.

He chuckled. "Alright, if you *must* know."

"I must." I raised a brow.

He got up, then turned his chair around so that he could straddle it, resting his arms along the top of it.

"It was no secret that Oeric valued knowledge above all else. It's the thing that kept him going, wanting to learn everything the Nine Realms and beyond had to offer him. That search inevitably led him to Eiði, where he met with one of the lesser-known gods, Marron.

"Marron was the God of Wisdom and Knowledge. During the Vætt, Áræði War, Marron's head had been severed by one of his own people. Oeric watched and waited until nightfall where he picked up Marron's head to take back with him to his tent. Through many songs, herbs, and embalming, Oeric managed to preserve Marron's head and then soon after, Oeric could converse with the Vætt even though he was just a head.

"Thanks to all the magic that the All-Father used, he was able to keep Marron with him at all times, with the Vætt offering advice on occasion. However, Oeric had grown weary of keeping the head with him and thus gave Marron to someone to call his own. In this case, he was placed beneath the Yggdrasil where a well had been built to house the droplets.

"The well became known as the Mímisbrunnr, or 'Well of Knowledge.' Those who drank a single sip from the well would become just as wise and knowledgeable as Marron. Over time, many gods sought out Marron to barter with the Vætt so that they too could wield knowledge lost to gods and mankind. He refused them time and time again until no one but Oeric would visit Marron.

"One day, when Oeric was having a most troubling day, he went down to see Marron and ask for guidance. As the Vætt had served the All-Father for thousands of years, Oeric had grown considerably close to the Vætt, even going so far as to call him a friend. Unfortunately, Oeric never ceased in his quest to find and obtain knowledge, so when he learned of the well's properties, he asked Marron to take a sip of the sacred water.

"Marron refused and sent Oeric on his way. For many days and many nights Oeric would come back to ask the Vætt to allow him to drink from the well. After several long conversations, Marron finally succumbed and allowed Oeric to drink from the well. However, to do so, he would need to sacrifice something dear to him. For Oeric, he had two eyes and thought that since he had two, he wouldn't need the second and so, he carved out his eye and tossed it into the well as the sacrifice."

My eye throbbed, and I couldn't help but run my hand along my face with a shiver, closing my eye so that I could feel it and make sure that it was still there.

Kol raised a brow. "There's more to this story."

I blinked. "More?

He nodded. "Care to hear the last of it?"

"Lay it on me," I said with a nod.

"After Oeric gained the knowledge from the well, he was said to gain premonitions and memories of those who came before him. One of the memories showed him the use of runic magic, but they were nothing more than fragments from various other gods. It was then that he wanted to learn how to use runes to create magic like they had. Ironically enough, they weren't gods that could use the runic magic, but the Norns—the three sisters of Fate.

"For this to happen, he decided to be worthy of such magic he opted to hang himself for nine days on the branch of the Yggdrasil. He did not eat, drink, or sleep for those nine days. The tree, however, decided by the fifth day that Oeric still was not worthy of such power and so, he sought to take more drastic measures. He stabbed himself with his most prized spear.

"One the eve of the ninth day, Oeric had gained what he so desperately craved. His sacrifice was enough that he was able to use the runic magic like the Norns. He then became the most feared god in all the Nine Realms."

Oeric sought knowledge so badly that he was able to lose an eye and hang himself for nine days. I shivered.

To get anything and everything he wanted, he sacrificed himself time and time again just to become the smartest man alive. However, if the Norns were the first to use the runic magic, then why did those old texts say that the first Völva was a Valkyrie? I shook my head; there was so much I still had to learn.

Kol cleared his throat. "You should get dressed. It's nearly time."

I sighed. "This better be the last party we go to," I told him.

He laughed. "If only that were true."

FORTY-NINE

I t was strange to think that in less than twenty-four hours I would be stealing Inkeri's Apple. Kol and I had yet to discuss how we would begin to even steal the apple, let alone the fact that they regenerate every two days.

Hopefully there would be enough time after this party for the both of us to talk more about it later and plan.

Just like last night, Oeric wasn't around, but his wife was. The only difference this time was the fact that the party was going when it hadn't been last night.

I easily spotted Eirik in the crowd. He made it hard not to notice him with his entourage of women and the hatred he kept for me. I did my best to pay him little mind as Kol threaded our hands and led me deeper into the party.

Carin, Ivar, Roar, and another god stood in a circle, laughing and talking. Kol tugged me over to them, my feet catching on my skirts as we neared.

The new god was someone I hadn't met yet, but he was just as tall as all the others. A characteristic I'd come to learn that came with being a god. His skin was dangerously pale, almost translucent, with hair that was long and braided down his back. His eyes were purple, and when he smiled at me, I took notice of his golden teeth.

"Njal." Kol's smile was tight-lipped, his eyes scrunched up at the corners. "It's nice to see you again."

The Watchmen of the Gods.

So, this was the god who watched over the Bifrost and kept the realm safe from harm. He was also the last of the Eleven Main Gods that I had yet to meet. How fitting now that I was going to meet him before one of my last days here.

"Kol." Judging by the slight frown on his face and the way he didn't seem interested in the God of Tricks, it looked as if Njal didn't seem too pleased to see him. "Come to cause more trouble?"

"As much as I would like to," Kol teased, "I'm quite busy at the moment."

Njal raised a brow, noticing me for the first time with a small smile. "Is that so? Is it because of that beautiful woman you have beside you?"

I grinned back at Njal, elbowing Kol in the side. "If only he would acknowledge that fact."

"Ha." Njal laughed. "She's got a mouth on her."

"If only she would use it less often." Kol rolled his eyes as he steered me away from the group, rubbing his side where I had elbowed him to emphasize his point.

My smile grew the longer we were together, and I was beginning to have some fun like the rest of them. I drank, ate, and danced to my heart's content. That is, until a certain dark-haired Annelisse came over with Eirik in toe.

Kol noticed them the same time I did, his displeasure written all over his face.

"What do you two want?" Kol's tone was hard and filled with steel as he slid toward me like I needed his protection.

Forcing him to the side, I watched the two gods as they halted in front of us. I didn't need Kol's protection; I could take care of myself. Sure, I couldn't use my magic in this room, but I had a sharp blade that was made for carving out the eyes of gods.

There was a gleam in Annelisse's eye, and a mischievous smirk to Eirik's lips. The air seemed to change, the tension in the room growing so taut that I could cut it with a knife.

Eirik was the first to speak, but he was mostly directed towards Kol. "I wanted to apologize for what happened a couple of days ago. Father demanded me to come and talk it out with you. Man to man."

The way he talked made me feel uneasy. I wasn't sure why, but there was something about this that rubbed me the wrong way.

If Kol noticed, he didn't say as he inclined his head towards Annelisse. "So why is she here?"

Annelisse right eye twitched at his comment, her lips twisted into a grimace. "Astrid and I got on the wrong foot when we first met."

"So, you came to apologize to her too?" Kol didn't seem convinced.

She nodded. "Yes. If she's going to be living here after to-morrow, it would be best if we all buried the hatchet altogether. Best not spend an eternity hating each other."

Kol eyed them carefully, his right foot tapping as he watched them in silence. I reached out, tugging on his sleeve. There wasn't anything right in this situation, but it would be best not to make it seem like we were arguing.

Already I could feel eyes on us, and I wasn't sure if they were just Oeric's Shadows or other people and gods entirely.

"They have a point," I lied. "It would be nice to bury the hatchet. I'd hate to argue with family."

Annelisse's smile was wicked as she grabbed my elbow, forcing me over to her so that she could loop her arm through mine. "Excellent. We'll be back. You two have fun."

Kol's expression darkened, but he didn't argue as he stalked off towards the other end of the room. I wasn't stupid; I knew what they were doing. Intentionally keeping us apart. For what, I wasn't sure, but it wasn't not like they could do anything to us in this room full of people. Still, being separated from Kol sent me on edge. Thank the gods I had my dagger with me.

Annelisse led me further into the foyer until I could no longer see Kol in the throng of people. She led us towards the front door, where it was propped open, the cool wind of the night drifting inside. I sighed as it touched my skin, sending gooseflesh along my arms.

I dug in my heels as she tried to get me closer to the door and she halted, letting my arm go. "This is far enough."

Annelisse crossed her arms. "Why? Afraid I'll do something to you?"

Silence stretched on for a few moments, neither of us speaking a single word as we continued to stare at anyone and everything that wasn't each other. Finally, after almost two minutes of not a single word being spoken, I took the first initiative.

"You said you wanted to speak to me?" I asked her.

"Right." She didn't meet my eye. "I just wanted to apologize for what I said and did."

"All is forgiven." I turned around to leave, but she grabbed my wrist, holding me in place.

Okay, now I *really* wasn't a fan of what was going on here. The separation, the keeping me close to the door. It all seemed rather... odd, to say the least. Why would they draw us apart? Unless they had planned something on their own and I was walking right into a trap. Luckily, I wasn't playing along to their whims but my own.

I opened my mouth to say something else when I heard a voice outside calling my name. I paused, not sure I heard that right until I heard it a second time.

"*Astrid.*"

Annelisse inclined her head so that I was looking at her instead of the door. "What are you staring at?"

I blinked. "I thought I heard my name."

"*Astrid.*"

I turned away from here. Was that Inkeri's voice? I hadn't seen her since coming down here, but that was definitely her voice, and it was coming from outside.

Annelisse walked in front of me, brows furrowed. "Where are you going?"

I gave her a pointed look. "What are you talking about? Inkeri called my name. I'm going out to see her."

Annelisse's expression flickered from confusion to sympathy. "I didn't hear anything."

Now it was my turn to look confused. "What do you mean you didn't hear that?"

"*Astrid! Come outside.*"

"See?" I pointed outside, seeing a glimmer of her golden head as she wandered around the people milling around. "I'll be back."

Annelisse grabbed my arm, stopping me in place. "I didn't hear anything, Astrid. Are you okay?"

I wretched my arm free, taking a few steps towards the door. "I'm fine."

She followed me, much to my displeasure. "It's not safe outside," she said to me. "I'll come with you."

I glanced back at her. "I don't need your help. Besides, I can take care of myself."

"Astrid—"

"Bye, Annelisse."

She stopped following me, but her confused expression remained as she turned on her heel to walk back inside.

Rolling my eyes, I stood on my tipped toes to gaze around the heads of the people filing in and out of the palace. Inkeri mentioned that she hated crowds, and if she had called for me to come outside, it would make sense that she would be out back in the forest we walked through the other day. She did say that it was one of her favorite places in Ásjá.

Peeking over my shoulder to make sure Annelisse had indeed gone back inside, I walked behind the palace without looking back.

FIFTY

T he night air was brisk, but it sent a warmth through me as I gazed upon the stars and the landscape. Taking a deep breath, my feet propelled me forward as I navigated around the other people that were out and about for the party.

Checking over my shoulder more than once, I continued on the path that led towards the forest, thankful that I had a moment to get away from Annelisse. Thinking about her gave me a headache.

I wished more than anything to have Fenrir by my side. Throughout this whole ordeal, he was just staying in the room, almost like an afterthought in my mind. My Fen would never be an afterthought, but I couldn't have him with me during this time here. If I had any relatives, I would have left him with them instead of having him around me waiting for us to go do something other than walks around the palace grounds.

Once this was over, I would make sure that both Fen and me would go on many, many more adventures. I knew how to travel between the realms now, and since he now had that earring on his ear, he could follow me wherever I went.

For now, though, we would need to wait until I secured Inkeri's Apple and make my trade to Oeric.

I halted by the entrance to the forest. Turning around, I began to scan the vicinity. There was no one around the entrance, but those who were outside the palace were far too occupied with the festivities for them to notice me. Inkeri wasn't here, but she may have gone further into the forest than I originally thought. Glancing over my shoulder to make sure that I wasn't being followed, I strode into the darkness.

Shadows enveloped me from all sides, almost like a vice trying to draw me into a spider's web. My mind clouded as I walked, not exactly sure why Inkeri would have gone into the forest this late at night.

I'd heard her call my name, but with the crowd of people gathering around, it was pretty hard for me to decipher where her voice had come from until I had seen her golden hair disappear behind the palace towards the forest. Perhaps she needed to check on her magical tree but needed a companion to go with her, and when I hadn't responded, she probably decided it was better for her to go by herself rather than wait around for me.

The further I walked, the harder it became for me to get a good glimpse my surroundings.

I'd only been here once and even then, I wasn't paying too much attention to what was around me. The only thing that I remembered was that no matter how far I walked into this forest I could still see the palace behind me. Maybe I *was* going in the right direction.

After a few moments, I decided to slow my steps to glance around. I hadn't encountered Inkeri yet, nor had I spotted her footsteps in the dirt.

Could I have been mistaken about hearing her call my name? Perhaps I had only imagined seeing her walk behind the palace?

Shaking my head, I stopped. I should go back, but I couldn't make my legs move. I'd made it this far, so perhaps I could continue on until I found that tree that would take me to Inkeri's Orchard.

Biting my lower lip, I forced my legs to move further in. Inkeri had told me that it took her apples two days for them to regrow and for her to harvest them. What if... what if that had been a lie? I had no reason to believe that she would lie to me about something she trusted me enough to show me. However, that was the thing. Inkeri trusted me wholeheartedly, and we'd barely known each other but two to three days at most.

Clicking my tongue, I pushed those thoughts in the back of my mind, focusing on trying to find that tree I had marked just the other day.

Clearing after clearing, tree after tree, and I still hadn't come across that same clearing and tree that Inkeri and I had been at before. I reached another clearing, prepared for it to end in failure so that I could turn right back around and head back. Surely by now Kol would have noticed my absence and come looking for me.

Striding towards each tree, I squatted down to run my hands along the bark, feeling for that familiar X that would mark the tree that Inkeri had used her magic on to create that door.

Each tree I touched left me frustrated and hollow, as each one didn't hold that indent I'd made.

Walking to the last of the trees in the clearing, my eyes swept around, searching. There, almost undistinguishable from the bark, was that X I'd created.

Elated, I rested my hands along the tree, fingers splayed and eyes closed. Replaying the other day when Inkeri and I were here in my mind, I racked my brain, thinking of the word she had used to create the portal.

"*Nál*," I tried.

The wind rustled slightly, but after a moment, nothing happened. That wasn't the word. There were so many runic words that could be used, and yet I couldn't remember a single one of them, as I didn't speak the ways of old.

Wait a minute... the word Inkeri had used had started with an "M". What was it again? Mark?

No, it was something similar to that word, something spoken in the old language. Placing my hand back on the tree, I closed my eyes a second time.

"*Mǫrk*."

The wind tore through me at breathtaking speed. I whipped my head to the side from the onslaught of the gust, trying to calm my heartbeat as the trees in this clearing began to change before my very eyes like they had before. The wind died down as the trees shook violently, jutting up high into the sky as their roots spiraled together, weaving that same familiar bridge that glowed like the color of the rainbow.

The image materialized like a ripple in a pond, the area beyond the bridge morphing into that same familiar tree with the stone bench beneath it.

This was it.

The place Inkeri took me to, the place where the apples would regenerate for further harvesting.

Once I stepped through this portal, there was no going back. Not only would the magic in my ring unravel, but so too would the relationship I had with Kol. I wouldn't tell Oeric that it was Kol who had sought me out back in Röskr. No, I would tell him that I had seduced Kol and made him privy to my whims.

Stepping through the portal, the warmth in this new place made me shiver. It was also bright out, like time did not reach here, leaving the night at bay.

The vines wrapping around the bench withered slightly, slithering off it to make enough room for me to sit down.

Unfortunately, I wasn't here for the pleasantries. Glancing around the area to make sure I was truly alone, I walked up to the tree. Unlike before when I was here with Inkeri, there was no fruit growing.

Panic set in as I walked around the tree, looking for signs that an apple may sprout forth.

She'd told me two days, and I told myself that there could be a chance, however slim, that one would grow before then. I rounded the tree several times with no success. Sighing heavily, I sat down on the bench, head in my hands.

How stupid could I be? To come here in the dead of night knowing there was a party going on in full swing beyond this place? By now Annelisse would have gone to Kol to try and seduce him herself. I was certain by now Kol would have grown tired of both Annelisse's advances and Eirik's constant yammering for him to come seek me out.

He wouldn't know where to find me, and even if he did, it would draw unwanted attention.

Pinching the bridge of my nose, I rose from the bench, turning around with my tail between my legs and preparing to head back as a failure. Raising my leg to jump through the portal back to the other realm, the sound of a wind chime made me stop in my tracks. It sounded like it came from behind me.

Waiting a moment longer, the wind chime noise came a second time. Turning back, my eyes widened when a small, golden apple began to grow.

With each beat of my heart, the apple grew until the branch began to sink lower and lower still. I didn't have an ash box like

Inkeri, but I had some clothes that might provide me with enough room to house this large apple.

Stepping over the writhing roots below me, I reached up, taking the apple as it fell into my hands, the branch shaking as it rose back in place.

The apple rested in my palms, heavy and solid. It was golden, and dew clung to the sides of it, the stem and one leaf still intact. Pulling out my shirt, I tried to stuff it down where my bra was, but it was far too big. I had to come up with something, otherwise this would be another thing I'd have to think about.

Setting the apple down on the bench, I took note of my surroundings. There wasn't anything around me that I could use to hold the apple in. Maybe that's why Inkeri had that ash box. Maybe it was imbedded with magic so that the apple would become the size of the normal fruit and be enough for her to carry in a box rather than out in the open.

I had no box, no satchel, and no one around me to help. I finally got what I was searching for this entire time, but now that I had it, there wasn't anything I could do with it. If I had some cloth or some—*cloth*.

That's it!

Reaching down, I retrieved my dagger from my boot, then pulled the hem of my dress out as far as it could go as I began to cut the fabric with my weapon.

With parts of my dress in hand, I used it to carefully wrap up the apple. It was still far too big to place anywhere, but at least now it was easier to say that it wasn't anything interesting, just a ball of cloth. Pft, yeah right. It wasn't the smartest plan, but at least it was something.

Setting the apple aside, I stepped up to the tree, placing my hand on it. Remorse tugged at me, the tree quivering like it already knew what was about to happen.

I can't do this.

Stepping away a few paces I stared up at the tree. I couldn't destroy this tree. In doing so, I could be killing off the gods— Kol and Inkeri especially. I hadn't spent time with the others to really get a feel for them, but they welcomed me with open arms, nonetheless.

However, this was a tree, and that apple no doubt had seeds in it. I wasn't positive, but it was enough for me to go back to the tree with my palms touching the bark.

"*Fiðri.*"

The runes on my arms blazed to life beneath my glamour, the deep shade of crimson glowing so brightly it was almost blinding. Magic poured out of me in waves. A small, simple cinder was all it took, igniting the tree into a fiery blaze. The flames rose, engulfing everything in the torrent of heat and flame.

"I'm sorry."

I didn't look back as I grabbed the apple and jumped through the portal to the other side.

FIFTY-ONE

My knees touched the ground first, followed by my hands and the apple that toppled from my grasp, rolling away from me.

I reached for it, stopping short when the wrapped fruit hit a foot and ceased rolling.

Swallowing, I glanced up to see Annelisse. Her hands on her hips, smile wide and cruel, her eyes glinted with glee as she bent down to take the apple from the ground, holding it up.

"And what do we have here?" she mused.

Rising to my feet, the ground began to quake. The trees unrooted themselves from each other, going back into the ground to reclaim their natural poses. My dagger was already in hand, ready to use if I needed it too. In truth, however, I didn't need my dagger to be a deadly force.

I had my Seiðr.

Annelisse's eyes slid towards mine, boring into me with intensity. She frowned as she tossed her braids to the side. "*This* is what you truly look like? I'm not the least bit impressed."

I didn't need to look at myself to know that I had lost my glamour. Still, I couldn't help but glance down at my arms to see my runic tattoos were back where they belonged. There was a freeing feeling knowing that I was truly myself and not hidden behind the fiery-red-haired Astrid.

She cocked her head to the side. "I'll admit, I never would have guessed you held the blood of a wolf. Makes sense with that wolf you have as a companion and the crescent moon on your forehead. Just like the great Wolf of Darkness Hati herself."

I took a step towards her. "Give me back the apple."

She tsked. "I don't think so. You see, we knew who you were the entire time, dear little wolf. It's been a part of the plan for a while now. This,"—she held up the apple—"is my ticket back into Oeric's good graces. As for you, I'll leave that up to Eirik."

The grip on my dagger tightened as I took a step towards her, raising my weapon to throw at her hand.

A high-pitched caw came from behind me, wings hitting me in the face as a beak clamped down on my fingers, the dagger falling from my grasp and to the grass.

"*Fiðri*," I cried out, arms shooting up to protect my face from the onslaught of claws. Fire erupted in my palms, but the raven didn't relent in his barrage of attacks.

"Oh, no you don't." Annelisse held out her hand. "*Lúði.*"

My flames sputtered out, extinguishing almost instantly as a blue, hexagonal shield came around to protect the raven from my flames. The raven held back for a second, and that was all the time I needed as I dove forward, rolling towards my dagger.

My fingers gripped the handle, turning as a boot connected with my midsection. Flung backwards, I rolled away until my back hit a tree with a thunk.

"*Fuck*," I cursed, arm wrapping around my middle, vision swimming. Boots crunched on the grass, tips by my face as whoever it was crouched down in front of me.

Cold steel touched my chin, forcing me to look up into Eirik's eyes, a cruel smile on his lips. "Oh, you poor thing." He shook his head. "You look a little worse for wear."

He reached out to touch my cheek, but I wouldn't give him the satisfaction of touching me without giving him something in return. I bit down on his hand until I tasted blood.

"You *bitch*." Eirik reared back, slapping me in the face hard enough to make my teeth rattle.

Shit, he really had a good arm. Blood pooled in my mouth, and I spat it out, glaring at him.

Swearing, he grabbed my hair, yanking me forward as he gave me another swift kick in the middle, making me gasp for air before he flung me into the tree. My magic swirled inside me, begging to be let loose.

There wasn't much I could do with Annelisse standing right there. She would no doubt use her protection magic on me a second time to protect Eirik. However, I had to try.

I gripped Eirik's arms. "*Fiðri.*"

The flames were on him in an instant, but just as quickly as they erupted, they were extinguished by Annelisse's magic. Eirik slammed my head into the tree, making it vibrate, black dots popping on either side of my vision.

"Can I go now?" Annelisse whined at him. "I did what you asked."

Eirik didn't even give her a glance as he responded, "Do what you wish. There won't be much else left of her when we're done."

She shrugged, tossing the apple in the air to catch it. "Right. I'll tell Kol of his fiancés horrible, gruesome death."

Grabbing me by the throat, Eirik lifted me up, putting pressure into my windpipe. "You're useless."

The only sound that came out was a gargle as his hold over my throat tightened.

He brought me closer, our noses almost touching. "*Powerless.*"

I was not useless.

I was not powerless.

I was Eira.

I was a woman to be feared.

I was the daughter of the Wolf of Darkness.

And I would make these gods fall.

"Well?" He raised a brow. "Have anything to say?"

His grip loosened on my throat for a moment so that I could catch my breath.

I said only three words. "Go to hell."

Kicking out with my right foot, it connected with his stomach. He sputtered, caught off guard as I next landed a blow with my left foot. His grip on me loosened enough that I was able to drop from his hold to the ground, hand over my throat with the other held out and poised toward Eirik.

"*Skoða.*"

Water spouted out my open palm, tidal waves hitting him square in the chest, sending him flying backwards into a tree.

The raven came for me, soaring with wings flung on either side, talons poised and ready for my eyes. The hand over my throat released, and I held it out to say, "*Skoða.*" Another wave hit the raven, capturing the bird in the torrent of water, choking him.

Preoccupied with the raven, I returned my gaze to Eirik only to see him already gone, my water hitting the tree where he had been.

"I've had enough of this." Arms wrapped from behind me, choking me. I sputtered, my magic dying almost instantly.

"Not so tough now, are you?" he seethed in my ear.

"*Eira!*"

Eirik's expression darkened as he yanked us up, turning the both of us around with my dagger now poised at my heart. "About time you showed up. And here I thought you didn't care about humans."

Kol's attention was solely on Eirik, but one glance in my direction was all it took for his expression to quickly shift to rage. "Let her go."

"*Kol.*" My eyes pricked with tears, but I refused to let them fall.

"*Eira.*" Eirik tasted my name on his lips, but it sounded wicked on his tongue. "So *that's* her real name."

"I'm not playing games, Eirik," Kol warned. "Let her go now, and no one will get hurt."

Eirik's laugh was loud and manic. "You can't hurt me. Nothing can."

"I wouldn't be so sure of that." Kol reached into the sheath at his waist, pulling out a dagger that was similar to my own with obsidian embedded in the steel.

"You think a *dagger* will save her?" Eirik scoffed. "Think again."

"It's all I'll need."

Eirik dragged me with him, walking in a circle towards Kol, but the God of Tricks didn't falter or move as he watched Eirik, not once looking at me. "What do you think my father will say about what's happened so far?" he mused. "He'll want to know why a thief was brought to the Realm of the Gods to steal something that keeps us alive. Keeps *you* alive."

"There are other beings in the Nine Realms that would pay a hefty price for one of those golden apples," Kol replied simply.

"Without the apple," Eirik continued as if Kol hadn't spoken, "you'd die like a mortal human. Is that what you want? To die like those who can't live past the age of eighty? Why would you risk everything for this girl? A girl that was born from the loins of certain destruction?"

Kol's eyes met mine. "Because there are things worth fighting for."

"*Love*," Eirik spat. "You can't honestly tell me that you love this woman." He shook me to emphasize his point. "She's human, Kol. Their purpose is nothing compared to ours."

Kol didn't respond, not at first. I was having a hard time believing that Kol was in love with me. There had been no indication thus far other than some intimate moments we'd shared, but other than that, there was nothing more.

However, I couldn't help the gravitational pull that always tugged me in his direction since the moment we'd met all those weeks ago. I couldn't deny the way he had looked at me back in the elven forest, relieved to see me alive and fearful of what could have happened. I saw it in the way he gave me those kisses, in the way he touched me like I wasn't some fragile bird.

"You wouldn't know what love was if it hit you in the face," Kol taunted. "You think with the wrong head."

Eirik snarled. "Why you—*fuck*!"

He grunted, throwing me aside. Gasping, I flopped to the ground like a fish, gulping in lungful of air.

My vision swam, black dots dancing along my vision. Coughing, I forced myself to roll over to see what was going on.

Fenrir had his fangs sank deep into the god's leg, tugging with all that he had in him. Kol was beside me, resting a hand on my shoulder, mouth moving, but I couldn't hear him. Blood rushed into my ears as I regained oxygen.

Eirik raised his dagger, arching it downwards, catching Fenrir in the shoulder. Terror filled me, seeing my best friend in danger.

My wolf yelped but didn't release his hold. He clamped down harder, eliciting a scream that tore through Eirik's chest. He couldn't be killed, but at least he could feel pain.

He slashed at Fenrir again, and this time my wolf released the god, jumping back. Blood oozed from the wound in his shoulder, but my companion showed no signs of stopping as he lunged towards Eirik.

Kol still tried to talk to me, but I was glued to the scene before me, hoping that my Fen wouldn't hurt himself anymore.

Kol noticed where I was looking and moved away from me to help Fenrir. The next scene was as if in slow motion, the air rushing into my lungs as I reached for Fenrir.

Eirik kicked my wolf aside, his—*my*—dagger embedded into Kol's shoulder. The God of Tricks didn't slow, didn't even flinch from the pain as he propelled himself forward, arching his arm to stick his dagger into Eirik's chest.

At first, Eirik didn't register that he was stabbed, blinking in confusion as he glanced down to see the dagger embedded all the way up to the hilt. He smiled slowly as he pulled Kol closer, blood trickling from the side of his mouth.

"Painful." He grimaced. "But you can't kill me. Nothing can."

Kol's brows drew upwards. "Is that so? Maybe you should take a deeper look."

Confused, Eirik looked down again as Kol removed his hand. Wrapped around the hilt of the dagger was a green bracelet wound tightly. Eirik's eyes went wide as recognition tore through him, his eyes turned towards Kol's.

"Mistletoe." Eirik's smile was filled with pain now, his shoulders quavering.

Mistletoe.

That's the thing that Kol had mentioned to me some time ago. It was what he told me would kill Eirik. At the time, I had been confused. Perhaps he had said something half-asleep, but that wasn't the case. The mistletoe plant was the thing that could kill Eirik.

"You see,"—Kol twisted the dagger upwards—"your mother was very forthcoming to the old gentlemen she met some time ago. Told him that she thought the mistletoe was too small and insignificant to harm anyone."

Blood bubbled on Eirik's lips, his eyes glinting with hatred as he bared his teeth. "Well," he coughed, "I hope you enjoy the wrath that my father will elicit from my death."

"Don't worry." Kol drew out the dagger, indifference on his face. "I'm already prepared."

Eirik laughed, but it held no humor as he crumbled forward, falling to his knees. He continued to laugh and laugh and laugh until he couldn't hold himself up any longer, slumping face-first into the ground.

Fenrir limped over to me, whining. Tears fell down my cheeks as I wrapped my arms around his massive neck, burying my face in his fur.

He winced when my arm touched his shoulder and I pulled back, placing my hand on his wound.

"*Hvíld.*"

Fenrir's injury knitted back together within a matter of seconds. All that remained was a scar and the dried blood that was crusted into his fur. I would need to scrub that later.

Kol stood over Eirik's body for a moment longer than necessary before he kicked dirt over the god and came over to me. Stashing the weapon in his jacket, he ran his hand along my body.

"*Hvíld,*" he whispered.

"Kol I—"

"Don't say anything." He wrapped his right arm around my back while his left dipped under my legs, hoisting me up.

I frowned, pushing on his chest. "I don't need to be carried. I can walk."

He didn't respond as he carried me towards the entrance of the forest. "I've no doubt. But you've led me on a wild goose chase, and now that I've found you, I'm not letting you go. Rest."

I wanted to argue with him, but exhaustion pulled and tugged at my limbs, and I snuggled deeper into his warmth, hating myself for loving the way his chest was hard and sturdy as an oak tree.

For once, I did what I was told and closed my eyes into oblivion.

FIFTY-TWO

I awoke with a start, my entire body aching like I had just gotten the living shit beat out of me. Oh wait, I did. Rolling over, I felt around the bed to find it empty. Fear settled in my bones at what just happened.

Eirik was killed by Kol's hand, and now Annelisse knew my identity.

Raising my head, my eyes scanned the room to see Fenrir asleep on the windowsill like he was guarding the room by watching through the windowpane.

Kol was sitting on the couch, his back towards me as he peered into the fire that was blazing in the hearth.

I sat up, the blankets tucked around my waist. I was dressed in a white nightgown, almost see-through, and I was wearing nothing but underwear.

Facing flushing, I tried not to imagine Kol's hands over my body as he tried to get my blood-ridden clothes off me before slipping me into this gown. Shaking my head, I pivoted off the bed, padding over to him on silent feet. Of course, nothing got past him. He turned his head slightly.

"If you're trying to slit my throat in my sleep," he said, "you'd need to be a whole lot quieter than that."

I huffed, ignoring his teasing tone as I walked around the couch, sitting on the other end as far away from him as I could. I couldn't bear looking at him in this moment because, in the end, it would be my downfall.

He sat forward, elbows on his knees, hands clasped together and resting his chin on them as he stared at the fire. "I risked a lot going after you."

I swallowed. "I know."

"No," he sighed. "You don't."

My chest puffed up in defiance. "I could have handled them myself."

It was a lie. I knew it, and he knew it. If I had the upper hand, then maybe I would have succeeded. But they were the ones who got the drop on me, and because of that I could have—*would* have—died by Eirik's hands if Fen and Kol hadn't come to rescue me.

A lump formed in my throat when I noticed the scar on Kol's right shoulder, right where Eirik had stabbed him.

I crawled over to him, lightly touching his injury. "Does it hurt?"

He raised a brow. "Well, it doesn't feel good."

I winced, reaching out to rest my hand on his shoulder. "I can use my magic. Here, let me—"

"Eira." He captured my hand, bringing me closer, our faces now inches apart and our noses dangerously touching. His gaze met mine. "You could have died today."

I swallowed thickly, trying to make the lump in my throat go away. I turned my head. "I know."

"Don't," he whispered, taking my chin to turn me towards him. "Don't turn away from me."

My eyes flicked to his. "I'm sorry, Kol."

"Just don't do that to me again, you hear?" He dragged me to him, almost throwing me on his lap as his arms encircled me, holding me closer.

My heart swelled with emotion, my eyes misting up from the way he said those words. Almost like he *cared* about me. I sniffed. "I do nothing but bring darkness to the ones I love."

He chuckled. "You and I are one in the same." Kol's grin was electrifying. His fingers wrapped gently around my chin, forcing me to gaze into his eyes. "We thrive in the darkness, my little hellfire."

I shivered at hearing that nickname. Gods, it sent me spiraling as I hopped fully onto his lap, wrapping my arms around his neck to bring my lips to his. Kol stiffened for a moment, hands at his sides, but after the confusion subsided, he raised his arms, gently holding me to him as he kissed me back. His hand strayed lower, resting on my ass, his fingers running along my skin.

"The apple!" I gasped, remembering and breaking the moment. "I almost forgot. I—"

Kol didn't skip a beat as he reached out to the end table beside him where my satchel rested, unclicking the top to show me the apple covered in my dress's cloth. I sighed in relief.

"Happy now?" he chucked, running his fingers along my lower lip, nose, and cheeks.

My face heated. "Maybe."

Taking my chin, he brought me back to him, capturing my mouth with his. One hand rested on my ass, caressing it, as the other snaked upwards to cup one of my breasts through the thin fabric. I gasped, the motion making my mouth open wider, his tongue snaking it to explore mine. His thumb ran over my sensitive nipple, sending a shiver down my spine.

My hands ran along his chest, loving the feel of his rock-hard abs beneath my fingertips. It was enough to send me in a frenzy as I grabbed the edges of his shirt, lifting them up slightly. He stopped me, holding my hand as he broke our kiss.

"There's no going back," he whispered to me. "If we do this—"

"Shut up and kiss me already."

Kol dipped me, planting those lips over mine, devouring me. I helped him remove his shirt, and he didn't waste a single second as he tore through my dress, exposing me.

His kisses trailed along my neck, nipping and sucking gently before seeking down along my collarbone and lower still. His hot breath sent a wave of desire through me as his lips took in my nipple, running his tongue along it and sending me into pure bliss.

He held me steady, nibbling along my supple nipple before paying attention to my second, giving it the same treatment.

Heat pooled in my belly, a fire that needed to be extinguished, a douse of water to quench my thirst as he held me to his chest, angling us so that he was on top of me on the couch. His knee slipped and he went forward, his face hidden in my neck.

I giggled. "I don't think this couch will fit the both of us."

"Hm."

Kol gripped me close, wrapping my legs around his waist he hoisted me up, carrying me across the room to the bed.

He tripped over the blanket I'd thrown off me previously, turning around so that he fell backwards with me on top of him. Giggles erupted from me, and his deep chuckle reverberated off, sending me toppling forward.

Kol's smile faded, his expression softened as he reached out, curling a strand of my black-silver hair. "I really love this color on you," he breathed.

Leaning forward, I kissed him, taking his bottom lip between my teeth to gently tug. "Show me."

In one swift motion he had me flipped over onto my back, his hands fumbling with his pants to strip them off. I reached down to help take my own off, but he stopped with me a steady hand, slowly pushing me back onto the pillows.

"Give me a moment," he whispered. "I want to savor this."

I didn't argue with him—couldn't. Kol's mouth expertly ran along my body. His kisses sent a thrill through me, made my knees weak.

My entire being felt energized. His fingers tugged on my hair, kissing me deeply. He slipped a hand between my legs, his palm hot against my core. If I wasn't wearing underwear, I would have come undone the moment he touched me.

Rolling my head back, I let out a little moan as his hands touched the most intimate part of me. He rose onto his knees, slipping off his underwear. I clambered up on my elbows, eyes wide at the sight before me.

By the grace of the gods, this man was…

I licked my lips, not paying attention as he slid my panties off, revealing me to him in all my glory.

Kol's own gaze remained on my body, scarcely breathing. He dropped down to give me a kiss, but I wasn't going to let him take all of the control. Tucking my leg beneath his, I used my strength. Kol, caught off guard, flipped from my movements, with me now straddling him.

I grinned down at him, his hands on either side of my hips looking just as amused as myself. "I never took you to be the dominant type."

"And I never took you to be so submissive," I teased back.

He sat up, the motion allowing him to slip inside me. A gasp escaped my lips. It had been quite some time since I'd been with a man and for the life of me, I never knew what I was missing.

Kol guided my hips along him slowly, his fingers digging into my flesh. Placing a hand on his chest, I forced him to lie back down, riding him. Dropping his head back, Kol closed his eyes as he let me do what I wanted to him.

The heat inside me exploded, my entire body on fire as the need to continue overwhelmed me. I felt like I had shattered into a million pieces and then been stitched back together as Kol shifted, rolling us so that he was on top of me again. He grabbed my arms, holding them above my head as he swayed his hips, thrusting into me with a force—a need.

Kol dipped his head, kissing me tentatively. He gripped my bottom lip between his teeth, tugging it to send gooseflesh to rise along my arms.

"My turn," he breathed.

Holding my wrists in one hand, Kol thrusted into me, the first few slow and steady, but with each thrust he pushed deeper and harder until he was slamming into me, making the bed bounce and shake. With his free hand, he used it to tease my breasts, tugging and running his fingers along my nipples before he groaned, returning his hand back to my wrist.

That same tingling sensation washed over me. It started at my heart and dropped with each thrust until it reached my navel.

Kol ground into me heavily, a gasp escaping me as the walls around me crumbled, sparks flying in my eyes as I reached my climax. Warmth spread through me from Kol, searing me from the inside out as he pressed his lips to mine, kissing me like I was the air he needed to breathe. He rode his own climax, his hips forceful as he slowed down.

Sweat beaded along his brow as he pulled out, grabbing me and flipping us over. He was on his back with my head on his chest, legs spread out over his. His chest rose and fell, eyes half lidded as I used my index finger to run along his abs.

Kol captured my fingers, kissing them before he grabbed my face, kissing me again and again.

I was in utter bliss and wanted more of this man than I ever thought possible. I shouldn't crave his touch, shouldn't want more than just a few caresses and kisses—but I did. More than anything in the entire Nine Realms.

I wanted more.

I wanted to know what it would be like to have Kol, to be wanted by someone that wasn't out to hurt me.

What would it feel like to love? I thought I knew love once, but that time never compared to what I felt in this very moment. Kol's touch elicited love and devotion, something I never thought I would ever have. For now, though, I would enjoy this moment for what it was worth because soon, it would be nothing but a distant memory.

FIFTY-THREE

The sound of Kol's light snoring almost put me to sleep. I forced myself to stay away, to keep my eyes open no matter what. I was alive and so was Fenrir and Kol.

We'd done it. We'd secured Inkeri's Apple.

I sat up, running a hand along my face as I turned to Kol's beautiful, naked sleeping form. Desire flared to life at seeing his exposed body, but I stamped it down.

I had an exchange to make.

Throwing the covers off me, I swiftly went to bathroom to change. I didn't have time to shower, so I would do that once I got home. It wouldn't be long before then so I could cleanse myself of Kol's fragrance, among other things later.

Fen lifted his head when I entered the room, huffing as he dropped from the sill to prance over to me.

Running my hand over his head, I grabbed my boots, lacing them on tightly. Flicking open my satchel, I made sure that the apple was there before I closed it back up, slinging my bag over my shoulders. I checked the mirror to make sure my glamor was in place before walking over to the door, I glanced behind me one last time.

I memorized the planes of Kol's features, right down to the serpent tattoo on the right side of his face before I opened the door and slipped out into the corridor.

Fenrir walked out before me, turning around to wait for me as I closed the door. I waited a few moments making sure that my rooting around hadn't woke him. A loud snore came from beyond the door, and I sighed in relief. He was still asleep. Good.

Grip tight on the satchel, Fenrir and I made our way down the hallway. I knew my way around this place enough that I wouldn't get lost too much. All I would need to do is find one of Oeric's Shadows and convince him to lead me to the All-Father.

Simple enough plan so long as it worked.

Stepping carefully through the palace was easier said than done. Each time I heard a creak or a snore, I would hide in the shadows hoping that no one had seen me.

Fenrir's steps were lighter than my own, the predator in him helping him through most of the situations I'd gotten us in over the last several years.

Right, back to the task at hand.

The foyer where the parties were held was quiet and devoid of life. This was also the only place that I'd ever seen the Shadows or heard them up in the ramparts. Pushing the door open, I walked into the foyer.

Darkness surrounded me on all sides, but the flapping wings above indicated the ravens were indeed here.

"Muninn? Hugunin?" I called.

There was a rustling followed by a string of curses, and a raven appeared, flapping just enough so that we were eye level. His beady black eyes were tired but filled with irritation at being woken up this late in the night.

"Muninn?" I tried.

"Hm," the raven huffed. "If you're going to be staying here, you should learn who is who."

"Hugunin," I surmised.

He nodded. "Now, what do you want?"

I raised my chin. "I need to speak with the All-Father."

Hugunin cocked his head to the side, assessing me further. Distrust filtered in his gaze, but it was quickly replaced with indifference as he turned. "Follow me."

Holding onto the satchel as tightly as I could, I followed Hugunin through the foyer to the end of the hall where there was a door hidden behind some curtains. He tapped on the handle, flapping away. Taking that as a hint, I turned the knob and opened the door, gazing up at a staircase that led further up into the palace.

"The All-Father is normally in his study," Hugunin told me. "These steps will lead you to him."

I turned to him, narrowing my eyes. "You're not coming with me?"

He huffed. "I'm not privy to most information. I may be a Shadow, but I prefer to keep my feathers attached, thank you. That being said, I don't wish to be around when he discovers who you are, Eira."

I paused. "You... you know who I am?"

Hugunin didn't respond as he turned and flew back up to the ramparts. I wanted to call him back, wanted to know just how exactly he knew me or about me. Tapping my foot in irritation, I decided to push that thought away for now and continue on with my plan.

Taking the steps two at a time, Fen and I ascended the stairs until we reached a door at the very end of the staircase. Opening up the satchel, I rested my hand inside, relieved to find that the apple was still there.

This is wrong, I told myself as I raised my knuckles to knock. *Turn back.*

"You may enter."

I froze, knuckles still poised to knock on the door. Did he—?

"I know who you are. You don't need to knock." Oeric's voice was filled with authority.

Swallowing, I pushed open the door and stepped into the room. This room was almost a carbon copy of the office of the Jarl's back in Röskr. It was still crazy to me just how alike they were. It was a little unsettling.

The All-Father sat at his desk, a map of the Nine Realms stretched out over the top of it. A holder for his ink and quill rested beside it. A window to the right overlooked the Realm of the Gods, the left riddled with parchments in old tongue and sketches of monsters I'd never seen. A six-tiered bookshelf rested behind him, filled with books that were far older than the ones back in the library below.

Oeric set down his quill, gesturing for me to sit across from him. Hesitating, I took one final glance around the room to make sure that there wasn't any immediate danger. Although, being in Oeric's presence itself was all the danger I had to hide from. Taking my seat, I placed my satchel on my lap.

Oeric smiled, but it didn't quite reach his eye. "What can I do for you, Astrid?"

Swallowing, I dug into my satchel placing the wrapped-up apple on the surface. "An exchange."

He raised a brow. "Exchange? Of what exactly?"

Reaching forward, I removed the cloth from the fruit, exposing its golden brilliance to the room. Oeric's eye never left mine as I continued to unravel my exchange. Amusement flickered over his features as he sat back, arms folded over his chest.

"I want the power to bring my mother back." I raised my chin, hoping I seemed as defiant as I felt.

Oeric studied me for a moment, his eye roving over my face, the apple, and then back again. He sighed. "You want to exchange one of Inkeri's Apples to bring back your mother?"

"Yes."

He chuckled, shaking his head. "You do realize that more grow every two days, right?"

"I do." I narrowed my eyes. "However, from what I saw, there won't be any more of those apples growing for as long as the gods shall live."

Oeric's expression didn't change as he walked around the desk. He walked over to his closet, opening up to reveal a similar ash box that Inkeri used, except this one was three times as large.

He settled it on the desk, resting his massive hand along the top of it. "Do you really think that I wouldn't know, Eira?"

"I—" I paused.

Did... did he just call me Eira? But that could only mean—

"I've known about your little plan for eons." Oeric pushed himself from the desk, his eye gleaming with malice as he reached out to open up the ash box. Dozens of golden apples rested inside it, apples that would no doubt hold seeds to grow an entire orchard rather than the one.

Shit.

He closed the box, leaning against the desk. "You see, Eira. I've known about this day for quite some time. I prepared myself for it. The day Kol brought you to the palace was the day I knew exactly who you were."

Don't say it, I thought.

"Eira Stormbreaker, Daughter of Hati, one of the Wolves of Darkness." He paused for dramatic effect before he continued. "You see, I knew about you long before you were ever even born. The daughter of darkness that would help bring forth the age of Ragnarök. I will admit,"—he gestured around the room— "I never thought you would have the balls to come and face me in the first place. I misjudged you, Eira."

"What do you want?" I snarled at him.

There was nothing that I could do to escape this situation. This was the All-Father, the father to all the gods in the Nine Realms. This would have worked if he didn't have that stock of apples and he would have been willing to barter. Instead, Oeric knew my move before I even made it. Did he really have premonitions or were they actual tales of the future? Either way, I was fucked.

"You see," he said with a cruel smile, "there's nothing I want. Not really. Perhaps if you had been successful in this endeavor, I would have been willing to barter with you. However, as I can see you have nothing else to offer me, I'll just take matters into my own hands."

I raised my chin defiantly. "If you're going to kill me, just do it."

"Oh, I'm not going to kill you," Oeric told me. "The thing about you is, you're not *natural*, Eira. You're the daughter of Hati, and she created you as a way to destroy the gods with those runes in your skin. Runes, I might add, that were stolen directly from me."

I frowned. "You can't steal runes—"

"I own them," he growled. "I own everything in the Nine Realms. Everything. Mind, body, soul. Nothing escapes my notice, and until I can find a way to rid your body of those runes, you will do as I say."

"And if I don't?" I questioned him.

"Then you will live out your days in Móðr."

The Underworld.

I rose. "Then it looks like you're going to have to imprison me because I'm not fucking doing that."

Oeric's face was grim as he snapped his fingers. "Roar. Carin. Ivar."

The three gods materialized, standing on all sides of me. The All-Father nodded at them as he walked back to his desk, settling in as he placed the apple I had stolen back into the ash box.

"Take her."

Rearing forward, I spat at him. "Fuck you!"

The grip on me tightened as they dragged me out of Oeric's office and down the stairwell. I fought, clawed, kicked to no avail.

Even Fenrir was captured, muzzled with steel and shackled so that he couldn't move as they continued to drag us. Upon seeing me, Fen tried to wrangle himself free. Ivar withdrew a dagger, slicing my wolf to make him obey. I opened my mouth to scream, hoping that Kol come rescue us, but Ivar reached out to slap me in the face.

"Kol won't hear you," he sneered.

I struggled some more as they continued to lead me from the palace and out into the fresh air. The sun was beginning to crest the hills, signaling the morning hours as the sky was painted with fiery pink and red, mingling together with the clouds that breezed on by.

"You'll regret this!" I spat at them. "Don't you know who I am? What I am?"

"We're well aware, As—*Eira*," Carin corrected herself.

"A wolf of darkness," Roar replied sadly, his eyes taking on a faraway look.

"A blight for the Nine Realms," Ivar commented, forcing me forward.

We crossed the bridge where Kol and I had come from, shoving me onward towards the tree that was marked with the sigil that would take me to Móðr. Carin placed her hand on the tree, speaking the words that would spell my doom.

"*Nál.*"

A portal opened, rippling into a snowy scene that held no warmth whatsoever. I cringed, but it didn't do me any good as they thrust me inside, following right in behind me. I turned as the portal began to close, sealing me in a new place of darkness.

To Be Continued

*In book 2 of **The Daughter of the Wolf** Duet:*

A God's Demise

ACKNOWLEDGMENTS

This book tested me in all the right ways. *A God's Promise* began as a passion project after a few days of playing God of War. I always held a love for Norse Mythology and spent so much time and energy on everything I could learn. The world, myths, legends, everything that I could get my hands on I sure did. I only wished I could devour more.

I would like to thank my beta readers. Without all of you, this story wouldn't be what it is today. I want to name each and everyone of you, but there's so many, but you all know who you are and how awesome you are!

I would like to thank my ARC readers for taking the chance on me and Eira. Your reviews and love keep me going and inspire me to continue writing each and everyday. I hope one day I can return the favor for the kindness you've all shown me.

To my Developmental Editor, Jennifer. I couldn't have done this without you. Your feedback was everything I needed and more. I will always, and I mean, always, choose you and thank you for each and every page you've given me.

To my Proofreader, Ashley, you're a rockstar! Your edits are invaluable to me and you make my books shine on the page. Without you, I don't think A God's Promise would have been as great as it is now!

To my cover designer, Saint Jupiter. You turned my idea into a breathtaking cover—one that I never thought possible. The apple, the gold, the fall leaves, everything about this cover just screams to me and it's so beautiful. I can't wait to come back and have more covers done from you.

To my map designer, Cartographybird, you always do such a stellar job with the fantasy maps! You turn my squiggled lines into something worthwhile. I love the two versions of The Nine Realms you helped create for me.

To my character artist, Karoline, I am in love with all the artwork you've created for A God's Promise. I'm so lucky to have them scattered throughout this novel and I cannot wait to start more projects with you.

To my husband. You surprise me time and time again whenever I need help. You're the mythology wizard, and you helped me create this world and helped me with the lore, myths, and legends.

PLEASE WRITE A REVEIW

Hello, and thank you for buying my book! You're amazing, and I cannot tell you how much I appreciate your support. A review would be wonderful, and I would love you all the more for it, as every review helps me a little bit, and I love reading them all!

THE NINE REALMS OF AUÐIN

Röskr: Realm of the Humans

Ásjá: Realm of the Áræði

Skóð: Realm of the Dwarves

Gørsimi: Realm of the Giants

Rök: Realm of Fire

Sókn: Realm of Ice, Snow, and Mist

Móðr: Realm of the Dead

Möl: Realm of the Elves

Eiði: Realm of the Vætt

THE MAIN CITIES

Ellriheimr: The main city in Röskr.

Allrland: The main city in Ásjá

Smíðajǫrð: The main city in Skóð

Niðrifold: The main city in Gørsimi

Einnbiǫð: The main city in Rök

Mærvegr: The main city in Sókn

Myrkrheimr: The main city in Móðr

Ljósvegr: The main city in Möl

Kynfold: The main city in Eiði

TERMS & MEANINGS

Hvíld—Heal

Fiðri—Fire

Hræzla—Invisibility

Skoða—Water

Nál—Transport

Seiðr—Magic

Völva—Norse word for "Seeress"

Vætt –Vanir gods

Áræði—The Aesir God

Auðin—The Nine Realms

Máni—Moon

Vé—Old Language for "Open"

Mǫrk—Old Language for "Mark"

Mímisbrunnr—The Well of Marron

Lúði—Protection

THE ELEVEN GODS

Inkeri—Idunn

Magnar—Thor

Kol—Loki

Oeric—Odin—Also known as the "All-Father."

Carin—Freya

Eirik—Balder

Ansa—Frigg

Ivar—Freyr

Njal—Heimdall

Tyra—Hel

Roar—Vidar